Murd
Margins

"[A]n irresistible cozy mystery that
will delight your imagination."
—*New York Times* bestselling
author PAIGE SHELTON

MARGARET
LOUDON

BERKLEY

$7.99 USA
$10.99 CAN

S > EAN

ISBN 978-0-593-09926-1

ALSO BY MARGARET LOUDON

The Open Book Mysteries
MURDER IN THE MARGINS

WRITING AS PEG COCHRAN

Gourmet De-Lite Mysteries
ALLERGIC TO DEATH
STEAMED TO DEATH
ICED TO DEATH

Cranberry Cove Mysteries
BERRIED SECRETS
BERRY THE HATCHET
DEAD AND BERRIED

Farmer's Daughter Mysteries
· NO FARM, NO FOUL
SOWED TO DEATH
BOUGHT THE FARM

Murder, She Reported Series
MURDER, SHE REPORTED
MURDER, SHE UNCOVERED
MURDER, SHE ENCOUNTERED

WRITING AS MEG LONDON

Sweet Nothing Lingerie Series
MURDER UNMENTIONABLE
LACED WITH POISON
A FATAL SLIP

Murder
IN THE
Margins

MARGARET LOUDON

BERKLEY PRIME CRIME
New York

BERKLEY PRIME CRIME
Published by Berkley
An imprint of Penguin Random House LLC
penguinrandomhouse.com

ISBN: 9780593099261

First Edition: October 2020

Printed in the United States of America
1 3 5 7 9 10 8 6 4 2

Book design by Gaelyn Galbreath

This book is dedicated to Reg—the best canine companion a writer ever had. You were always at my side or by my feet. I will love you forever, and I will miss you forever, buddy.

ONE

❧

If Penelope "Pen" Parish had known how useless a master's degree in Gothic literature would turn out to be, she would have opted for something more practical instead—like accounting or mortuary science. After keeping herself somewhat afloat for several years with a hodgepodge of temporary jobs like waitressing and data entry, she'd hit upon a solution.

Instead of studying other authors' Gothic novels, she would write one of her own.

She'd subsequently spent every bit of her spare time in her attic garret—okay, a fifth-floor walk-up with drafty windows—with her fingers on the keys of her used laptop, surrounded by empty takeout containers, channeling her favorite Gothic authors—Mary Shelley, the Brontës, and Ann Radcliffe. By adding a touch of horror à la Stephen King, she had managed to produce a book the critics called a "unique, fresh twist on the classic Gothic novel."

You could have knocked her over with a feather when *Lady of the Moors* became a bestseller.

And therein lies the rub, as Hamlet opined.

Publishers have a habit of expecting their authors to follow up one bestseller with another. And Penelope Parish was suffering from a terrible case of writer's block.

She thought of that old saying, "Be careful what you wish for." The truth of that old saw had certainly hit home. She'd done her share of wishing as she'd slogged through her first manuscript—and there were entire days if not weeks when it was definitely a slog. She'd dreamed of all the things every writer does—book signings, coast-to-coast book tours, hitting the bestseller lists, royalties pouring in to swell her dwindling bank account.

And while it hadn't been *exactly* like that—her publisher had nixed the idea of a coast-to-coast book tour—some of it had actually come true.

And it had given Penelope a terrible case of nerves. She'd been raised with the strict New England ethic of hard work and was quite accustomed to it—holding down two jobs while getting her degree hadn't exactly been a picnic—but sometimes hard work wasn't enough. Ever since her success, she'd forced herself to sit in her chair at her desk with her fingers on her laptop keys for hours on end, but the words had refused to come. She'd hit a writer's block the size of Rhode Island.

Salvation had come in the form of a writer-in-residence position at the Open Book bookstore in England. She'd seen the ad in the back of the *Writer* magazine and had impulsively applied.

The application had been curious to say the least—filled with unusual and admittedly creative questions.

If you could be any character in fiction, who would

you be? That had taken some thought on Penelope's part, but finally she had put down Bridget Jones. Because Bridget's friends and family liked her *just the way she was.*

Penelope's mother and sister were constantly trying to turn her into something she was not—a polished, put-together career woman balancing life and work as easily as a Cirque du Soleil performer juggled balls. Her friends were forever urging her to get it together and move on with her life. Yes, Bridget Jones it was.

If you were a type of food, what type of food would you be?

Penelope had thought long and hard about that one, too, and had finally come up with her answer—pizza. Everyone liked pizza. It was unpretentious. It was comfort food and always made you feel better. You could have it any way you wanted—with or without pepperoni; sausage; mushrooms; onion; green peppers; or even, if you insisted, pineapple.

Penelope had sent off the application without any great expectations. And for the second time in her life, you could have knocked her over with a feather when the letter came—the e-mail actually if you want to split hairs—announcing that she'd won.

It had seemed like a heaven-sent opportunity—the quiet of a charming English village where she could write in peace in exchange for running a book group and a writers group and anything else she could think up to enhance the bottom line of the Open Book.

And the chance to get away from everyone's expectations—her mother's, her sister's, and even her publisher's. It had crossed Penelope's mind that her decision might have looked to some as if she was running away but she immediately dismissed the thought. She was having an adventure and wasn't that what life was meant to be?

Penelope had thought of herself as well prepared for life in an English village. She was an avid reader of British authors—she knew her Miss Marple inside and out—and she never missed an episode of *The Crown* or *Victoria*.

She didn't expect to be homesick. Homesick for what? An unsatisfactory romantic relationship? Her overpriced Manhattan walk-up?

There'd been objections, of course. The road was never smooth sailing as far as Penelope was concerned. Her sister, Beryl, insisted that this "sabbatical," as she called it, wasn't going to get Penelope a career. Despite Penelope's publisher springing for a full-page ad in the *New York Times*, her sister didn't consider book writing a viable occupation. According to her, what Penelope ought to do was apply for an academic position at a prestigious university.

Penelope's mother had objected, too, telling Penelope that she'd never meet anyone in Britain, and, even if she did, all the men there had bad teeth and if she thought she was going to meet Prince Harry or any prince at all, she was sadly mistaken. And as far as breaking into British society was concerned, she could forget all about that. Besides, what about her boyfriend, Miles?

Miles had seemed mildly put out that she wouldn't be on hand to grace his arm at the annual Morgan Fund investor's dinner, but in the end he was the only one who didn't vigorously object to Penelope's upping stakes and moving overseas.

Fortunately Penelope was used to doing things that others objected to—she'd been doing it all her life—so that didn't stop her from accepting the Open Book's offer.

No, she was going to make a go of this opportunity, because really, she had no choice. And—she could hear her grandmother's voice in her head—*the Parishes aren't quitters.*

And thus it was that Penelope had arrived on the shores of Merrie Olde England with her laptop and her battered suitcases and how she now found herself driving down the wrong (wrong in her opinion, anyway) side of the high street in Upper Chumley-on-Stoke two weeks later.

Today Chum, as Upper Chumley-on-Stoke was affectionately known to its residents, was a beehive of activity. Tomorrow was the annual Worthington Fest.

Banners, adorned with the Worthington crest and announcing the fest, hung from every streetlamp along the high street and fluttered in the mild breeze. It was a brisk October day, but the sky was cloudless and the sun warmed the air enough so she could get about nicely with just a light coat or a heavy sweater.

Upper Chumley-on-Stoke was a charming village within commuting distance of London. It was the real deal—a well-preserved medieval town that even the bright, shiny new Tesco and the curry takeaway on the outskirts of the city couldn't spoil. The quaint cobblestoned streets were the delight of tourists even if they were a nuisance to the residents who found them rough going in any footwear other than thick-soled walking shoes.

Buildings of brick worn over the years to a rosy hue followed a bend in the road until they petered out and gave way to a narrow road bordered by hedgerows that cut through the grassy green fields beyond and into the countryside.

Penelope found the town enchanting. She felt as if she

had stepped into a storybook and even the inconveniences didn't bother her—WiFi that was spotty at best, narrow streets instead of wide modern roads, an absence of large chain stores and shopping malls save the Tesco that had opened in recent years.

The Open Book was equally enchanting. It was fusty and musty in the best possible way with books spilling willy-nilly from the shelves and arranged according to Mabel Morris, the proprietor's, unique shelving system, which Penelope soon discovered made finding a volume more of a treasure hunt than the usual cut-and-dried affair.

There was a low ceiling crisscrossed with wooden beams and a large diamond-paned front window where Penelope could imagine Charles Dickens's newly published *A Christmas Carol* might have been displayed while men in greatcoats and women in long dresses walked up and down the sidewalk outside, occasionally peering through the glass at the array of books.

Penelope negotiated the roundabout at the top of the high street and was admiring a red sweater in the window of the Knit Wit Shop when a horn blaring close by made her jump.

She returned her attention to the road and was horrified to see another car coming straight at her. She jerked the steering wheel, overcorrected, bumped up over the curb, slammed on her brakes, and came to a stop within an inch of a cement planter filled with bright orange and yellow mums.

Her heart was beating hard, her palms were sweaty, and there was a haze in front of her eyes.

The other car, a Ford, had stopped in the middle of the road and the driver was now standing next to it.

Penelope took a deep breath, opened her door, and got out.

"What do you mean driving down the wrong side of the street," she said, still slightly breathless, as she approached the other driver.

The driver looked amused. He wasn't handsome but had a kind, open face that was very appealing. He was an inch or two shorter than Penelope's six feet. Penelope had sprouted up early and there had been hopes that she would follow in her mother's and sister's footsteps to model; but although she was attractive enough, the camera didn't love her the way it did them. Besides, Penelope had no interest in parading around having her picture taken.

The fellow still looked amused. She knew she needed to rein in her indignation but it was her default setting and not easy.

"You scared me half to death," she said, pushing her glasses back up her nose with her finger.

"You're American," the fellow said. He had a slight Irish lilt to his voice.

Penelope raised her chin slightly. "Yes." She was about to say *what of it* when a horn honking made her jump.

A line of cars had formed behind the driver's Ford Cortina and a red VW Golf was attempting to pull around it.

Penelope's hand flew to her mouth as the realization hit her. "*I* was on the wrong side of the road," she said in a horrified voice.

"Exactly."

"I'm so sorry. I forgot . . . I thought . . ." Penelope stuttered to a halt. "I'm so terribly sorry. You're not hurt . . . or anything . . . are you?" She swayed slightly.

"I'm fine," the fellow said, his face creasing in concern. "But I'm worried about you."

"I'll be okay." Penelope took a deep breath. "It's only that I think I forgot to eat lunch."

It used to drive Penelope's sister crazy that she had to constantly watch her diet to maintain a slim figure, while Penelope could go a whole day without even thinking about food, then devour a meal worthy of a linebacker and still never gain an ounce.

"As long as you're sure . . ."

Penelope waved at him. "I'll be fine." She gestured toward the cars lined up down the road. "You'd better get going. That mob looks ready to attack you."

He smiled. "I guess I'd better."

Mabel Morris, whose Miss Marple–like appearance and demeanor belied her former career as an MI6 analyst, was behind the counter when Penelope pushed open the door to the bookstore.

She was all rounded curves and had fluffy white hair that tended to want to go every which way and pale powdery skin. Her blue eyes, however, had depths that suggested she wasn't unacquainted with tragedy and the seamier side of life.

"My sainted aunt," she said when she saw Penelope, "you look like you could use a good strong cup of tea."

"A shot of whiskey is more like it," Penelope said as she slumped against the counter. "Not that I'm in the habit of drinking in the middle of the day."

"This is strictly medicinal." Mabel pulled a bottle of Jameson and a glass from under the counter. She poured out a generous splash of whiskey and handed it to Penelope. "Drink up and then tell me what's having you look like Hamlet's father's ghost."

Penelope tossed back the whiskey and sighed as the warmth traced a path down her throat, to her stomach, and out to her limbs. She felt her shoulders and neck relax and her agitated breathing slow.

"I very nearly had an accident," she said, putting her glass down on the counter.

Mabel inclined her head toward the glass. "Another?"

Penelope shook her head. "Not on an empty stomach."

"You haven't eaten?" Mabel looked alarmed.

"I'll be fine," Penelope reassured her. "Thank goodness the other fellow was able to stop in time."

"What happened?"

Penelope sighed. "I'd like to say it was the other driver's fault, but I'm afraid I forgot where I was and ended up on the wrong side of the road." She felt her face color. She didn't like making mistakes.

"This is how many near misses now?" Mabel turned and put both hands palms down on the counter. "Maybe you should consider giving up the car. You can walk to the Open Book and if you need to go any farther than that, you can hire a taxi."

"That's very tempting," Penelope said, briefly reliving the horror of seeing another car headed straight at her. She raised her chin. "But I'm determined to nail this driving on the other side of the road if it's the last thing I do."

Mabel raised an eyebrow. "That's what has me worried— that it will one day *be* the last thing you do."

Gladys Watkins wandered up to the counter. She handed over a copy of romance novelist Charlotte Davenport's latest, *The Fire in My Bosom,* which featured a rather long-haired, bare-chested man on the cover and a damsel whose look of considerable distress seemed to match Gladys's own.

"I can't begin to imagine what the queen thinks of it," Gladys said as Mabel dropped some coins into her outstretched palm. "I imagine the poor thing is simply beside herself."

"One can't quite imagine the queen being beside herself," Mabel said, as she turned toward the register and ripped off the receipt. "She's made of sterner stuff than that."

"That's certainly true," India Culpepper said. She'd casually sidled up to the counter in order to join the conversation. "What with all that nonsense about Charles and Camilla she's had to endure. You know, stiff upper lip and all, that's her majesty's motto."

"Yes, no doubt that's embroidered on the throw pillows in the drawing room at Buckingham Palace," Mabel said dryly.

"High time the Duke of Upper Chumley-on-Stoke settled down," Gladys said, her brow furrowed fiercely. "Driving up and down the high street in that sports car of his and getting drunk at the Book and Bottle causing no end of embarrassment to the royal family. He's very nearly forty after all."

"It's the red hair." India nodded sagely. "Everyone knows gingers are bound for trouble. Comes from his father's side. His great-grandfather was known to cheat at cards and"—she lowered her voice—"run around with loose women."

Penelope frowned. "Oh, pooh. That's an old wives' tale. Redheads aren't any more prone to getting into trouble than anyone else."

India looked far from convinced.

Penelope quashed the sudden desire to dye her brown hair red to prove them all wrong—although she was hardly the right person to challenge their assumption. Her father had often said that trouble was her middle name.

"But an American!" Gladys said, clutching her book even more tightly to her ample bosom and piercing Penelope with a laser-like stare.

Penelope stood up taller and straightened her shoulders. "Americans have become quite civilized, you know. We don't live in covered wagons anymore."

Gladys sniffed. She was as round as an apple with a ruddy complexion and large, guileless blue eyes.

"I agree with Gladys," India said, looking quite surprised that for once she and Gladys found themselves on the same page. "Most unsuitable. Of course, Arthur is barely in the line of succession, but *still*." She said that last as if it was her final word on the subject and *that was that*.

India was *to the manor born* as the saying goes, and even though the family fortune had slipped through numerous fingers before reaching her in a significantly diminished amount, she comported herself as the aristocrat she considered herself to be.

"And not just an American," Gladys was continuing, "but Charlotte Davenport—an American romance novelist." She said that last as if it left a bad taste in her mouth.

India stared rather pointedly at the book in Gladys's hand, but the significance of India's glance was lost on Gladys.

"Charlotte Davenport is actually quite a lovely person," Pen said firmly.

Gladys's eyes goggled. "You've met her?"

"As a matter of fact, I have," Pen said. "It was at a writers' conference—my first. I was positively terrified and Charlotte very graciously took me under her wing. She was already a bestselling author and my book hadn't even come out yet. I was scheduled on a panel she was moderating—I don't even remember what the topic was but I do remember being horribly nervous." Penelope shuddered to think about it. "I developed a sudden case of stage fright when someone in the audience asked me a question and Charlotte managed to coax an answer out of me."

"Still . . ." India let the word hang in the air.

Mabel turned to Penelope and winked. "How is the book coming? Do tell us."

Penelope suddenly found three pairs of eyes trained on her. She was more than grateful for the change of subject, but she really wished it had been changed to something other than her nearly nonexistent book.

"It's coming," she said as firmly as possible. "I just need to find a reason to compel my main character, Annora, to go against all her best instincts and search this creepy castle basement alone in order to find a chest that's hidden down there."

Penelope thought of some of the pickles she'd gotten herself into growing up—climbing a tree and then not being able to get down, sneaking out her bedroom window the time she was grounded and falling off the roof and breaking her ankle, hitchhiking home her freshman year in college with a knife she'd taken from the cafeteria for protection—but even she knew better than to go into a basement alone with a killer on the loose.

"That's a tough one," Mabel said.

Penelope nodded. "Tell me about it! I can't have a heroine who is TSTL."

This time three sets of eyebrows were raised in unison.

"Too stupid to live," Penelope explained. "It's the sort of thing that makes a reader want to throw the book across the room."

"Quite." India fingered the yellowing pearls at her neck.

Penelope looked at her watch. "Ladies, it's almost time for our meeting of the Worthington Fest marketing committee. Shall we sit down?"

"Regina's not here yet," Gladys looked around as if expecting Regina to magically appear in a puff of smoke. "She's always late." She made a sour face.

"Let's get settled. I am sure Regina will be along shortly."

Penelope herded everyone to the table and chairs Mabel had set up in a cozy nook at the back of the store. Penelope used it for her writing group although her book group tended to array themselves in the mismatched overstuffed chairs and sofa that Mabel had also furnished the nook with.

The Open Book was to have a stall at the fest, and Penelope had offered to head the marketing committee with the help of India and Gladys. Regina Bosworth was the chairwoman of the fest itself.

"Shall we start without Regina?" India said, looking around the table for confirmation.

"Let's give her a few more minutes," Penelope said decisively.

It was now nearly ten minutes past the hour. Penelope opened her mouth to begin the meeting, but just then a voice rang out from behind one of the stacks.

"I'm here. I'm coming."

Regina rounded the corner, flapping her hands furiously. "So sorry, ladies, couldn't be helped. I've had such a busy morning. There's masses to get through yet before the Worthington Fest opens tomorrow. The Duke of Upper Chumley-on-Stoke had me positively running off my feet."

Penelope noticed India roll her eyes. Hardly anyone referred to the duke by his title—around the village he was Arthur Worthington or simply Worthington and was often greeted familiarly by the patrons of the Book and Bottle, where he was known to regularly pony up for a round or two, as *Worthington, old chap.*

He and India were vaguely related. Penelope couldn't remember how, but she thought it was through India's mother's line. Of course, while India lived in somewhat straitened circumstances in a cottage on the grounds of the estate, Worthington had inherited the castle itself along with a substantial amount of money.

Regina took her seat. She straightened the Hermès scarf at her neck—the queen had one just like it, she never failed to point out—opened her Louis Vuitton handbag, and spread out her things—an expensive notebook with an embossed leather cover and a blue lacquered Mont Blanc fountain pen.

"Now, Penelope," Regina said in an officious tone, "would you like to make your report?" She folded her hands on the table in front of her.

India and Gladys turned to Penelope expectantly.

"You've all seen the banners along the high street," Penelope began and the others nodded. "We've placed posters in all the shops along the high street as well."

Gladys nodded. "We have one in our window."

Gladys's husband owned the Pig in a Poke, Upper Chumley-on-Stoke's butcher shop.

"And Regina was brave enough to volunteer to be on our local BBC radio station to talk up the fest," Penelope said. "Brava, Regina."

"As if she would have turned that opportunity down," India whispered to Penelope.

Regina looked around the table and beamed at them. "Thank you. Thank you." She cast her eyes down demurely. "And," she said, pausing dramatically, "our little fest has been written up in the *Sun.*"

Gladys gasped and clasped her hands to her chest. India looked equally startled. Stories from their little corner of the world rarely made it into the national papers.

Regina preened. "Gordon—that's my husband," she said to Penelope, "places a lot of ads with the *Sun* for his business. He pulled some strings and well . . ." Regina batted her eyelashes.

She reached into her purse, pulled out a copy of a newspaper, and placed it on the table. She thumbed it open to the fifth page and tapped a headline with a crimson-manicured fingernail.

"Here it is. 'Upper Chumley-on-Stoke to hold its annual Worthington Fest on Saturday. Hosted by the Duke of Upper Chumley-on-Stoke and his American fiancée, the fest is an annual event'—well, you can read the rest yourselves." She turned the paper around so the others could see.

A stock photo of the duke and Charlotte Davenport taken at some other event was included with the article. Penelope had seen Worthington from a distance once or twice as he sped through the village in his vintage Aston Martin but had never gotten a close-up look at him.

He had a roguish air about him—in the photograph at least—with blue eyes that twinkled beneath thick, straight brows and a mouth that looked to be curved in a perpetual half smile—as if he was privy to an especially delicious secret.

Charlotte looked every inch the duchess she was about to become in a pale pink dress with a full skirt and lace bodice. Her blond hair was in a sleek bun at the nape of her neck and she carried a tiny clutch bag in one hand. Her other hand—with its four-carat diamond solitaire—was laid lightly on the duke's arm.

"I still don't know why Worthington chose that woman," Gladys said, tapping Charlotte's picture.

"Well," Regina said, raising an eyebrow, "they're not married yet, are they? Anything could happen."

Regina folded the newspaper back up and tucked it in her handbag, and they went back to the business at hand, finishing up their meeting half an hour later. Regina gathered her things together and immediately took off at a trot, yelling over her shoulder that the duke was waiting for her and she simply mustn't be late. Everyone stood in a cluster as they listened for the sound of the door closing behind her.

"That woman becomes more insufferable by the day," India said. "Nouveau riche," she declared as if that explained it.

"I don't know why Worthington chose her to be the chairwoman of the fest," Gladys grumbled, her expression stormy.

"Quite," India said. "I understand that competition for the position was dreadfully fierce among the ladies of Chumley."

"She probably badgered him until he cried uncle," Penelope said.

India made a sound like a snort.

"I wonder what she meant about Worthington and Charlotte not being married yet," Penelope said. "It almost sounded like she was hinting at something. As if she knew something."

Gladys laughed. "What could Regina possibly know about it?"

"I don't know." India frowned. "But Regina collects secrets the way some people collect stamps. And she's not afraid to make use of them either."

TWO

It was a minute or two after five o'clock when India and Gladys left the Open Book.

"I'll go hang the closed sign, shall I?" Mabel said as Penelope sank into one of the Open Book's armchairs.

Penelope glanced out the window. Traffic on the high street was slowing down; the sun was setting and dusk was beginning to descend, creating pockets of shadow in the doorways and under the trees. The streetlights were winking on and nightlights twinkled in most the shops across the street.

"Here we go then," Figgy said, wheeling over a tray from the Teapot, the Open Book's tea shop. A china pot swathed in a flowery quilted cozy sat on top along with three cups, three saucers, and a plate of cheese and pickle and egg salad sandwiches. On the lower level of the cart were delectable-looking slices of orange and cardamom cake fanned out on a platter.

Lady Fiona Innes-Goldthorpe, as she had been chris-
tened, had had the nickname of Figgy bestowed upon her
at a Girl Guide camp when her mother had marked her
uniforms and towels with her initials—*F.I.G.* She and Penelope had hit it off immediately.

When Mabel had first seen the two of them with their
heads together she'd muttered, "Uh-oh, here comes trouble."

Figgy had black hair that was spiked with gel on top,
two earrings in each ear, a stud in her nose, and a tattoo
of a peace symbol by her ankle. She had been doing a bit
of catering and had dreamed of opening a tea shop. Mabel
had offered to rent her space inside the Open Book. Everyone agreed that there was no better combination than a
nice cuppa and a good juicy novel.

"So how is the book coming?" Figgy said as she poured
out the tea.

Penelope made a face. "I suppose you could say it's
coming."

"It should be quiet enough for you," Mabel said, "now
that Ruth Goldstone and that crazy Chihuahua of hers
moved out of the place next door."

Mabel had loaned Penelope a small cottage a bit of a
ways down the high street but within walking distance of
the Open Book.

"Oh, it's quiet enough," Penelope said.

She was used to her walk-up on East Eighty-seventh
Street in New York City, where cars roared down the
street all night long, people shouted to each other at two
o'clock in the morning as they headed home from the
bars, and dogs barked whenever the mood struck them.

Figgy handed out plates and Penelope helped herself to
a cheese and pickle sandwich, a combination much be-

loved by the British and which she was slowly coming to appreciate herself.

Mabel looked over at Penelope. "How are you getting on, then? Settling in, are you?"

Penelope laughed. "Sometimes I feel a little bit like an exhibit in a museum or a rare animal in a zoo. People seem to find Americans terribly exotic. That surprises me because I always thought our two countries had so much in common." Penelope popped the last bite of her sandwich into her mouth. "I mean, we've given you fast food and you've given us David Bowie and the *Great British Baking Show*." She made a face. "I suppose it's hardly a fair trade." She smiled. "I don't blame you for being resentful."

"You're a novelty, that's all," Figgy said. "Most of the residents of Chum have been here for generations. Some of them have never been to London even though it's only a little over an hour on the train. There isn't much diversity. Give them time to get to know you."

"They certainly seem to resent the fact that Worthington is marrying an American. They almost make it sound as if she's some sort of alien from outer space."

Mabel laughed. "They're just jealous. Every mother of girls for miles around has fantasized that their daughter would be the one to capture Worthington's heart. They'd be grousing just as much if he'd picked someone from London or Cornwall or Wales."

"That's certainly true," Figgy said as she nibbled on the corner of an egg salad sandwich. "My mother still harbors the hope that I'll snag someone with a title. When she heard I was going to be living in the same town as Arthur Worthington, it only added fuel to her fire. I wouldn't be surprised if she has a whole trousseau tucked away somewhere for me embroidered with *Duchess of Upper Chumley-on-Stoke*. She was positively gutted when she read about his engagement in the *Sun*." She made a sad face. "I don't know what she's going to think when she finds out about Derek."

"I thought your parents knew about Derek," Mabel said.

"They do." Figgy began shredding the edge of her napkin. "Only I sort of glossed over a few things when I told them about him. Like the fact that his father is Pakistani and his last name is Khan."

"So what?" Penelope said. "It's your life."

"And Derek is a lovely person." Mabel reached for another slice of cake.

Figgy blew out a huge breath and her bangs fluttered in the air for a second.

"He is. And it certainly doesn't matter to me. But my parents?" She rolled her eyes.

"I thought he was terribly charming," Penelope said. "I'm sure your parents will love him."

"I hope so," Figgy said, but her tone was glum.

Mabel stretched out her legs. "Tomorrow is the big day. I hope everything goes well."

"No reason it shouldn't," Penelope said, helping herself to another sandwich. She'd suddenly realized she was starving. "We've got the books all packed and ready to go. The stalls have already been set up on the Worthington grounds, and the weather reporter is predicting sunny skies and exceptionally mild temperatures."

"I've ordered another shipment of Charlotte Davenport's latest," Mabel said. "I should imagine we'll sell all our current stock at the fest tomorrow. Nothing like being engaged to a duke to turn your book into a bestseller," she said dryly.

"To be fair," Pen said, "Charlotte was a bestselling writer long before she ever became engaged to Arthur Worthington." She turned to Figgy. "I met Charlotte at a writers' conference and thought she was charming."

"I've met her, too. She did a book signing here," Figgy said. She turned to Mabel. "Remember? I agree—she was perfectly lovely—so gracious and charming. I can see why Worthington has fallen for her."

"Apparently the queen was rather taken with her as well, much to everyone's surprise." Mabel crumpled up her napkin and dropped it on her plate. "I understand she gave her blessing to the match quite willingly—not that Worthington needed it, but he respects her opinion." She smiled, deepening the crinkles around her eyes. "Of course, Worthington is a favorite of hers. The queen always did have a soft spot for bad boys."

"Regina hinted that the wedding might not come off," Penelope said, wetting her finger and picking up the crumbs on her plate. "And India said something about Regina collecting secrets."

Mabel looked startled. "I can't imagine what kind of secret Regina could be privy to, but she'd better not do anything to interfere. Worthington is utterly besotted with Charlotte. He wouldn't take kindly to it."

Penelope enjoyed the crisp autumn breeze coming in through her partially opened window as she drove down the high street, which was quiet with that hush peculiar to small towns after dark. Lights were on in the

Book and the Bottle however, and when the door swung open, a wave of animated voices rushed out.

Penelope pulled up to the curb in front of the cottage where she was staying, parked the car, and patted herself on the back for having traversed the quarter mile from the Open Book without once wandering across the line onto the other side—the wrong side—of the road.

The cottage was quintessentially English—covered in ivy and with two rooms up and two down. It was small but Penelope adored its coziness—the enormous open fireplace in the living room, flanked by bookcases, the rough-hewn beams in the low ceiling and the bay window that afforded her a view through the lace curtains of the comings and goings on the high street.

She felt a sense of calm and ease that loosened her tense shoulders as she opened the front door. A loud meow greeted her and Mrs. Danvers, her tuxedo cat, rushed from the shadows to weave in and out between Penelope's legs.

Penelope bent down to scratch her back, and Mrs. Danvers arched luxuriously beneath Penelope's fingers.

Penelope turned the light on in the kitchen, plugged in the electric teakettle, and grabbed a mug from the set of sturdy crockery stored in an old wooden dresser against one wall.

She'd always been a coffee person—setting her coffee maker so that it would begin brewing the minute her alarm went off—but since living in England she'd discovered the calming and restorative benefits of properly brewed tea.

Mabel had been appalled the first time she'd seen Penelope casually plunking a tea bag in a mug of micro-waved hot water and had shown her the correct way to make a good pot of English breakfast or Earl Grey.

The kitchen was cozy with an ancient Aga belching warmth, a rough farmhouse table, and a row of herbs in terra-cotta pots blooming in front of the window.

While the water for her tea heated, Penelope went upstairs to get her laptop. She had a small bedroom upstairs, a bathroom and a second room that was barely bigger than a closet and which she used as a sort of study, although more often than not she set up shop in the living room in front of the fire.

She went back downstairs, Mrs. Danvers by her side, and out to the kitchen. She took the kettle from the counter, poured a bit of hot water into her mug, swirled it around, and dumped it out. Now that her mug was nicely warmed, she filled it with water and dropped in a tea bag to let it steep.

The girl from the village who came in to clean had laid logs in the fireplace. Penelope lit a match and held it to the pile of kindling. It burst into flame and soon the logs began to catch. She stood for a moment enjoying the warmth.

Then, with a certain amount of reluctance, she fired up her laptop. She still hadn't solved the dilemma of getting her heroine Annora to go down to the deserted castle cellar.

Maybe if Annora heard something—something that compelled her to go investigate? Mrs. Danvers jumped up onto the couch and snuggled into the crook of Penelope's arm. The cat then reached out a velvet paw and tapped the space bar on Penelope's laptop.

That was it! Penelope thought. What if Annora heard a cat crying? Surely she would feel compelled to investigate. The kitten might be trapped or injured, and Annora was a girl with a kind heart who would hardly leave a poor helpless animal to fend for itself and possibly even starve to death.

Penelope began typing furiously, her spirits rising with every stroke of the keys. There was nothing like solving a problem in your work in progress to lift your mood.

She was nearly finished with the scene when a ping announced a text message on her phone. Penelope stifled a sigh of frustration. She should ignore it and plow on with her work.

But she couldn't.

She pulled her phone from the pocket of her sweater and clicked on the message.

Hey babe, she read, do you miss me yet? LOL.

Penelope made a face. It was Miles Smythe, her on-again, off-again boyfriend. Her sister, whose husband was a stockbroker and who lived in an enormous and expensively decorated house in Greenwich, Connecticut, couldn't understand why Penelope didn't work harder at her relationship with Miles. After all, in her sister's words, *he was quite the catch.*

Miles was, to be fair, the manager of a highly successful hedge fund, made a salary nearing seven figures, lived in a penthouse apartment in Chelsea, played a mean game of racquetball at the New York Athletic Club, and had season tickets to the Yankees.

Penelope could see how her sister might think Miles was a more appropriate partner than the circus performer she'd nearly run away with when she was sixteen or the tattoo artist she'd taken up with in college.

But despite dating Miles for nearly a year now, Penelope remained somewhat ambivalent about his charms. She liked him well enough, but his idea of a good time was a cocktail party in the Hamptons with all the right people and hers was curling up on the sofa with a good book and a carton of Chinese takeout. Her sister insisted that opposites worked well together in a relationship, the one bringing yin to the other's yang, but Penelope wasn't so sure.

She had hoped that this separation would help her to decide one way or the other. Unfortunately it seemed as if absence was not making the heart grow fonder. As a matter of fact, it was more a case of out of sight, out of mind.

She texted with Miles for several minutes and when he asked how the book was coming, after sending numerous texts telling her about how much money he'd made trading stocks that day, Penelope told him it was coming along fine—that the change of scenery had been just the thing she'd needed.

When the exchange ended, she wondered why she had lied to Miles. Why hadn't she told him about her struggles with her manuscript? *Because you know he was only asking out of politeness*, a little voice inside her head whispered. *He really doesn't care.*

She ought to break it off with him and put him out of his misery. Not that he was miserable—it was more like the thought of him was making *her* miserable. Her fingers hovered over her cell. She couldn't do it. Breaking up with someone via text would hardly get Miss Manners's approval. She'd have to brave him in person.

She'd do it the next time she saw him. Whenever that would be.

Penelope went back to her manuscript, but the texts from Miles had ruined her mood. She glanced at the word count at the bottom of the screen and shuddered. At this rate, she'd never make her deadline.

She was about to shut down her computer when she decided to check her e-mail. There were the usual sales notices from stores she frequented, spam from a strange man in Nigeria claiming to have money for her, and an ad for dentures, which she hoped she would never need.

She was about to breathe a sigh of relief when a new e-mail popped up. It was from her publisher. She felt her stomach drop. Maybe it was just her editor saying hello?

Penelope positioned her cursor over the e-mail, closed her eyes, and clicked open. She took a deep breath, counted to ten and opened her eyes.

The e-mail was, indeed, from her editor. Only she wasn't asking after her health or asking how was the weather in England.

Bonjour,

Although I suppose it's already evening there. Checking in to make sure you're on track to meet your deadline. Marketing has a whole campaign ready to go and it's epic. Color me excited! How is England, by the way? XOXO Bettina

Penelope glanced at her word count again and felt her stomach drop even further.

THREE

❧

Worthington House, as it was officially called, was actually a castle but in typical English understatement was known by the more diminutive term of *house*. It was situated on a slight rise above Upper Chumley-on-Stoke and was a proper castle with turrets, towers, lookouts, and all manner of things save an actual moat. The moat had been filled in several centuries earlier and turned into a vast, broad lawn where a huge white tent now stood.

Penelope sensed the buzz of activity even as she turned into the drive leading to the car park behind Worthington House. The car park had been installed to accommodate the tourists who paid nineteen pounds each (twelve pounds for the disabled) to tour the house's main floor.

Today Worthington House was open to all those who had paid their ten pounds to enter the fest grounds. The proceeds would go toward the beautification of Chumley's high street with items like boxwood wreaths hung from the lampposts at Christmas and baskets dripping with flowers in the spring and summer.

Penelope managed to squeeze her ancient MINI Cooper in between a behemoth Range Rover and a 1957 Aston Martin with a minimum amount of sweat and a maximum amount of swearing. She eased open her door—the spaces were close—and slid out. She locked the doors and headed toward the fest grounds.

As the writer in residence at the Open Book, she had been invited to give a talk in the Worthington House great hall on the *Castle of Otranto*, a literary classic and one of the first and finest Gothic novels. The vast Worthington collection included a signed first edition and would be on display in the Worthington House library during the fest.

A feeling of unease gnawed at Penelope's stomach. She hadn't made much headway on her own novel that morning—a mere five hundred words of which she'd ultimately deleted over two hundred.

Her talk wasn't scheduled until just before lunch, and in the meantime, she would be helping out at the Open Book's stall on the front lawn of Worthington House. Mabel had selected a number of novels to sell at their booth: bestsellers, tried-and-true classics, crime fiction, and of course the latest romance by Charlotte Davenport.

The sun was bright and Penelope was glad to duck into the shadows under the tent. Volunteers were bustling about with great purpose, setting up tables and bringing in merchandise. The vicar's wife was putting out the baby items including booties, hats, and receiving blankets that she had spent the winter knitting to sell at the fest.

Gladys Watkins and her husband had a booth, too. They were selling Gladys's homemade Cornish pasties.

They were always a huge hit and people were known to stand in line for over an hour to buy one.

Regina ricocheted around the grounds like a ball in a pinball machine. She smiled benignly at the vicar's wife's table as if she was bestowing the royal warrant, raised a well-plucked eyebrow in disapproval at poor Gladys who had already managed to soil her apron, and flapped her arms at another vendor whose preparation was lagging in Regina's estimation.

Half the tent was taken up with a makeshift tearoom. Figgy had set up tables and chairs, and a line run from the house provided power for her electric teakettles. Several carts—filled with scones, cucumber sandwiches, and fairy cakes on plates festooned with paper doilies—sat at the ready.

Penelope waved to Figgy, who was wrestling with a large cardboard box of sugar packets.

She put the cardboard box down on a table and waved back. Penelope began to walk in her direction.

"Gorgeous weather, isn't it?" Figgy said. "One year it positively poured cats and dogs—ruined the whole day."

"Girls," Regina called and they both jumped.

Figgy groaned. "Here comes Regina. She thinks she's so la-di-da, but she's merely pretentious."

"This is no time for a chin wag," Regina crowed as she reached them. "The gates will be opening any minute now and everything must be in tip-top shape. We don't want to disappoint the duke, do we?"

Penelope and Figgy made exaggerated sad faces. "No," they murmured in unison.

Regina glanced around the tearoom and smiled broadly. "You've done a lovely job, Figgy. Absolutely lovely. Very elegant."

"Just when you've decided she's absolutely odious," Figgy said as Regina walked away, "she says something nice and makes you think maybe she isn't so bad after all." She looked after Regina. "She once bought a silk scarf for Violet, the vicar's wife. Violet was chuffed to bits to have something so nice. She usually buys her clothes at Oxfam or jumble sales."

Penelope watched as Regina grabbed the arm of a man walking by. She seemed to be giving him what for. He had a hangdog expression that made Penelope feel quite sorry for him.

"Uh-oh," she said, pointing to the man. "Looks like someone has gotten Regina's dander up." The man had a bristly mustache that made Penelope think of a British army officer from colonial days.

"Poor thing," Figgy said. "That's Gordon Bosworth, Regina's husband. Regina leads him around by the nose. I don't know why he puts up with it."

"It does look like she's got him by the short hairs," Penelope said as she watched Regina shake her finger in front of her husband's face.

"Regina desperately wants him to be something he's not. He's made pots of money with his company—something to do with supplying uniforms for factory workers—but that's not good enough for her. She imagines herself married to someone who works in the city or is a barrister and a member of the Inns of Court. She feels she's been quite ill used that she can't call herself *Lady* Bosworth."

Penelope watched as Regina dragged her husband away. She turned to Figgy.

"Will Worthington be here?"

"I'm sure he'll make an appearance at some point.

With Charlotte on his arm, no doubt. That should really thrill the crowd. They ought to put him behind a curtain and charge fifty pence a peek."

Penelope laughed and glanced toward the gates to Worthington House. She cocked her head in that direction. "Looks like the hordes are about to be let in. We'd better man our positions."

"Yes," Figgy said. "Brace yourself for the assault."

P enelope spent the morning helping Mabel at the Open Book's stall. It had been busy and they'd completely sold out of *The Fire in My Bosom.*

Penelope glanced at her watch. "It's almost time for my talk."

"You go on, then," Mabel said, tucking a wayward strand of hair behind her ear. "I'll manage just fine."

Penelope felt like a fish swimming upstream as she made her way through the crowd, which seemed to be flowing in the direction of the tearoom, anxious for a cup of tea and a bite to eat.

She headed toward the house and around to the side where visitors had been directed to enter for their tours. India was at the door, waiting to take her turn as a guide.

"Ready for your talk, are you?" she said as she led Penelope into the great hall.

Penelope's jaw dropped in awe. The room was enormous and quite forbidding.

Colorful heraldic banners hung from poles along the walls and on ropes from the vaulted ceiling. Logs were laid in an open fireplace large enough to accommodate an ox, and Penelope imagined a fire would be most welcome even during the summer. A chill emanated from the black-and-white flagstone floor and a draft leaked into the room from around the wavy glass in the high arched windows.

The heels of India's pumps tapped briskly against the floor as she shepherded Penelope through the great hall, down a corridor lined with dark oil portraits of past Worthington family members, and into the library.

It was another forbiddingly large room lined with bookcases that reached nearly to the ceiling. A stone fireplace was against the far wall and stiff-looking upholstered chairs were scattered about. A dark oil painting of a bloody battle and a man skewering an enemy soldier with a sword hung over the fireplace.

Penelope looked around and shuddered. "It's hard to imagine curling up in your pajamas with a good book or tuning in to the latest episode of *Dancing with the Stars* in this room."

India gave a polite laugh. "Worthington's living quarters are far more comfortable and far more modern. I heard he used Ben Pentreath who did Apartment 1A in Kensington Palace for the Duke and Duchess of Cambridge. Although I should imagine that Miss Davenport will want to put her own stamp on things when she officially becomes the Duchess of Upper Chumley-on-Stoke."

Folding chairs were arranged in neat rows, and in the center of the room was a glass case on a stand. Penelope peered into the lit interior where the Worthington copy of *The Castle of Otranto* was reverently displayed on a ruby-red velvet cloth.

India walked toward the front of the room. "We've put the lectern here. Will that be all right? Or would you rather have it elsewhere?"

"That's fine," Penelope reassured her as she took off her glasses and polished them on her shirttail.

The frames were large, square, and a dark tortoise. Penelope's sister had encouraged her to get contact lenses but Penelope didn't like the idea of poking herself in the eye with a piece of plastic. Besides, she thought the glasses made her look more serious.

She took out her notes to go over them one more time. She was confident of her material—less confident in her ability to deliver it. It was one thing to speak to a group of Gothic novel enthusiasts and quite another to keep a more diverse audience entertained.

Soon the first few people began to shuffle into the room. Penelope glanced at her watch. Five more minutes. She hoped she'd have a bigger crowd than this.

A minute later a whole group of people arrived and began to choose seats. Penelope recognized the headmistress of the Oakwood School for Girls, a boarding school just outside of Upper Chumley. She was a frequent visitor to the Open Book.

Slowly the rows of chairs filled with people, leaving only a vacant chair here and there. Penelope smiled at the audience, spread out her notes, cleared her throat, and began.

"*The Castle of Otranto* by Horace Walpole is considered to be the first example of the Gothic novel," she said. "Walpole was the fourth Earl of Orford and had a very interesting career."

Penelope was just beginning to work up a head of steam when a frantic scream rang out.

Along with everyone else in the room, she turned toward the door, in the direction from which the sound had come. Within seconds there was another scream and the sound of footsteps thundering down the corridor. The noise was cut off, became a gurgle, and finally ended in silence, which was almost as startling as the scream had been.

Everyone was catching their breath when Gladys hurtled into the room. Her normally ruddy complexion had been drained white. She stared at the audience gathered for Penelope's talk, her milky eyes wide and bulging.

"There's a body," she said finally, her breath coming in gasps. "I went down to the basement to get some more pasties from the freezer the duke is letting us use for the fest. I couldn't hardly believe me eyes." She burst into tears.

Penelope managed to hide her own shock at Gladys's announcement and instead went over to her and put her arm around her. "You poor thing."

"There's a body," Gladys said, giving a loud hiccough. "It's her. She's dead."

And she burst into tears again.

"She's going to faint!" someone yelled.

Penelope took Gladys by the arm and lowered her into a chair.

"Put your head between your knees," India commanded, coming up behind Penelope.

Her tone of voice was bracing as if that would help Gladys pull herself together and stiffen her upper lip.

Penelope crouched down so that she was nearer to eye level with Gladys, patted her knee reassuringly, and looked up. "Can someone fetch a glass of water?"

She thought longingly of Mabel's bottle of Jameson tucked under the counter at the Open Book. That was what Gladys really needed.

A chair scraped against the floor as someone got up

and started toward the door. "There's a lemonade stand outside. Will that do?"

"A good strong cup of tea with plenty of sugar would do better," India said to the young man. "See if you can bring a cup, would you?"

She waved a hand at the young man and he took off at a trot.

Penelope wasn't sure what it was that Gladys had seen, but she was quite certain it couldn't have been a body. Whose body? And why on earth would there be a body in Worthington's cellar? Surely Gladys was imagining it.

"Maybe we should go check the basement ourselves?" Penelope hoped she wasn't being TSTL. She'd saved her protagonist Annora from that fate—was she heading into danger herself?

"Excellent idea," India said.

She appeared to be disappointed at not having thought of it herself.

"Follow me," India said as she swept toward the door.

Penelope followed in her wake. In spite of her bravado, she felt a quiver of unease that grew as India led the way down a corridor and to a heavy oak door set in the stone wall that led to the cellar.

She pulled it open.

"Do be careful. The stairs have been worn down over the centuries and are quite uneven."

The air became cooler and damper the lower they descended, and Penelope wished she had a sweater to drape over her shoulders. She was beginning to regret all the Stephen King books she'd read as a child under the covers with a flashlight when she was supposed to be sleeping.

The basement was surprisingly clean and well kept—no cobwebs hanging from the arches or dust blowing across the floor in the draft. It was well lit with electric lights in sconces along the walls and pendant lights hanging from the ceiling.

"Electricity was installed by the sixth Duke of Upper Chumley-on-Stoke in 1887," India said as they walked along. "And I believe it was Worthington's grandfather who installed the wine cellar," she said as they passed a recessed area where racks of wine were visible through a wrought iron grate. "Worthington himself is quite a connoisseur."

Penelope peered through the grate at the bottles. What she knew about wine could be summed up in two words—red and white. Whenever she bought a bottle for herself, she was more concerned with the numbers on the price tag than the year of the vintage.

"The kitchen used to be down here as well. Of course it was moved upstairs decades ago. Today's help wouldn't be content finding themselves working in the cellar. Back then, they were grateful to have a job, and now it's all protests about salaries and working conditions and who knows what else."

India took a step and suddenly slipped.

Penelope grabbed her arm. "Are you okay?"

"Quite, thank you. I seem to have stepped on something."

India bent down and picked up a small bead. She held it between her thumb and index finger.

"What is it?" Penelope said.

India put the bead in the palm of her hand. "It looks like a pearl. It's from a piece of jewelry belonging to some bygone Worthington ancestor no doubt." India tucked it into the pocket of her skirt. "No sense in leaving it on the floor where someone else might step on it and fall."

They continued their search, peering into all the corners and the darker recesses between the arches but still didn't see anything resembling a body unless you counted a suit of armor and even Gladys wasn't fanciful enough to have convinced herself that that was a human body, although Penelope took the precaution of lifting the visor and peering inside just to be sure.

"I wonder what it is Gladys mistook for a body," Penelope said as they stopped in front of a large walk-in freezer.

"I can't imagine," India said. "Nothing seems amiss." She frowned. "Is that door slightly ajar?" She pointed to the thin line of light outlining the edge of the freezer door and tut-tutted under her breath. "Gladys must not have shut it properly."

"I'll get it." Penelope stepped forward, put the flat of her hand against the door, and pushed. She turned toward India. "The door won't close. Something must be in the way."

She grabbed hold of the handle. The door was indeed somewhat ajar. She pulled it open all the way. The bright light inside the freezer made her blink for a moment and she didn't, at first, realize what she was looking at.

"Good heavens!" India exclaimed, her face suddenly drained white. She looked at Penelope. "It's Regina Bosworth. What on earth is she doing in the freezer?"

"I don't know," Penelope said, her voice quavering slightly. "But I do believe she's dead."

FOUR

꿍

S he can't be." India bent and patted Regina on the cheek. "Come on, Regina. Wake up. Are you feeling unwell? Have you fainted?" India gasped. "Is that blood?" She straightened up and staggered back a step, pointing at the blood pooled alongside Regina's body. "It looks as if Regina's been shot. How on earth . . . it must have been some sort of accident."

India's pale skin had turned even paler and her hands, with their brown spots and prominent blue veins, trembled uncontrollably.

Penelope felt her head swim and for a moment, the room appeared to be swirling around her. It made her feel sick to her stomach. She was grateful she hadn't eaten anything recently. She had anticipated all sorts of adventures in England—finding a dead body hadn't been one of them.

When the spinning sensation stopped and her stomach

settled down, Penelope began looking around. "But there's no gun," she said. "If she accidentally shot herself, there'd be a gun nearby, wouldn't there? It would have fallen from her hand when she collapsed."

"Yes, of course," India said. "You don't suppose . . ."

"Someone has to have shot her," Penelope said bluntly. "And then taken the gun away with them."

"That means . . . murder," India whispered, her voice quavering.

Penelope looked down at Regina's lifeless body crumpled in the freezer. She hadn't particularly liked the woman—Regina had been insufferably bossy, snobby, and opinionated—but certainly she didn't deserve to die like this. No one did.

Penelope broke out in a cold, clammy sweat. She started shivering and had to clench her teeth to keep them from chattering. It was one thing to read or even write about murder and quite another thing to come across a real dead body. Nothing could prepare you for that.

For a moment she and India were immobilized by shock and then they both started talking at once.

"We'd better—" India began.

"I think we should—" Penelope said at the same time.

India swayed slightly and Penelope looked at her in alarm.

"Are you okay?"

"Yes. Quite. A bit of a surprise that's all. One doesn't often find a corpse stuck in a freezer."

"We should call the police," Penelope said. She pulled her cell phone from her pocket, punched in the numbers, and crossed her fingers. She let out a sigh of relief when the call went through. She waited but the phone at the

other end rang and rang. Where was all that British efficiency, she wondered?

"There's no answer," she said to India. "Someone always answers nine-one-one calls."

"Is that what you dialed? Well, no wonder you're not
getting an answer. That's in America. Here we dial nine
nine nine for the police."

Penelope punched the numbers in on her cell, explained the situation to the dispatcher at the other end
when she answered, and then clicked off the call.

"They said someone would be here shortly."

"We'd better go upstairs, then," India said, giving Regina's body one last glance, "and make sure no one comes
down here and tramples the scene."

Penelope was startled. She didn't expect someone like
India to be conversant with police lingo and the words
sounded strange coming from her. People had hidden
depths, she reminded herself.

"It's probably best if we tell everyone there's been a
slight delay," India said, "and send them back to their seats.
I'm sure the police will want to speak to them or at least
take their names and addresses."

"I agree. And the less said about the incident the better."

"Yes. It's probably best if we simply say there's been
an accident." India shuddered. "I can't imagine the panic
if we mentioned the word *murder*."

A buzz of voices, sounding like a swarm of bees, rose
from the anxious crowd clustered in the hall when Penelope and India emerged from the cellar.

"There's been an accident," India announced in imperi-
ous tones that even the queen would have envied. "Nothing
to be alarmed about." She held up a hand as the crowd be-

gan to murmur in louder tones. "The authorities are on their way. There will be a slight delay in Miss Parish's talk. If everyone would please go back to their seats."

The crowd hesitated, whispering among themselves and shifting from foot to foot, until a young man in a navy blazer with a name tag pinned to his lapel came along and shooed them all back toward the room like a sheepdog herding its flock.

India looked around. "What's happened to Gladys? Surely the police will want to talk to her."

Violet Thatcher, the wife of the vicar of St. Andrew's, drifted toward them. She was thin to the point of being gaunt, with sparse curly hair and clothes that looked as if she'd put them together from a jumble sale, which she most likely had.

"Poor Gladys," she said when she reached them. "I got her a nice hot cup of tea but it was impossible to calm her. She was hysterical." Violet made a face. "She never did have much self-control. In the end, we decided it was best to summon the ambulance that Worthington had arranged to have stationed outside the fest in case of an emergency. They've taken Gladys to hospital. They assured me that they would be able to give her something there to soothe her nerves."

"Yes, of course," India said. "Quite. Excellent idea."

Penelope was amazed at how quickly India had regained her sangfroid. Leave it to the British to keep a stiff upper lip. She herself felt a bit wobbly in the knees. She would have liked to sit down, but if India could handle this, so could she. She didn't want to be seen as a namby-pamby American.

"I imagine they'll be sending Constable Cuthbert around," India said.

Penelope frowned. Surely they were going to need someone with more experience than a mere constable. Walking a beat was hardly preparation for dealing with a murder.

And the fact that he was named Cuthbert did little to convince her of his competence. The name brought a mental picture to mind of one of those roly-poly toys that popped back up every time you knocked it down. Penelope had barely formed the thought when a rotund man in a crisp blue uniform stepped somewhat hesitantly into the room. He was bald, with an impressive handlebar mustache and a belly that strained the buttons of his shirt. He smiled as he approached them and Penelope noticed he had a sizable gap between his two front teeth. It was as if the vision in her head had suddenly materialized.

"Good day, ladies," Cuthbert said, bowing slightly at the waist. His words came out with the hint of a whistle as air rushed through the space in his teeth. "I understand there's been some sort of accident in the cellar?"

"You might say that, yes," India said rather dryly. "I do think the situation calls for a detective, though."

"Detective Maguire should be along shortly." Cuthbert looked around. "Meanwhile, I'll guard the door to the cellar, shall I? Make sure no one tries to slip down there."

Constable Cuthbert plodded down the hall toward the cellar door. A few people were still milling around but when nothing more exciting happened, they soon became bored and went back to their seats in the library.

Penelope was beginning to wonder how much longer before the detective arrived when a man came walking down the hall toward them. Penelope squinted. He looked vaguely familiar but that didn't seem possible given that she knew so few people in Chumley. Perhaps she'd passed him on the street or stood in line in back of him at Tesco?

His face came into focus as he got closer and Penelope finally realized where she'd seen him before—standing next to his car after he'd had to slam on his brakes to avoid her MINI because she was driving down the wrong side of the road.

She felt her face begin to burn but forced herself to hold her chin up. Perhaps he wouldn't remember the incident or perhaps he wouldn't recognize her.

"You're the girl who nearly ran into me the other day," he said as he came up to them. "At least we're not meeting head on this time."

So much for that, Penelope thought.

"Is this another one of your victims?" He grinned and gestured toward the cellar door where Constable Cuthbert was patiently standing guard. He rubbed a hand over his face. "I'm sorry. That wasn't fair. I'm Detective Brodie Maguire." He held out his hand.

He wasn't a particularly tall man, but his hand was large and easily enveloped Penelope's own. His palm was warm and she realized that hers had turned to ice. He shook Penelope's hand, then turned to India and took hers.

He had light brown hair with a reddish tint that was close cropped on the sides but long enough to curl slightly on top and at his neck and a face that crinkled when he smiled. Penelope noticed again that, despite not being in the least bit handsome, he was a very attractive man.

She was also grateful for his presence. She was more than ready to hand everything over to the police and get herself a nice cup of strong tea—preferably spiked with something like Mabel's Jameson.

"I'm afraid I'm going to have to ask you to wait," he said, looking at Penelope and India. "I'd like to view the scene first and then I'll have some questions for you, if you don't mind." He frowned. "You did find the body, is that correct?"

"Not exactly," India said. "That would be Gladys. Gladys Watkins. Her husband is Bruce Watkins who owns the Pig in a Poke on the high street here in Chumley."

Maguire nodded. "I'll need to talk to her."

"I'm afraid she's been taken to hospital," India said.

Maguire looked alarmed. "Was she injured?"

"Not at all," India assured him. "She became hysterical and needed treatment." India's tone of voice made it clear that she herself would have stayed calm under similar circumstances.

"I see," Maguire said.

"We'll be waiting in the small office off the library if that's all right with you," India said. "We've kept everyone in the library in case you need to speak to them." She turned to Penelope. "Let's go sit down,"

Penelope had no objection to following India into the office, where she sank into one of the armchairs. A musty smell rose from the cushions and she fought back a sneeze.

"What's this I hear about a body?" Arthur Worthington suddenly strode into the room.

His hair was redder than in the pictures Penelope had seen of him and he looked every inch the English country gentleman in a tweed jacket with a mossy green sweater vest underneath.

India immediately jumped to her feet. She smoothed out her skirt.

"Regina Bosworth has been found shot in the cellar.

The police are here now. Constable Cuthbert is guarding the door and Detective Maguire is surveying the scene."

"Good heavens!" Worthington ran his hands through his hair. "Was it some sort of accident? You don't mean she's dead, do you?" He turned to India, a panicked look on his face.

"I'm afraid she is. There's no sign of the gun. It appears as if she may have been murdered."

"Murdered!" Worthington exploded. "I know the woman was an infernal pest but for someone to murder her . . ."

"She must have had enemies?" Penelope said.

Worthington whirled around, a curious look on his face.

"I wouldn't really think so, would you? I mean, I know women have their little tiffs over things, like who stole whose recipe for sticky toffee pudding or who was flirting with whose husband at the Women's Institute gala, but one hardly murders someone over something that trivial."

India gave him a dark look. "I don't know. . . . I remember reading a story in the papers about a woman who killed her daughter's rival for a spot on a cheerleading squad. That was over in America, of course." She looked at Penelope.

As if strange things only happened in the United States, Penelope thought. She wanted to bring up Jack the Ripper, but then thought better of it. It might seem churlish.

"Let's hope the police find the culprit quickly," Worthington said, running his hands through his hair again as he paced back and forth.

Penelope would come to recognize it as a gesture he habitually made when nervous.

"I do hope this doesn't upset Charlotte too much,"

Worthington said, almost to himself. "She's very sensitive. And what with the stress of the wedding and all . . ."

He stopped pacing and looked at Penelope as if he'd suddenly noticed she was there.

"This is Penelope Parish," India hastened to explain. "She's the writer in residence at the Open Book. She was meant to give a talk on *The Castle of Otranto*."

"Yes, of course," Worthington said, nodding at Penelope.

"Excuse me." Detective Maguire stepped into the room.

"Brodie, old chap," Worthington said. He slapped Maguire on the back jovially. "Surely you can sort all of this out without creating a fuss."

Maguire smiled. There was a weary look in his eyes. "I'll do my best."

"Good man." Worthington slapped him on the back again. He glanced at the Breitling Aerospace watch on his wrist. "It's almost time for Charlotte and me to make an appearance at the fest. I assume you can carry on without me?" he said to Maguire.

"I'm afraid I will need to speak to you."

Worthington looked momentarily put out. "Very well, then," he said in rather icy tones, "I'll be waiting for you in my study." He strode from the room leaving behind the faint citrusy scent of his bespoke Floris cologne.

Maguire waited until Worthington was gone, then turned to Penelope and India.

"Do you mind if I sit down?"

They shook their heads.

He pulled the desk chair over, turned it around, and straddled it. He leaned his arms on the back and looked at Penelope and India and raised his eyebrows.

"India Culpepper," India said, sitting even straighter in

her chair. "I've been a resident of Upper Chumley-on-Stoke all my life. Arthur Worthington is a distant cousin."

Maguire inclined his head. "I see." He turned to Penelope.

"Penelope Parish," Pen hastened to say. "I'm the new writer in residence at the Open Book here in Chumley. I only arrived a couple of weeks ago."

"I just have a few questions for you ladies," Maguire said. "So it was Gladys Watkins who found the body? What was she doing down in the cellar?"

"Gladys and her husband have a booth at the fest every year selling Cornish pasties," India said. "They're quite famous for them."

Maguire smiled. "I'll have to try one."

"There's a freezer in the cellar where they keep their stock—Gladys spends a good month making up the pasties for the fest. And even then they always run out before the day is over. She went down there to get another batch. They have a portable oven in their booth where they bake them fresh."

Maguire nodded. "Any idea what Regina Bosworth was doing down there?"

Pen shook her head.

"I have no idea," India said. "But she is . . . was the chairwoman of the fest, so perhaps she was checking on something."

"I assume the two women knew each other?" Maguire smiled. "I've only been here six months myself—transferred from Leeds. Long story." His face clouded over. "Everyone seems to know everyone here."

"They were acquainted, yes," India said, her tone guarded. "Not socially, of course, but Gladys was on the marketing committee for the fest—not that she was particularly useful—but she did persuade that husband of hers to hang a banner in their shop window. So their paths crossed, but as I said, it wasn't anything more than that."

"It sounds, then, as if it's unlikely Regina went down to the cellar to search Gladys out."

"I don't know," India said. "She might have—to discuss something in relation to Gladys's booth perhaps." A look of shock crossed India's face. "You're not thinking that Gladys might have killed Regina? Because that's not possible."

Maguire smiled. "You'd be surprised what people are capable of and some of the ridiculous motives that drive people to murder."

Penelope thought of Gladys with her round and perpetually flushed cheeks and large guileless eyes. It was impossible to imagine her killing a spider let alone a human being.

India shook her head vehemently. "Not Gladys. No. She would never . . ."

Maguire shrugged. "Did Regina have any enemies?"

India cleared her throat and looked at Penelope. Penelope knew what she was thinking.

"How shall I put this? I don't know that I would call them enemies exactly." India fiddled with a button on her cardigan, avoiding Maguire's eye.

"Frenemies, then?" Maguire raised his eyebrows. "Isn't that the term they use nowadays?" He looked at Penelope and she nodded.

"I've never heard that before," India said. "What does it mean?"

"It's a combination of the words *friends* and *enemies*," Penelope said. "People who act friendly toward you but don't necessarily have your best interests at heart."

"I see. I rather like that." India smiled. "Yes, that describes Regina's relationships perfectly. As Worthington said, people found her to be a pest, not to mention bossy and often condescending. But I doubt anyone seriously contemplated murdering her."

"Except it appears that someone did murder her," Maguire said.

FIVE

❧

"What on earth is going on? Do you know?" Mabel said when Penelope finally returned to the Open Book booth. "I saw the ambulance go streaking toward the castle and then Constable Cuthbert arrived. Has someone taken ill?"

Penelope explained about Gladys finding Regina's body in the freezer in the cellar, dead from a gunshot wound.

"How terrible! Was it an accident? So many accidents these days—especially with all those young whipper-snappers coming out from the city to hunt on the weekends and with so many of them barely knowing which end of the gun is which. There was bound to be a tragedy sooner or later."

Once again the horror of the situation washed over Penelope and she sank into one of the folding chairs they'd brought from the shop.

"Are you okay?" Mabel said. "Feeling a bit peckish, are you?"

"It's not that." Penelope rubbed her temples. "There was no gun anywhere near Regina when Gladys found her. The detective thinks she was murdered."

"Good heavens," Mabel said, plopping into the chair next to Penelope. "I don't believe we've ever had a murder in Chumley. At least not in recent times. I didn't particularly like Regina, but how horrible to have your life cut short like that." She clenched her fists in her lap. "I do wish I'd brought that bottle of Jameson with me." She gave a little smile.

"So do I," Penelope said.

They saw Figgy coming toward them holding a dish in her hands.

"Why the grim faces?" she said. "The fest's going quite smoothly, don't you think? Although I did notice that the ambulance suddenly took off. Someone fainted or had chest pains I should imagine. It happens every year." She put a plate down on the table where Mabel had set up a cashbox and a pad of receipts. "I've brought you some potted shrimp sandwiches to nibble on and some petits fours. You all must be starving by now."

Penelope suddenly realized that she *was* starving and reached for one of the tea sandwiches.

"So tell me. Do you have any idea what's happened?" Figgy said.

Once again Penelope explained about finding Regina dead in the cellar.

Figgy's already pale face became paler. "Do you think Regina's husband, Gordon, finally had enough? She's henpecked the poor man for years. Perhaps he snapped." She twisted one of the earrings in her ear. "Frankly, who could blame him?"

"The detective who questioned us asked if Regina had any enemies. Poor India seemed at a loss as to what to say." Penelope finished her sandwich and reached for another.

"That's no surprise," Mabel said. "One doesn't want to speak ill of the dead but in this case . . ."

"I'm knackered. I've got to get off my feet for a few moments." Figgy grabbed another folding chair and sat down. She glanced over her shoulder at her makeshift tea shop. "I've left things in Jasmine's hands. I think that girl is one sandwich short of a picnic. She can barely make change. But it looks as if nothing is on fire—at least not at the moment." She blew out a breath of air, ruffling her short bangs.

"Do you really think Regina's husband might have killed her?" Penelope said.

Mabel snorted. "I almost hope he did. I should imagine it would have given him some sense of satisfaction. But I doubt it. He's much too mild mannered."

"Who else, then?" Figgy said. "Some random stranger?"

"The detective asked about Gladys, since she's the one who found her." Penelope brushed a crumb from the corner of her lip.

"Poppycock," Mabel said, reaching for a vanilla-iced petit four and popping it into her mouth. "If Gladys was going to murder anyone, I'm pretty sure the bookies would give it two-to-one odds that it would be that husband of hers."

"Oh?" Penelope raised her eyebrows. "What's wrong with Gladys's husband?"

Mabel sighed. "He's something of a tyrant. He dictates Gladys's every move. He wouldn't even let her join the church choir although she has a lovely voice and enjoys singing." Mabel licked a bit of icing off her finger. "Fortunately Gladys has her romance novels to take comfort in. I gather Bruce—her husband—doesn't approve of them, but it's the one thing she's put her foot down about."

Figgy swatted at a fly that seemed determined to make a nest in her hair. "What about Regina's husband? Do you think he had a bit on the side and maybe wanted to get Regina out of the way?"

Mabel burst out laughing. "Gordon?" She wiped her eyes with the hem of her blouse. "Sorry, but I can't begin to picture Gordon stepping out on Regina. For one thing, he'd be much too terrified of what she'd do if she found out."

"I don't know," Pen said, stretching out her legs. "I can sort of picture a poor henpecked husband taking up with some very kindly woman—pretty and on the plump side—and who cooks for him and pampers him a bit."

"I'm sure he'd love something like that," Figgy said, picking up the now empty sandwich plate. "And maybe now that Regina's gone, he'll be able to find someone."

Mabel nodded. "Bachelors aren't exactly ten a penny in Upper Chumley-on-Stoke although we seem to have more than our share of unmarried women. He'd be quite the catch despite his potbelly and receding hairline. Any living, breathing single male around here is considered a good catch. By tomorrow women will be bringing him casseroles by the dozen."

"Of course it might have been an intruder who shot Regina," Penelope said. "She surprised them and they shot her."

"What would anyone want to steal from the Worthington's cellar?" Figgy said. "There's probably nothing but dust balls down there."

"He has quite an extensive wine collection," Penelope said. "India pointed it out to me when we were down there."

"Or," Mabel added, "they broke into the cellar and were planning on making their way upstairs. I'm sure there's plenty worth nicking up there."

Figgy jerked a thumb over her shoulder. "I saw a whole bunch of coppers arrive a few minutes ago. I imagine they are searching Worthington House right now. Maybe the murderer is hiding in a closet or something." She shuddered.

Figgy glanced over her shoulder and her expression changed to one of alarm. "It looks as if the tea shop is getting busy. I'd better get back and lend Jasmine a hand or who knows what might happen. The poor girl is easily flustered."

"Thanks for the sandwiches," Mabel said. "They were just the ticket."

A few moments later, a tall, well-built woman in jodhpurs and gleaming leather boots approached the booth. "Good morning, ladies," she said in posh tones. She turned to Penelope. "I don't believe we've met."

"Evelyn, this is Penelope Parish. She's our new writer in residence at the Open Book," Mabel said. "Pen, this is Lady Evelyn Maxwell-Lewis."

Evelyn held out a hand. It was large—almost manly—with short, unpolished nails. There was a gold signet ring on her pinkie.

"Call me Evie," she said. "Everyone does." She smiled at Penelope.

Just then another woman approached them, her face stretched into a smile. She'd broken off from her two companions who were waiting for her at a distance.

"Georgina, is that you?" she said, smiling at Evelyn. "I'd recognize you anywhere. It's me. Bunny Churchill." She touched Evelyn's arm. "We were at St. Agatha's together. Surely you remember."

Evelyn shook her head. "Unfortunately, I'm afraid you're mistaken. I don't believe we've ever met before. I'm Lady Evelyn Maxwell-Lewis."

"I'm terribly sorry. It's just that you look so much like her. Granted, I haven't seen her in over twenty years." The woman laughed.

Evelyn inclined her head and smiled.

"How odd," she said to Mabel and Penelope when the woman had left. She shrugged. "Mistaken identity, I guess."

She tapped the cover of a book on display. "I thought I'd pick up Charlotte's latest book. Arthur is sure to ask me if I've read it when I see him tomorrow night. He positively dotes on Charlotte." She laughed. "He's had his share of affairs. We were all surprised when this one stuck." She frowned. "I just hope she isn't after his money."

The words *It was a dark and stormy night* ran through Penelope's mind as she sat in the living room of her cottage, a fire blazing in the hearth, her computer in her lap and rain streaming down the front windows. It was nearly as dark as night although unlike in that overworn phrase, it was actually only mid-afternoon.

It was Sunday and even though the Open Book was open from noon until five o'clock, Mabel had said she could manage by herself. Besides, she had a young student who wanted to earn some pocket money who came in to help on the weekends.

Pen was engrossed in writing an exciting scene in her manuscript where Annora was lost deep in a dark wood without even moonlight to guide her. Penelope knew, even though Annora didn't, that the bad guy who was after her, thinking she held the key to a mysterious locked door, was silently creeping up behind her, his night vision as sharp as any nocturnal animal's.

Pen couldn't help but think of poor Regina and how terribly frightened she must have been when she realized she was alone in the basement with a killer.

The thought actually made the hair on Penelope's neck stand up; and when there was a sudden noise overhead, she jumped so hard she nearly knocked her laptop to the floor.

What was that? Did Mrs. Danvers jump off the bed upstairs?

Penelope heard an irritated meow and realized Mrs. Danvers was not upstairs at all but sitting on the other end of the sofa, her tail hanging over the edge and swishing back and forth.

She turned the light on as she mounted the stairs. She remembered how, as a child, she'd been convinced that lamplight could chase monsters away—especially the ones she was positive lived under her bed.

She was nearly to the top of the stairs when she heard a squeak—like a door whose hinges needed oiling— slowly opening.

Penelope paused for a moment, her foot suspended over the next step. What on earth was that?

Surely there was a reasonable explanation. She would probably find that one of the windows was open and the wind was being playful, sending a door swinging back and forth slightly. As it was, it seemed as if the wind was attempting to shake the cottage on its very foundation.

There was no reason to be alarmed, Penelope told herself.

She looked all around—under the bed, in the closets. She poked in the dark corners of the room and behind the furniture but could find no explanation for the noises. Had she imagined them?

Writing about Annora's predicament in the dark forest and thinking about Regina's murder must have put her imagination in overdrive.

She couldn't help but wonder, as she walked back down the stairs, if writing romance would have the same effect and perhaps conjure up a Prince Charming.

She certainly didn't consider Miles to be her Prince Charming. Pen realized she hadn't talked to him for several days and she felt guilty for ignoring him. She picked up her phone and punched in his number, but her call went unanswered.

And now she felt even guiltier because the only emotion she felt was relief that he hadn't picked up.

R ain was still coming down in buckets the next day.
    "Good thing we aren't holding the fest today," Mabel said, watching the rain batter the bookshop windows.

The temperature had dropped dramatically from the day before and the store's ancient radiators were clanging and banging and belching out warm steam. The day was dark with heavy clouds, but all the lights in the Open

Book were on and Penelope felt as if she was in a warm, cozy cocoon.

She was waiting for her book group to arrive. They'd chosen to read *Rebecca* by Daphne du Maurier—one of Penelope's favorite Gothic novels.

India arrived first—shaking out her umbrella over the mat by the front door and brushing the rain from the shoulders of her coat.

"Beastly weather," she said as she stepped into the shop.

"Figgy is brewing some tea for us. You look like you could use a cup," Mabel said.

India's sharp features were pink from the cold. She hung her raincoat on the coat-tree by the front door. She was well armed against the chill in a boiled-wool jacket; a heavy plaid skirt; thick, cabled stockings; and stout walking shoes.

India settled herself in one of the armchairs. "What a day we had Saturday," she said. "A murder at the Worthington Fest. Most unseemly. It's never happened before, and I, for one, hope it never happens again."

"Yes," Mabel said. "I'm sure Regina would be mortified if she knew. The poor thing had prepared for every contingency except her own murder."

The bell over the front door tinkled and Gladys walked in. She'd obviously dashed across the street without bothering with an umbrella since rain had plastered her hair to her head and was dripping off her nose.

"Gladys, dear, how are you? You gave us all quite a fright the other day," India said.

Gladys blew out her cheeks. "Bruce was none too pleased that I'd been taken off to hospital and he had to man the booth by himself."

"I can imagine," India said dryly.

"He carried on about it for a good hour that night until I told him that I'd never be able to get on with making his tea if he didn't quiet down. After the day I'd had, the last thing I needed was his aggro." She blew out her cheeks again.

The bell tinkled once more and Violet Thatcher pushed open the door. She drifted in like the fog, silently and slowly. She was even thinner than India and her sparse fluffy hair made her look like a wraith. She sank into the armchair next to India with a sigh. She unbuttoned the top button on her coat but didn't take it off and instead huddled inside it.

"I've just been round the shops," Violet said when she'd gotten settled. "And the talk is all about the fest and poor unfortunate Regina's murder." She knitted her gnarled hands together. "I lit a candle for her at Evensong last night and Robert said a prayer for her at this morning's service." She shook her head. "Such a tragedy."

Figgy bustled over with a rolling tea tray set with porcelain cups and saucers, a sugar bowl, milk pitcher, and slices of lemon.

"And I've made some fresh Eccles cakes for you," she said, putting a plate down on the low table between the chairs and sofa. "Given everything that's happened, I thought we could all do with a bit of cheering up."

Violet sniffed. "This sort of thing wouldn't have happened if it wasn't for that woman Worthington's taken up with. Maybe now the queen will step in and say something. I'm sure a word of advice in his ear wouldn't go amiss."

"You can't possibly be saying that you think Charlotte

Davenport had something to do with Regina's murder," Mabel said.

Violet fussed with one of the buttons on her coat. "She is American, you know," she said as if that settled it. "They do things differently over there."

Pen felt her hackles rise. She and Figgy exchanged a glance. She thought of Mrs. Danvers and how all her fur stood up when she was offended by something. Now she knew how her cat felt.

She tried to stifle her emotions. Her job at the Open Book wasn't to alienate customers, and she didn't want to put Mabel in an uncomfortable position. Still, she was quite positive that steam was coming out of her ears. She was surprised the others couldn't see it.

"We may do things differently," Penelope said in as pleasant a tone as she could muster, "but we don't necessarily stoop to murder."

"Really, Violet," India said in exasperation.

Violet put a hand over her mouth. "I didn't mean . . ."

Penelope took a deep breath the way she'd learned to do in yoga class and managed a smile in Violet's direction. "Of course."

The door to the store opened again and three people walked in, collapsing their umbrellas and stashing them in the stand Mabel had cleverly placed by the door. Penelope assumed that given the weather in England, it probably got a lot of use.

The three—two women and one man—walked over to where Penelope and the others were gathered.

"Are we late?" one of the women chirped as she took off her scarf and folded it.

The sole gentleman smiled and smoothed his mustache

with his index finger. Despite his decidedly civilian gray wool pants, cream colored V-necked sweater, and blue-and-white checked shirt, Penelope had no doubt that he was former military. It was obvious in his bearing and the way his hazel eyes took in everything without appearing to.

The two women jockeyed for a seat next to the lone man who had introduced himself as Laurence Brimble. Penelope noticed Mabel raise her eyebrows and roll her eyes.

"That was certainly a bit of excitement Saturday," the older blond woman said. "You don't expect to have a murder at the Worthington Fest. I wonder when the police will find the person who did it."

Brimble made a sound like a grunt.

"I knew Regina," the dark-haired woman in the polka-dot raincoat said. "She had a way of making enemies for herself. The last time I talked to her"—she lowered her voice slightly—"she said she knew something about that woman Worthington is engaged to, Charlotte Davenport. She wouldn't tell me what it was but she hinted that it would create a huge scandal if it got out."

The blond gasped. "You don't think Charlotte Davenport killed Regina?"

The brunette raised her eyebrows and shrugged her shoulders. "Who knows? I do know everyone is talking about it. No one seems to know where she comes from or who her family is or really anything about her at all."

"I hope Worthington isn't being played for a fool," Violet piped up.

"All speculation," Brimble said brusquely, running a finger over his mustache again. "Let the police do their work. They'll find out who did it in due course. And if we don't get started with our book discussion, we'll be here till seventeen hundred hours."

His two companions glared at him.

Penelope cleared her throat. "Good idea." She nodded at Brimble. "Let's discuss our book," she said, automatically seguing into what she thought of as her lecture voice.

The discussion, which started out quite robustly, eventually degenerated into a heated debate over who should play the characters in *Rebecca* if the movie was remade with half the group voting for Helen Mirren to play Mrs. Danvers and the other half favoring Judi Dench for the part.

Violet was in the midst of arguing for Helen Mirren when the front door opened. Everyone stopped talking at once and turned in that direction.

A young woman walked in and looked around as if she was searching for something—not a book since she didn't even bother to approach the nearest shelves. She was wearing a tightly belted trench coat over a dark pantsuit and black high-heeled pumps and had her blond hair pulled into a low ponytail. She looked as if she meant business despite her ethereal good looks.

Mabel, who had been standing on the fringes of the book group, broke away. She smiled as she walked toward the young woman.

"May I help you? Are you looking for something in particular?"

The girl's head snapped around when she heard Mabel.

"Yes, actually you can help me, I hope. I'm Katie Poole. I'm Miss Davenport's assistant."

By now the book group was silent and straining to hear the conversation.

"I've been told that I would find Penelope Parish here."
She pulled a pale blue envelope from her purse. "Miss
Davenport would like me to deliver this to her."

Gladys had been casually leaning back in her chair in
order to better hear the conversation. "Why on earth
would Charlotte Davenport need an assistant when
Worthington has a house full of servants?"

"A lot of them help authors with things like social me-
dia now," Penelope said as she got up.

She walked toward Mabel and Katie. "I'm Penelope
Parish."

Katie gave a quick smile and held out the envelope.
"This is for you. Miss Davenport asked me to deliver it
to you."

"Thank you," Penelope said.

"She'll be waiting for an answer," Katie said when Penelope didn't immediately open the envelope.

Pen slid her finger under the flap and pulled out a note
written in a very feminine hand on lightly scented blue
cardstock. The letters *CED* were entwined in an elaborate
monogram at the top.

Penelope was curious. She couldn't imagine why Charlotte would be writing to her. Perhaps she remembered
Penelope from the writers' conference they'd both at-
tended? Pen read the note. It seemed that Charlotte was
inviting her to tea that afternoon at four o'clock at
Worthington House.

SIX

❧

"I wonder why Charlotte is inviting me to tea. I'm surprised she's even remembered me," Penelope said later when she and Mabel were alone in the shop. They were unpacking a carton of books that had just arrived—a new novel being touted as the next *Harry Potter*. Penelope was looking forward to reading it to see if it lived up to the hype.

"As a courtesy? Because you're a fellow American? And you did say that you'd already met each other." Mabel had been bending over the carton. She straightened up and put a hand to her back. "The nobility tend to view themselves as unofficial ambassadors. Perhaps Charlotte is taking up the mantle early."

"I've never been to tea before," Penelope said, brushing a Styrofoam peanut from her sweater where it had stuck. "Will this be what you English call high tea?"

Mabel laughed and shook her head vehemently. "A

common misconception that people across the pond have. No, high tea is what workers and laborers call what I suppose you would term supper. It's a heartier meal eaten after the workday. Beans on toast, bangers and mash, steak and kidney pie, and things like that. What you're going to have is afternoon tea."

"I have to admit to being a little nervous," Penelope said. "What if I make some huge faux pas? You English have a way of making us Americans feel terribly gauche."

"I don't think you have anything to worry about. Besides, Charlotte is American. This is all probably new to her, too." Mabel bent and slit open another carton. "Put your napkin in your lap, keep your feet off the table, and you should do fine. Just remember—don't drink your tea with your pinkie in the air. That's considered pretentious."

Penelope laughed. "Got it."

"My mother used to take us to tea at Brown's Hotel in London. It's where Alexander Graham Bell made the first telephone call from Europe and Agatha Christie supposedly used it as inspiration for *At Bertram's Hotel*, although there's some dispute about that." Mabel pulled open the carton. "Mother would dress us up in our best clothes, and all the way there on the train she would lecture us on proper manners. We weren't to eat as if we were starving no matter how enticing the cakes and sandwiches looked. No clattering of spoons or teacups either." Mabel straightened up and blew back a lock of hair. "Did you know that in the eighteen hundreds women believed they could tell a lot about a potential mate by the way he handled his teacup? If he placed his spoon on his saucer incorrectly, he'd be written off."

"Now you're really scaring me," Penelope said.

"Times have changed. You'll be fine." She turned to Penelope and looked her up and down. "What are you going to wear?"

"Wear?" Penelope looked down at her sweater, leggings, and ankle boots. "Do I need to change?"

"You might consider it," Mabel said dryly.

Penelope mentally went through her closet. She hadn't brought that many clothes and the ones she had were all similar—worn, comfy, and familiar. She did bring the pantsuit she'd bought to wear to book signings. She supposed it would have to do.

W ish me luck," Penelope said to Mrs. Danvers as the cat wove in and out between her legs, complaining loudly that Penelope was leaving so soon again. "Your water bowl is full and so is your dish," Penelope reassured the cat. Mrs. Danvers did not look amused. As a matter of fact, she looked decidedly annoyed, narrowing her green eyes to slits and meowing her displeasure.

Pen reluctantly closed the cottage door behind her and headed toward her MINI, which was parked at the curb. She remembered how nervous she'd been when she'd gone to her first book signing but this was far worse. At least at the signing she hadn't had to worry about balancing a teacup and a plate and making sure she didn't spill the contents of either on what would no doubt be a priceless Oriental rug.

She turned the key, started the engine, checked the rearview mirror, and pulled away from the curb. It took all her concentration to keep the car on the correct side of the road and she forgot about being nervous until she was pulling through the gates of Worthington House when her nerves began twitching and twanging again like a fiddle being played in a bluegrass band.

The sight of Worthington House brought back the horror of Regina's murder, and Pen's hands were shaking on the steering wheel as she headed for the car park where visitors going on tours left their vehicles. A handful of cars were in the lot along with a tour bus with *Countryside Tours* written on the side.

Her next dilemma was how to get into the house. She couldn't picture herself marching up to the enormous front door and banging the knocker. How did one get into a castle, anyway, short of being catapulted in or charging the ramparts on a horse with a sword like in medieval times?

A small van pulled into the lot with *Sunshine Retirement Home* printed on the side. It came to a halt and six people got out—two white-haired ladies with canes, three with walkers, and a gentleman in a blue cardigan with a portable oxygen tank. They began walking toward the side door of the house where a sign was posted—*Welcome to the Worthington House Tour*. The hours were listed underneath in smaller type.

That was the entrance Pen had used the other day so she decided to join them. She followed them through the door, where an attendant was taking tickets and handing out brochures. Penelope waited while the brisk young woman, who had shepherded the group from the van into the house, spoke with the attendant.

Pen couldn't help wondering if the group would be as enthusiastic about touring Worthington House if they had been the ones to find Regina's dead body in the basement.

Then again, she supposed there might be a sort of ghoulish thrill in visiting the scene of a murder.

Penelope was about to tell the attendant that Charlotte was expecting her when someone called her name. She looked up to see Katie Poole crossing the room with a folder tucked under her arm.

She smiled as she walked over to Penelope.

"There you are," she said. "I hope you didn't pay for a tour." She smiled again revealing a dimple in her left cheek. "I was waiting for you by the front door, but when you didn't appear I thought you might have come to this entrance."

"I wasn't sure—"

"Please, don't worry about it. Come with me. Charlotte is excited to see you."

That took Penelope aback and she nearly stumbled. Perhaps Charlotte *did* remember her.

"Charlotte is dying to talk shop with you," Katie said. Her high heels made a tap-tap-tap sound as they crossed the marble floor. "She's been talking about it since she heard of your arrival."

It had never occurred to Penelope that she and Charlotte had anything in common. They both wrote books, of course, but Charlotte was engaged to a duke and Penelope . . . wasn't.

Katie led her down corridors where the walls were hung with dark oil paintings of men and women in eighteenth- and nineteenth-century dress and watercolors of pastoral settings with weeping willows and rambling brooks.

Finally they paused in front of a door. Katie knocked and then pushed it open. The room was empty.

Katie smiled reassuringly. "Charlotte will be down in a few moments. Please"—she swept a hand toward the sofa and chairs—"make yourself comfortable."

Katie left, closing the door behind her, and Pen began to look around.

The floor-to-ceiling windows were draped with moss-green curtains with ornate gold fleur-de-lis holdbacks. An Empire-style desk sat in front of them with a laptop in the center and a neat stack of papers to one side. Bookcases filled one wall, and opposite were two armchairs and a small sofa set around a low table.

Penelope couldn't help herself—she'd never been able to pass a bookshelf without checking out the titles. These seemed to be mostly volumes on the craft of writing—Penelope owned many of them herself—along with a generous selection of history books on the Regency period.

Penelope had just sat down when the door opened and Charlotte came in. She was wearing slim-fitting dark denim jeans, a luxurious black cashmere cowl-necked sweater with a heavy gold chain around her neck, and leopard print ballet flats. Her hair was down, the blond ends curling onto her shoulders. She smelled lightly of a flowery perfume.

Charlotte smiled. "I do apologize for being late." She gave Pen a quick hug, then took a seat on the sofa.

She had barely sat down when there was a tap on the door and a butler in a uniform resplendent with gold buttons came in, bearing an enormous silver tray set with tea things and a tiered serving dish holding dainty crustless sandwiches on one level and delicate pastries on another. He placed the tray on the table in front of Charlotte, bowed, and withdrew.

"Tea?" Charlotte said, picking up the teapot.

"Thank you."

Charlotte filled their cups and handed one to Penelope. The cup was porcelain and had a gold rim and a delicate floral pattern.

"I've come to love the English tradition of afternoon tea," Charlotte said, stirring sugar into her cup. "Although at first it quite intimidated me. I was terrified of doing something wrong or, heaven forbid, of dropping my cup or plate." She raised her teacup to her mouth.

Penelope felt herself relax. Charlotte was apparently still quite human after all.

"I've read your book," Charlotte said. "I thoroughly enjoyed it. I remember how excited you were about it when we met at that conference."

Penelope felt herself color. "Thank you. I'm afraid I haven't—"

Charlotte waved a hand and the enormous diamond on her left ring finger caught the light and sparkled brilliantly.

"Romance isn't everyone's cup of tea," she said, her eyes twinkling. She leaned forward and helped herself to one of the sandwiches. Penelope followed suit. It was cucumber and dill and quite delicious.

"Can I ask you something?" Charlotte said. Her eyes were fixed on Penelope.

"Yes, of course." Pen couldn't imagine what question Charlotte would have for her.

"Do you ever get writer's block?"

Penelope laughed and the cup and saucer in her hand began to rattle alarmingly. She remembered what Mabel had said about that and abruptly put them down on the table.

"That's how I ended up here," she told Charlotte. "I

was hopelessly blocked and thought perhaps a change of scenery would help."

"It's a relief to hear you say that," Charlotte said, toying with her necklace. "I've been feeling like a failure because the words have refused to come lately. I've spent countless hours staring at my computer screen, watching the cursor blink. I thought perhaps my muse had packed her bags and hightailed it back to the States." She laughed.

They talked books and writing for the next hour, until the teapot was empty and most of the pastries had been consumed.

"Can I ask you a favor?" Charlotte said suddenly. She leaned forward and her heavy gold necklace swung forward and clanged against the table.

Charlotte grabbed it with one hand as she leaned back again. She fiddled with the links, not looking at Penelope. Penelope thought she seemed nervous, which was surprising but also curious. What did Charlotte have to be nervous about?

"Everyone is talking about Regina Bosworth's murder," Charlotte said, frowning slightly. "Very few people have ever been this close to a murder. Certainly I haven't." She clenched her hands in her lap. "Arthur is particularly upset about it." She looked toward the window. "He feels a sense of responsibility since it happened here at Worthington House."

"I believe the murder has everyone upset," Penelope said. "You're right—it's not something we're used to dealing with."

"It's not only that. It's because . . ."

"Because?"

"Because I'm an American. I've heard that people want to blame me for it."

Penelope had a sudden horrible thought—what if people started blaming *her*?

Charlotte wiped a finger under her eyes. "It's not only because I'm an American but also because I'm marrying Arthur."

"That's ridiculous. You didn't even know her, did you?"

"Not really. I'd met her, of course, since she was in charge of the fest, but that's all. No, they're doing it because they want to get rid of me. Everyone wanted Arthur to marry a local girl and, if not that, at least some European royalty. That way they could console themselves with the fact that their precious daughters were never in the running in the first place. And here he's chosen me— a perfectly ordinary American woman."

Charlotte crossed her legs and one leopard print flat dangled from her toes.

"That's why I have a favor to ask you." She looked at Penelope, her eyes pleading.

"Yes?" Penelope raised her eyebrows.

"Could you try to find out who really killed Regina?"

"Me?" Penelope was taken aback. "But I have no idea how to go about it."

"You're the only person I can trust to be on my side. The townspeople are all suspicious of me although they seem to have taken to you."

"That's because I'm not marrying Arthur Worthington," Penelope said rather dryly, pleased to see that brought a small smile to Charlotte's lips.

Penelope didn't know what to say. It was an absurd request. There wasn't anything she could possibly do. And surely Charlotte didn't think the local gossip would be taken seriously? It didn't add up. She thought of what she'd been told about Regina—that she collected secrets. And that she'd discovered something that would cause a huge scandal—something that might put an end to Charlotte's romance with Worthington.

"I still don't understand why you think the police are going to accuse you of Regina's murder. Did Regina discover something that makes you a likely suspect?"

Charlotte jumped and her leg jostled the tea table. The cups and saucers rattled loudly.

"No, of course not." Her cheeks colored with indignation. "Why would you say something like that?"

Penelope suspected Charlotte wasn't indignant—she was scared.

Penelope held up a hand and made soothing noises.

"I didn't mean—"

"Of course you didn't." Charlotte smiled charmingly. "I'm sorry. It's the stress. It's my fault. I offended you. It wasn't intentional."

"I understand," Penelope said. "I'd be more than happy to see what I can do," she said, regretting the promise even as she made it. But Charlotte had helped her out of a jam once—admittedly a far smaller predicament than the one Charlotte now found herself in.

And it wasn't simply that Pen felt she owed Charlotte something—she actually liked Charlotte. Besides, the whole thing was stirring up her curiosity. More than once Pen's mother had reminded her that curiosity supposedly killed the cat. But once Pen had gotten the bit between her teeth, to mix metaphors, there was no stopping her.

Something was making Charlotte very nervous though— that was obvious. Regina knew something about her— something Charlotte didn't want known—Penelope was sure of it. But had it been enough to push Charlotte to murder Regina? Pen didn't think so.

Penelope decided she would do whatever it was she could to help the police find the real culprit—even if that was very likely to turn out to be very little.

SEVEN

❧

The sun was shining the day of Regina Bosworth's funeral, its rays warming the worn bricks of the façade of St. Andrew's Church. Leaves on the enormous oak tree, whose branches overhung the roof of the church and were a perpetual concern during storms, were just beginning to turn color.

There was a nip in the air and Penelope pulled her coat more closely around her as she followed Mabel into the church for the service. Gladys was sitting up front, a handkerchief already pressed to her eyes; and India was behind her, ramrod straight in the uncomfortable wooden pew.

Mabel poked Penelope and gestured toward Gladys with her head.

"Gladys is one of those people who cry at every funeral, whether they knew the deceased well or not at all. I can't think why she'd be all that upset about Regina's death. Regina always treated her with such obvious condescension."

There was a rustle of movement among those gathered and Penelope turned around to see Charlotte entering the church. Katie Poole was with her as well as a tall man in a dark suit who was so obviously a bodyguard he could have come from central casting.

"Nice of Charlotte to come," Mabel whispered to Penelope. "I believe Worthington is in London today or I am sure he would have made an appearance as well. He takes his lord-of-the-manor duties seriously."

A hush fell over the church as Gordon Bosworth walked out of a side door and slipped into a pew in the front row. A slightly plump young woman in an ill-fitting black dress followed him. They took a seat together and the young woman reached out and squeezed Gordon's hand.

"Who is that?" Penelope whispered.

"That's Gordon and Regina's daughter, Victoria," Mabel said, reaching for the nearest hymnal.

The doors at the back of the church opened, the congregation struggled to their feet, and the choir processed in singing "Great Is Thy Faithfulness" with abundant vigor if not corresponding skill. Regina's elaborate mahogany coffin was carried down the aisle and the vicar began the service.

"We have come here today to remember before God our sister Regina; to give thanks for her life; to commend her to God, our merciful redeemer and judge; to commit her body to be buried; and to comfort one another in our grief," he recited in a shaky voice.

Gladys continued to press her handkerchief to her eyes.

Charlotte was in a front pew with Katie, who appeared to be texting on her phone while the bodyguard stood against the wall in line with their pew, his eyes on the crowd and not the altar.

Penelope found her mind wandering to her previous day's conversation with Charlotte. Her promise to help track down Regina's murderer had been a bit rash but she hadn't wanted to disappoint Charlotte. After what Charlotte had said about being a suspect because she was American, Penelope had had a nightmare that night that a crowd of villagers had surrounded the bookstore demanding her head. She had woken up in a panicked sweat.

Before long the vicar was intoning the last words of the service. "'May God in his infinite love and mercy bring the whole Church, living and departed in the Lord Jesus, to a joyful resurrection and the fulfillment of his eternal kingdom.'"

The congregation responded with a resounding "Amen," Regina's coffin was wheeled out, and the choir began to sing "The King of Love My Shepherd Is." The congregation rose and slowly filed out of the church into the bright sunshine.

Penelope and Mabel walked down the worn stone path to the lawn where people were gathering. Gladys wandered over toward them, her handkerchief still in her hand.

"Lovely service, wasn't it? Regina would have been so pleased." She sniffed and pressed her handkerchief to her eyes. "Are you going to Gordon's for the memorial luncheon?"

"Yes. Figgy offered to help mind the store for us so we could go," Mabel said.

* * *

The Bosworths' house was in a new subdivision on the outskirts of town. Mabel drove down the winding streets while Penelope checked the address.

"It says Hampton Court House on Surrey Lane. There's no street number."

"Birnam Woods is the sort of subdivision where houses don't have numbers—they have names. The locals, led by Worthington himself, fought tooth and nail to prevent its being built. They already knew from the experience of other small towns like ours that the subdivision would attract a lot of wealthy upper-middle-class people who would speed through town in their fancy European sports cars but would do their shopping in London and not at the local merchants."

Mabel put on her blinker and turned down a road dotted with enormous houses, sweeping front lawns meticulously landscaped.

"I think this is it."

Mabel pulled up in front of a faux-Tudor extravaganza with mullioned windows and a lawn so perfectly groomed it looked as if it had been cut with manicure scissors.

The double front doors—indeed, the whole structure—reminded Penelope of the Grill and Brew restaurant in Connecticut where she grew up and where her date had taken her to dinner before the senior prom.

"Looks like they've got quite a good crowd," Penelope said as Mabel pulled over to the curb and parked the car.

"No one was going to turn down a free lunch along with a chance to ogle the interior of Regina's house. Chumley residents live for this sort of thing."

Mabel buzzed the car doors locked, and they crossed

the street and made their way down the slate path to the front door, where they were confronted with a massive gold knocker in the shape of the Tudor rose.

"Should we knock or just go on in?" Penelope said.

Mabel tried the doorknob. It turned and she opened the door. A wave of voices washed over them.

Guests were clustered in the living room, which had dark wood-paneled walls, dark woodwork, a beamed ceiling, and oversized furniture covered in dark red velvet. The only notes of bright color came from the flowers scattered around the room—stiff floral arrangements with cards tucked into their foliage that had obviously been sent to the grieving widower after Regina's death.

Gordon Bosworth looked none the worse for his grief. He was in the center of a circle of women, all vying to console him in his time of sorrow. One of the women seemed to be getting most of his attention. She was younger than the others, pretty, with an eye-catching figure shown to advantage in a low-cut blouse.

"Who is that girl?" Penelope whispered to Mabel, inclining her head toward Gordon.

"That's Daphne Potter. She's a waitress at the Book and Bottle. She and Gordon are quite friendly." Mabel put air quotes around the word *friendly*. "He stops in for a drink every night on his way home from work."

"I wonder if Regina knew."

"I'm sure she did. She knew everything—even things that didn't concern her and weren't any of her business. My guess is she knew perfectly well what was going on."

"Do you think Gordon and Daphne plotted to kill Regina so they could be together?"

Mabel laughed. "You've been reading too many books. Besides, I think the interest is all one-sided."

Pen watched Daphne and Gordon talking. She wasn't so sure. If Daphne was a barmaid, her life was likely to be less than luxurious. Perhaps she wanted what Regina had had—a big house, nice cars, and a husband with a good job.

People were drifting into the dining room, where the caterer had put out an impressive spread—a large roast, a ham, shrimp, a pasta dish, and cold salads—on the enormous trestle table. The Tudor décor had been carried through into this room as well with a huge wrought iron chandelier with faux candles, high-backed upholstered chairs, a massive dark wood sideboard, and a crewel wall hanging depicting the Tudor rose.

Gordon came up behind them as they were filling their plates. He pointed to the tapestry on the wall.

"Regina made that. She liked to do needlework while she watched the telly."

"It's lovely," Penelope said. "She was quite talented."

Gordon looked momentarily sad, as if the realization that Regina was gone had just hit him, but then Daphne came toward him and his expression lightened.

The baize door to the kitchen swung open and Penelope noticed Victoria, an apron over her black dress, helping the caterer arrange dinner rolls in a basket.

Mabel wandered off to talk to someone she'd recognized, and both India and Gladys were also engaged in conversations. Penelope didn't know anyone else so she took her plate out to the conservatory at the back of the house.

It was blessedly empty and quiet and she sat down at the small wrought iron table situated beneath a giant fern. The air in the room was warm and slightly humid.

Penelope felt as if she'd stepped into another climate. It reminded her of Florida and the trip she'd taken to Fort Lauderdale with some friends after college.

She was finishing her lunch when she heard a loud, disgruntled meow. She looked up to see a cat wandering toward her—a calico wearing a red collar with a bell on it. The cat jumped up onto the chair opposite Penelope and stared at her, slowly blinking its emerald-green eyes.

Eventually it seemed to tire of that. It jumped off the chair, stretched luxuriously, and wandered over to one of the potted plants and began digging in the dirt.

Penelope got up from her chair and called the cat.

"Here, kitty, kitty." She walked toward it. "Should you be doing that?" she said as dirt flew out of the planter onto the flagstone floor.

The cat looked at her and blinked slowly, then jumped out of the planter and began grooming itself.

Penelope glanced at the hole the cat had dug. Should she cover it up again or let Gordon deal with it? She looked closer and noticed that something was sticking up out of the dirt. Had the cat uncovered one of the roots? She didn't know much about plants beyond the fact that they needed sun and water, but she didn't think the roots should be exposed.

She started to smooth the dirt over the top of the planter when she realized that it wasn't a root—it was the tip of a very small notebook. She pulled it out and brushed the dirt off. It was no bigger than two inches by four inches.

How strange. Had the cat buried it there? Or had someone hidden it in the planter for some reason? She opened it to the first page.

She didn't know what she had expected to find—computer passwords, bank account numbers, the combination to a safe?

The first page—and subsequent pages—appeared to contain some sort of code. There were entries like $E = past$ and $D = money$.

Penelope didn't have a clue as to what these meant but she wondered if these notations could somehow be tied to Regina's murder. Maybe Regina was involved in some clandestine operation that no one else knew about. She thought of giving the book to Gordon but then changed her mind. What if it did have something to do with the murder and Gordon was a suspect?

She would give it to Detective Maguire instead. Perhaps he would be able to make something out of it. But first, she was going to photograph the pages.

Thanks," Penelope said as Mabel dropped her off in front of the police station, which was within walking distance of the Open Book.

"Good luck," Mabel said. "I'm curious as to what Detective Maguire has to say about your notebook."

Penelope closed the car door and stood for a moment in front of the police station. The building was old, like every other building in Upper Chumley-on-Stoke, and made of putty-colored stucco and dark wood timbers. Right by the front door was a blue lamp on a pole with *Police* written on it.

Penelope went inside and approached the front desk. The man behind it looked up.

"How can I help you, love?" He had a wide smile and a slight overbite.

"I'd like to see Detective Maguire, if he's in."

A door behind the reception desk opened and Maguire stepped out. He saw Penelope and smiled.

"This is an unexpected pleasure. I didn't think I'd see you again so soon. Is there something we can do for you?"

"It's regarding the Bosworth case. I have . . . something that might be useful," Penelope said. She suddenly felt foolish. What if Regina's notebook turned out to be nothing important at all?

Maguire raised his eyebrows. "Let's go into my office, then."

He led Penelope into a small room crammed with a desk, a wooden straight-backed chair positioned in front of it, and several filing cabinets. Stacks of paper were piled on every available surface. The blinds in the window were down, and Penelope noticed that several slats were bent.

Maguire sat behind his desk and Penelope took the chair in front of it. She pulled the notebook out of her pocket. A few crumbs of dirt still clung to the cover. She handed it to Maguire.

"I went to the memorial luncheon for Regina Bosworth today. I was sitting in their conservatory when their cat began to dig in one of the potted plants. It unearthed that notebook. I thought it might have some bearing on the case."

Maguire raised his eyebrows and opened the notebook. He leaned back in his chair as if he was getting ready to settle down with a good novel.

He flipped a few pages, sat back up, and scratched his

head. "What does this mean? It looks like code of some kind."

Penelope nodded. "Regina Bosworth was known for ferreting out people's secrets. I thought perhaps that notebook"—she gestured toward it—"contained code for some of the things she'd discovered."

Maguire chuckled and Penelope felt her face getting hot. Maguire wasn't taking her seriously and it was making her feel silly as if she were a child playing at being Nancy Drew.

Maguire closed the notebook. "More likely it's some sort of diary. I doubt it has anything to do with Mrs. Bosworth's murder; however, we'll look into it." He tapped the cover. "I hope you don't mind if I keep this?"

"Not at all." Penelope stood up. "Thank you for your time," she said rather stiffly.

"Would you like a cup of tea before you go?" Maguire said.

"Thank you, but I need to get back to the bookstore."

Penelope nearly ran out of the police station and by the time she arrived at the Open Book, her face was flushed and she was breathing heavily.

"What the dickens happened to you?" Mabel said when she saw her. "You look like all the furies in hell are after you."

"I showed Maguire the notebook. And he didn't take me seriously. I felt so stupid."

Pen felt her anger bubble up again.

"What did he say?"

"He said he didn't think the notebook had anything to do with the case. I got the feeling that he thought I was a hysterical female. Or worse, some sort of busybody with nothing better to do."

"If I learned one thing in my career as an analyst," Mabel said, coming out from behind the counter to put an arm around Penelope's shoulder, "it's that things always mean something even if we can't immediately figure out what that is."

"Is everything okay?" Figgy came toward them. She ran her hand through her hair, ruffling it even further.

Penelope explained about finding the notebook and giving it to Maguire.

"You did the right thing," Figgy said. "The police are always urging people to share any information they have about a murder case and that's what you did." She smiled at Penelope. "I think we could all do with a nice cuppa. Why don't I make us some?"

Mabel and Penelope joined her in the tea shop and waited while she prepared the tea.

"Here we go," Figgy said finally, putting a tray down on the table. She poured cups of Earl Grey and handed them around.

"Let's see the photographs you took of the notebook," Mabel said.

Penelope pulled them up on her phone and handed it to Mabel. She explained her theory that the notations possibly had something to do with the secrets Regina was in the habit of collecting—a way for her to make note of them but disguising the information in case someone found the notebook.

"If it doesn't mean anything, why would she have hidden the book in that planter?" Penelope said.

"I suppose she didn't want Gordon to find it, but how on earth would he have been able to make heads or tails of this?" Mabel said. "If this is a code, it's a strange one—combining single letters with whole words. Normally you would begin to decipher code by assuming that the single letters were the word *a*, since that is such a common one-letter word. And then you'd go from there—seeing if the three-letter words could possibly be *the*."

"What if the single letters were initials?" Penelope blew on her tea.

Mabel frowned. "That could be. As you said, with Regina's penchant for hoarding secrets, that notebook may very well have been her way of keeping track."

"What is the first entry in the notebook?" Figgy said, refilling her teacup.

Penelope took the phone and scrolled through the pictures. "It's a *D* followed by the word *money*."

"Could that be Daphne Potter?" Mabel said. "But why the word *money*?"

"Maybe that she's after Gordon's money?" Figgy said. "Perhaps Regina overheard something?"

"We may never know," Mabel said, "but it certainly is curious." She took the phone and scrolled through the photographs again. She pointed to an entry. "There's a phone number written here." She looked through the photos of the rest of the notebook's pages. "No other numbers, but there's an address here."

Penelope peered over Mabel's shoulder. "'Compton Lane, Northampton,'" she read. She pointed to another entry. "What's this? 'MM—OS—wed.'"

The phone began to tremble in Mabel's hand and her face turned white. She all but shoved the phone at Pen.

"Who knows what that infernal woman was up to? It probably means nothing. Best to forget about it."

Penelope tucked her phone back into her pocket.

"I'm sure the police will solve the case without our

help," Pen said soothingly. "Maybe then we can work backward and figure out what all that gibberish means."

That was rather odd, Penelope thought. Mabel had acted so strangely when she saw that one entry. Could it possibly be that the MM in Regina's notebook stood for Mabel Morris?

EIGHT

~⚬~

Penelope wasn't one to give up easily—although what she thought she could do when even Mabel, with her experience in MI6, couldn't decipher the code in the notebook, she didn't know.

Mrs. Danvers greeted Penelope with cool disdain when Penelope pushed open the door to her cottage.

"You're mad because I left, aren't you?" she said to the cat, scratching her under the chin.

Mrs. Danvers purred and arched her back. It seemed she was willing to forgive Penelope—at least for the time being.

It was chilly in the cottage. Penelope arranged some logs and some kindling in the fireplace and put a match to it. She patted herself on the back when it caught. She was finally getting the hang of this. She knelt in front of the fireplace warming her hands. A few minutes later the logs began to catch, and then they too began to glow.

Penelope's stomach rumbled and she paused to examine the sensation. She must be hungry. She glanced at the clock. Of course she was—it was nearly past dinnertime.

The night before she had made a pot of spaghetti Bolognese or what she'd learned the Brits called spag Bol. She was about to put her dish in the microwave when she heard a knock on the door.

Mrs. Danvers, who had been loitering in the vicinity of the food, made a mad dash for the living room. Penelope followed. She flung open the door. A woman was standing on the doorstep clutching a batch of brochures. She was slight with short brown hair in neat waves. Her skirt was either too long or too short to be fashionable and she smelled clean—like soap and laundry detergent.

She smiled hesitantly at Penelope and held out a brochure. "I'm Nora Blakely from the WI."

Penelope raised her eyebrows. "The WI?"

"I'm sorry. That's the Women's Institute—the Upper Chumley-on-Stoke chapter. I'm the treasurer."

Penelope hoped she wasn't collecting money for something.

The wind had picked up and was tugging at Nora's skirt and swirling leaves along the gutter outside Penelope's cottage.

"I'm sorry," Penelope said. "Won't you come in?"

"You're Penelope Parish, right?"

Penelope assured her that she was and Nora stepped over the threshold.

"What a charming room," Nora said, looking around. "And the fire feels quite lovely. It's become rather chilly out."

"Please sit down," Penelope said. "Would you like a cup of coffee?"

"No, thank you. I've just had my tea." She folded her hands and put them in her lap.

Penelope waited expectantly.

"I'm here to tell you about the Women's Institute," Nora said finally. "And to invite you to join the group to show our hospitality."

"Oh." Penelope was taken aback. "That's very kind of you. What does the Women's Institute do?"

Nora cleared her throat. "The organization was started to get women in rural communities and small towns like ours to produce food during World War One. Then we were provided with extra sugar, which was being closely rationed, during World War Two to produce jellies and jams with fruit that would have gone bad otherwise. We even received canning equipment from America."

She smiled benignly at Penelope as if Penelope had been personally involved in the donation.

"Now we've become a sort of radical group." Nora laughed at her own joke. "We've gotten involved in politics and all sorts of things."

"I don't know—"

"The queen is a member," Nora said as if that settled it.

"Could I look over the brochure?" Penelope said.

"Certainly." Nora folded her hands in her lap again. She appeared to be waiting for an answer.

"Can I let you know—after I've read the brochure?" Penelope said.

Nora looked startled. "Certainly."

"It's very kind of you to invite me," Penelope said again lest Nora think she wasn't grateful.

Nora nodded and got to her feet. "It's such a shame about what happened to Regina Bosworth. She was supposed to be our next president. I suppose we shall have to hold another election now." She paused and pursed her lips. "Unless the runner-up takes over the position. We shall have to check the bylaws."

She smiled at Penelope as they walked toward the door. Penelope saw her out and then closed the door. A thought struck her as she was putting her dish of spaghetti back in the microwave to heat.

Hadn't there been a notation in Regina's notebook for someone whose first initial was *N*? She put her plate on the kitchen table and went out to the foyer to retrieve her purse. She pulled out her phone and flipped through the photos. Yes, there it was: $N = Work = WI/Drink$.

N could certainly be Nora. She was obviously involved in the WI, if that stood for the Women's Institute.

But why the word *work* and what on earth did *drink* mean?

Penelope washed her dishes, dried them, and put them away. Unfortunately charm didn't come with a dishwasher but since she made very few dirty dishes, she really didn't mind.

She brushed her teeth, ran her fingers through her hair, put on her coat, and grabbed her laptop. Mrs. Danvers stared at her with disapproval from her perch on the arm of the sofa.

Penelope assured Mrs. Danvers that she would be back . . . eventually . . . and went out the door. Tonight was a special event at the Open Book. Cookbook author Evaline Foster was going to give a demonstration right in the store. Pen was looking forward to it.

The evening was chilly but cloudless with hundreds

of stars dotting the night sky. Penelope stood for a moment admiring them—without the light pollution of the big city it almost looked as if you could reach up and touch them.

She decided to walk to the Open Book. Mabel looked up when Penelope opened the door.

"That night air has done you some good, I see. It's put some color in your cheeks." She smiled. "You look healthy."

Penelope unwound her scarf, took off her coat and hat, and hung them on the coat-tree.

Mabel had set up folding chairs in a half circle in an empty area of the bookstore. A table in back of the chairs held copies of Evaline Foster's latest cookbook, *Cakes Fit for a King*. A long table covered with a white cloth was in front of the chairs. On it were bowls, wooden spoons, whisks and packages of McVitie's digestive biscuits.

Evaline was fussing over the arrangement and checking things off against the list fluttering in her hand. She was a plump woman with ash-blond hair set and lacquered into place in a hairdo reminiscent of the queen's. She was wearing a fawn-colored short-sleeved dress with a frilly white apron tied over it. There was a starburst broach pinned to her shoulder.

Figgy wheeled over a tea cart set with plates, cups, saucers, and two electric kettles.

"I've got two types of tea," she said to Penelope. "Earl Grey and Lapsang souchong. And we'll be serving Evaline's cake as well."

Evaline would be demonstrating one of the recipes from her cookbook and afterward she planned to sign copies for the Open Book's patrons.

India was the first to arrive followed by Shirley

Townsend and Tracey Meadows. Tracey was a new mother with a four-month-old baby.

"How is the baby?" Shirley took a chair, crossed her legs, and smoothed out her blouse.

"He's finally sleeping through the night. If you can call five hours through the night. Still, it's the most sleep I've had in months."

"Is Nigel minding him?"

"Yes. Under some duress, I might add. He kept trying to tell me he wasn't up to it, but I told him that as long as the baby was alive when I got home, it was a job well done."

Tracey pointed to the picture of the cake on the front cover of Evaline's book. "I'll have to stay away from that. I have to get serious about slimming. I need to lose the baby weight. There's a smart young secretary in Nigel's office and she's had eyes for him for ages now. I can't have him getting any ideas." She pointed to her blouse. "I'm still wearing maternity tops." She looked down and scratched at a bit of a stain near her shoulder. "Spit-up." She made a face.

"I should be on a slimming course myself." Shirley laughed and patted her stomach. "This might not have been the best demonstration to come to. I hear Miss Foster is going to show us how to make a chocolate biscuit cake."

"That cake is a favorite of the queen's," India said with authority as if she had inside knowledge of that fact and hadn't read it in *My Weekly* magazine. "She has it for tea every day until it's finished. They've even transported it to Windsor Castle for her."

"Here comes Helen Hathaway," Tracey said. "Hi, Helen." She waved at a petite silver-haired woman.

"There's going to be a demonstration on how to make a chocolate biscuit cake."

"I remember the one you made, Helen, for the Women's Institute tea when the Countess of Wessex came to visit our chapter," Shirley said.

"Yes. Wasn't that the time—"

"There was that incident with Nora Blakely? Yes."

"So dreadfully embarrassing," India said, clutching her pearls.

"What happened?" Penelope took a seat.

"Well," Shirley said in a tone that suggested she was about to impart a particularly juicy morsel of gossip. "Nora was known to . . ." She mimed drinking. "And it wasn't just the odd glass of afternoon sherry. She came to the tea completely sozzled and fell face-first onto the tea table." Shirley laughed. "Her head landed in a bowl of Eton mess if you can believe it!"

"Regina was beside herself," Helen said. "I thought she would have a stroke."

"Of course, it seems funny now," Shirley said, "but at the time we were all mortified. In the presence of the countess no less. We'd all been warned to be on our best behavior and then . . ."

"I heard she's gotten help," Tracey said. "My neighbor told me she saw her coming out of one of those Alcoholics Anonymous meetings." She picked at the spot on her blouse again. "They hold them at St. Andrew's, I think."

Penelope was surprised. She wouldn't have expected Nora, of all people, to have a problem with alcohol. She'd seemed so prim and proper.

"That's sad," Penelope said.

Shirley nodded. "It is. You never know what's going to drive a person to drink. I think it was that accident."

"What accident?" Tracey said.

A handful of other women had arrived by now and Evaline was standing behind the table, smiling benignly at everyone. She cleared her throat.

"Shall we begin?" She opened her cookbook to a glossy full-color picture of a cake and held it up for everyone to see. "Today we are going to be making a chocolate biscuit cake. It's a favorite of the queen's," she cooed. "It's what we call a refrigerator cake and is quite simple to make despite its royal pedigree."

Penelope wasn't paying attention. She was thinking about what Shirley had just said. What accident had Nora been in? And what did it have to do with her drinking? And did any of it have anything to do with Regina's death?

As soon as the demonstration was finished, and the ladies had eaten and fussed over Evaline's chocolate biscuit cake, Penelope retreated to her writing room. Mabel gave her a strange look as Pen sped past, her laptop under her arm.

Penelope wasted no time but got her computer up and running, clicked on her favorite search engine, and typed in some information. She bit her lower lip as she hit enter and waited for the near instantaneous results.

She scrolled through several entries until she came to a link to an article in the Upper Chumley-on-Stoke newspaper, the *Trumpet Herald*. She began to read. According to the article, a Nora Blakely of Evergreen Lane, Upper Chumley-on-Stoke, had lost control of her car on an icy road and had hit another vehicle head on, killing the other driver instantly.

Penelope leaned back in her chair. She could imagine that something as traumatic as that might drive someone to drink. Was that what had happened to poor Nora?

* * *

It wasn't until later, when Penelope and Mabel were helping Figgy clean up, that the penny dropped as Penelope's grandmother would have said. She abruptly put down the plates she was carrying and ran to get her purse.

"What's up?" Figgy said.

"You know that notebook I showed you? The one I found in Regina's planter?"

Figgy and Mabel nodded.

Penelope rummaged in her purse—a large, shapeless affair that she kept meaning to clean out. Where had her phone gotten to? She pulled out her wallet, a spare pair of glasses, one sock, and finally, there it was.

Mabel and Figgy gathered around as she thumbed through the pictures on her phone until she found the ones she'd taken of the notebook. Mabel put on her glasses, which had been resting on top of her head.

"See?" Penelope pointed to the entry $N = Work = WI/Drink$. They peered at the notation in Regina's fancy scrawl.

"I guess Regina knew that Nora drank," Figgy said. "But so did everyone else it seems, so it was hardly a secret."

Mabel rubbed her chin. "And WI? She's the treasurer of the Women's Institute but it's hard to believe Regina would have written these things down if that was their only significance—that Nora drank and was in the Women's Institute. Don't you think?"

Penelope tucked her phone back in her purse. "I suppose. But what do you think it means, then?"

Figgy paused with the plate of what was left of the cake in her hand. "What if Nora hasn't quit drinking? Maybe she's fallen off the wagon?"

"Do you think Regina was trying to blackmail her?" Mabel sounded incredulous.

"That does sound rather astonishing," Figgy admitted.

"Maybe Regina planned to use that knowledge to her own advantage somehow?" Pen said. The more she thought about it, the more logical the explanation seemed.

"Now that does make sense," Mabel said. "We just have to find out what that was."

Fancy a drink?" Mabel said as they were closing up the store. "You haven't been to the Book and Bottle yet, have you?"

Penelope buttoned up her coat as they stepped outside. The air was fresh against her face. She felt a sense of contentment she hadn't felt in a long time.

"Sounds good to me," she said as she and Mabel headed down the high street.

The wind had picked up and the wooden sign depicting a volume of Shakespeare and a bottle of lager hanging outside the Book and Bottle creaked as it swayed back and forth. They were about to pull open the door when someone from the inside pushed it instead. A man came stumbling out, his hat slightly askew and his jacket buttoned up all wrong.

"'Scuse me, ladies," he said and hiccoughed. The air filled with the smell of beer. He staggered down the street singing "God Save the Queen" at the top of his lungs.

A window above one of the shops opened and someone yelled, "Be quiet, would you? The wee lad is finally asleep."

"A bit the worse for wear," Mabel said, gesturing toward the fellow weaving his way down the street.

They stepped inside the Book and Bottle and Penelope paused to look around. The pub had beamed ceilings, old oak furniture, and gleaming taps behind a long wooden bar. It was warm, cozy, and snug.

Men in jeans and flannel shirts clustered around the bar, their hands around tankards of ale. A lively dart game was going on in the far corner and a young man with lank dark hair was pulling the handle on the slot machine—or the fruit machine, which Pen had learned was the British term. Judging by the set of his shoulders, Penelope guessed he wasn't having much luck. Several young couples were deep in intense conversation, holding hands across the table and oblivious to everyone around them.

Nearly everyone in the place turned around and looked when Penelope and Mabel entered.

"Don't worry," Mabel whispered to Penelope, "the novelty will wear off after you've been here a couple of years." She laughed. "I was deemed highly suspicious when I first moved here after I bought the Open Book, but I no longer hear whispers when I enter a room."

They found an empty table and sat down.

"What will you have?" Mabel said. "I suggest a cider. I think you'd like it."

Penelope readily agreed. She shrugged off her coat and unwound her scarf as Mabel went to the bar to place their order.

She recognized the young woman behind the bar who waited on Mabel—it was Daphne Potter who had appeared to be consoling Gordon Bosworth at his wife's memorial luncheon. She was wearing an old-fashioned barmaid's outfit with the obligatory low-cut puffed-sleeve blouse, a tight vest that accentuated her small waist and abundant cleavage, and a short frilly skirt. Her long dark hair was pulled back in a twist and there was a dark red ribbon woven through it.

Mabel soon returned, balancing two glasses on a tray along with a packet of potato chips.

"I've got us some crisps," she said, ripping open the bag and setting it in the middle of the table. She laughed at Penelope's blank expression.

"We call these crisps. I believe you call them potato chips?"

Penelope nodded. She took a gulp of her cider.

"Careful," Mabel said. "There's alcohol in that."

Penelope had been expecting the American version of apple cider and coughed and sputtered as the liquid burned its way down her throat.

"It's good," she said as she took another, more cautious sip.

Mabel played with her glass—turning it around and around in her hands. She turned serious and Penelope looked at her curiously.

"Thanks for coming out with me tonight," Mabel said. "Today is a difficult day for me." She took a sip of her cider. "It's the anniversary of the day we learned Oliver had gone missing."

Penelope cocked her head. "Oliver?"

Mabel laughed. "I wasn't always a white-haired old lady. I was young once and in love. Oliver Semenov was an MI6 operative. He was born in Russia but his family emigrated to Britain when he was a child. The fact that he could speak the language made him invaluable as a spy. We had nine months together before he was assigned to go undercover in the Soviet Union."

Mabel stared into the distance for several moments, then sighed.

"Somehow he managed to get messages to me to let me know he was all right . . . and to tell me he loved me." Mabel looked down at the table. She wiped a finger under her eyes and when she looked up, Penelope could see they were glistening with tears.

"One day the messages stopped. I didn't think anything of it at first—there were often long gaps when I didn't hear a thing. It wasn't always easy for Oliver to find a way to communicate that wouldn't jeopardize his cover."

Mabel picked up the empty crisp packet and began to pleat it between her fingers.

"But I began to sense that this time might be different. I don't know why. Intuition? A gut feeling? Months went by, then it was a year and then several years. It took a long time, but I finally gave up hope of ever hearing from Oliver again. They never did find out what happened, but it was presumed that he was dead."

"I'm so sorry," Penelope said. She wrinkled her brow. "Semenov? That name rings a bell for some reason."

Mabel looked startled. Her hand jerked and she nearly knocked her cider over.

"It's not a terribly common name—at least not in Britain. I doubt you've heard it before. Anyway," Mabel said, suddenly becoming brisk. "All that was a long time ago. I've recovered, although there are still those days when all the feelings come rushing back." She smiled. "It doesn't last for long. I'll be right as rain tomorrow." She finished the last bit of her cider. "Thanks for listening," she said. "I didn't mean to lay that all on you."

Penelope reached out and took Mabel's hands. "Don't

be silly. I'm glad I could be here for you. Anytime. Seriously."

Mabel smiled ruefully. "Somehow I never fell in love again. There were dates, even an affair that lasted almost six months, but in the end I guess I never really got over Oliver." She looked at Penelope. "I suppose I didn't want to." She laughed. "Silly me clinging to something that was over—something that could never be."

Penelope thought of her own love life—or lack thereof. Was she doing the same thing as Mabel—stringing Miles along so she didn't have to admit the relationship was a failure and look for someone else? She knew she had no intention of marrying him—not that he'd asked her but things seemed to be heading in that direction.

Miles had said he would come to Chumley to see her the next time he was in London on business and could spare a few days away from his job. She'd definitely tell him then that it was over between them. Keeping him hanging wasn't fair to either of them.

And then, without Miles as a safety net, perhaps she'd be open to meeting someone else.

NINE

⊸⊱⊰⊷

Penelope glanced at her computer screen and sighed. She had managed to get her protagonist, Annora, into the cellar where Penelope wanted her and where danger awaited her. She was now in the clutches of the villain. But how to rescue her?

Penelope was certain of one thing—Annora had to rescue herself—no Prince Charming riding in on his white horse to save her. Like life, Penelope thought. You couldn't depend on a man to define your life. You had to do it yourself.

Her mother claimed that Penelope's independent attitude would drive men away. Penelope didn't care—she didn't want a man who was threatened by her independence anyway.

She was about to close her laptop when she changed her mind. Ever since talking to Mabel earlier that evening, Penelope had been trying to remember where she'd heard the name Semenov before. Mabel was right—it wasn't a common name. But Penelope was convinced that she remembered it from somewhere.

She pulled up a search engine and typed in *Semenov*. The headline on the first article that appeared read "Surgeon Saves Wife of Prime Minister with New Cardiac Procedure." The name Semenov immediately caught Penelope's eye.

The surgeon, Ursula Semenov, had invented a new surgical technique, which she had used to treat the prime minister's ailing wife. Now that Penelope had seen the article, she remembered reading about the lifesaving surgery. No wonder the name had sounded so familiar.

She wondered if there was any relation between Ursula Semenov and Mabel's Oliver.

She did some more searching and discovered a longer article on Ursula Semenov. It talked about the surgical procedure she had pioneered, her early life in Russia before coming to Britain, her medical training. Suddenly the name Oliver Semenov popped out at Penelope.

She reached for her mug of tea and settled down to read.

The more she read, the more shocked she became. It turned out that Ursula and Oliver Semenov were husband and wife . . . and there was no mention of a divorce. There was speculation that Oliver hadn't disappeared in Russia but that he'd actually defected to his birth country.

So Mabel had been in love with a married man. Penelope grabbed her purse and pulled out her phone. There it was: MM—OS—Wed. Regina had obviously uncovered Mabel's secret. Had she tried to blackmail Mabel with it? Penelope couldn't imagine what Mabel could have done for Regina. Perhaps it was simply one of the secrets Regina kept in her back pocket in case it ever came in handy.

Penelope couldn't decide whether to mention her discovery to Mabel or not. What purpose would it serve? She thought about it as she climbed the stairs to bed and by the time she'd slid under the covers, she had decided she would keep the information to herself.

She was due at the Open Book shortly for the writing group she had started at Mabel's suggestion. She felt like a bit of a fraud running a group for writers when she was struggling so much with her own manuscript.

Penelope spent an extra couple of minutes making a fuss over Mrs. Danvers who purred loudly, arched her back, then suddenly stalked away, her tail in the air.

So much for that, Penelope thought, getting her coat out of the closet. It was another brisk day, and although the sky was overcast, rain hadn't been predicted. She decided to take a chance and walk to the bookstore again since she had to stop in at the drugstore and pick up some shampoo.

Penelope closed and locked the front door to her cottage, paused for a moment to admire her temporary home—she never seemed to tire of that—then began walking down the high street.

She passed Icing on the Cake—the bakery—and glanced in their window, where luscious-looking tarts filled with glistening berries and cakes with delectable frosting were on display. Her stomach rumbled and she realized she had forgotten to eat breakfast. The iced scones looked very tempting, but, as tempted as she was, she knew Figgy would have something for her at the bookstore. The Sweet Tooth candy shop was right next door and the window was filled with more scrumptious goodies and the smell of their homemade chocolates wafted out the door when a customer opened it.

The Upper Chumley-on-Stoke Apothecary was next to the Sweet Tooth. The rabbit warren of shelves behind the counter was original to the store, and, although modern improvements had been added along the way, the old wooden floor still creaked under foot.

Penelope found the shampoo display and was looking for the brand she wanted when she heard two women talking an aisle over.

"She was being quite forward," one woman said in offended tones.

Her companion murmured something Penelope couldn't quite catch.

"And at his wife's funeral, no less," the first woman added.

Penelope's ears perked up. Could they be talking about Regina's funeral? She found the bottle of shampoo she wanted but continued to linger, pretending she was looking at the various products.

"She's been after him for a time now," the other woman said. "And I blame Gordon for encouraging her the way he does."

They *were* talking about Regina's funeral. And Penelope had no doubt the woman they were criticizing for being *quite forward* was Daphne Potter.

"I thought Gordon was just being nice to her," the first woman said.

"Nice? You do know he gave her a car, don't you? I heard it from Lady Maxwell-Lewis when I was getting my hair done."

Penelope heard the other woman gasp.

"It was secondhand, of course, but in terribly good shape—a Vauxhall of some sort. I'm afraid I don't know my cars. It looked almost brand-new if you ask me. I've seen her driving around town in it as if she was the Duchess of Upper Chumley-on-Stoke herself!"

That was interesting, Penelope thought, as she paid for her purchase. So Gordon's interest had gone beyond just visiting the Book and Bottle for a drink every night. A car was quite an expensive present to give to someone—especially if that person was just a casual acquaintance.

Maybe there really was more to Gordon and Daphne's relationship than everyone first realized. Perhaps they were having an honest-to-goodness affair. Wouldn't that give Daphne a motive for murder?

D id you know that Gordon Bosworth bought Daphne a car?" Penelope said when she arrived at the Open Book.

"Yes," Mabel said. She was shelving some books that had been left out on the various tables scattered around the store. "It was terribly kind of him." She turned around to face Penelope. "I wouldn't read too much into it. Daphne's sister, Layla, is disabled—she uses a wheelchair. Some sort of accident, I believe. She's collecting insurance, of course, but she can't live on her own. Daphne takes care of her." Mabel hesitated, a hand on her hip, then put one of the books face out on the shelf. "Daphne's old car broke down—

it had been destined for the junk heap for a long time as it was and there was no putting another bandage on it to squeeze out a few more miles—and it was difficult for her to get her sister to her medical appointments, let alone take her for the occasional outing to break the monotony of being in the house all day."

Mabel smiled at Penelope. "Don't tell me you're still trying to solve Regina's murder? I would leave that to the police, if I were you. They probably already have a lot more information than we do. They have forensics and the like— things the police in Christie's Miss Marple books didn't have."

"Believe me, I'd be more than happy to leave it in Detective Maguire's lap. It's only that I promised Charlotte I would see what I could do."

"I can't imagine why Charlotte would think you'd have any better luck than the police."

"Neither can I," Penelope said, thinking of how little she'd been able to discover so far.

She was feeling rather discouraged when the members of her writing group began to arrive. Lady Evelyn Maxwell-Lewis was the first. She was wearing jodhpurs and tall leather boots again, and the faint odor of horse combined with fresh hay clung to her. Penelope had been surprised to find out that Evelyn was writing a Regency romance. All that bodice ripping and shirtless men with rippling muscles was so at odds with her cut-glass persona.

Nora Blakely was also in the group and was working on a children's book, which seemed fitting. Penelope thought her illustrations were quite good—fairytale-like watercolors—and she was hoping to guide Nora in writing a salable manuscript to go with them.

Two more members drifted in—both also writing romances—obviously a popular genre—but far more tepid and timid ones than Evelyn's.

They all took seats around the table at the back of the store. Nora took a notebook from her bag, placed it in front of her, put a pencil beside it, and folded her hands on top. Evelyn flung herself into a chair, pulled an untidy sheaf of manuscript pages from her purse, put them in her lap, and leaned back, crossing her long legs.

Figgy wheeled over a cart set up with an electric kettle and an assortment of tea bags and cups and saucers, and Penelope took that as a signal to begin. She cleared her throat.

Before she could say a word, Evelyn pushed back her chair. "I simply must have a cup of tea first. I hope you don't think I'm being rude, but I'm utterly parched. I took Brigadier out this morning for a long ride and he kicked up so much dust my throat feels like the Sahara."

The spoon tinkled against the cup as Evelyn stirred sugar into her tea. She glanced at Nora. "What is the Women's Institute going to do about the president's position now that Regina is no longer with us?"

"I can't believe she was elected," one of the other women murmured. "I know I didn't vote for her."

"Neither did I," Evelyn said. "But obviously others did. I imagine she would have been quite good at it—as well as insufferably bossy and condescending." She paused with her teaspoon in her hand, her mouth forming a small *o*. "Do you suppose the election results were tampered with?" She looked at the others.

"You mean by Regina?" Penelope said. "Would that have been possible? Surely someone else counts the votes?"

A flush had risen up Nora's neck to her face, which became mottled with red. "I count the votes," she said in a very small voice.

Evelyn raised an eyebrow. "And you couldn't have made a mistake?"

Nora shook her head. "No, I counted them twice to be sure."

She put her hands in her lap but not before Penelope noticed they were shaking slightly.

Had Regina convinced Nora to change the vote in her favor? But why would Nora agree to that? She thought back to the conversation she'd had with Mabel and India before the murder—about how Regina collected secrets. Maybe Regina knew something about Nora that persuaded Nora she had to do what Regina wanted. Mabel had said she didn't think it had anything to do with Nora's drinking, despite the entry in Regina's notebook—Nora's vice seemed to be a well-known secret. It had to be something else. Something Regina thought she could use against Nora.

P enelope realized that her diet of late had consisted mainly of food Figgy had kindly given her from the Teapot. She decided it was time to make herself a proper dinner for a change and at lunchtime she went across the street to the Pig in a Poke to buy whatever looked good— and that she could afford.

A sign in the window announced a sale on pork-and-leek sausage and boneless pork loin chops, and hung beside a large wooden cutout of a pink and smiling pig. Penelope wondered what on earth the poor pig had to smile about, given that it would soon find itself butchered into chops and roasts or stuffed into sausages and splayed out on a platter on someone's dining table.

Penelope pushed open the door. Large cuts of meat hung from vicious-looking hooks behind the long counter. The shop also carried poultry, and chickens with the heads still attached dangled between the cuts of beef. There was an outline of a pig on a poster on the wall with arrows indicating the different cuts of meat and another one on the opposite wall showing the different parts of a cow.

Gladys was behind the counter, handing a customer a brown-paper-wrapped parcel tied with twine. Her husband, Bruce, was in back of her, cutting a beef tenderloin into plump filet mignon steaks. He had broad shoulders and a thick neck dotted with short bristly hairs. His neck was a dusky red—as if he'd been sunburned. His gray hair was cut close to the scalp and was receding on the sides.

Gladys's plump face broke into a smile when she saw Penelope. "Hello, love. What can I get for you?"

"I don't know," Penelope admitted. "I've decided to cook myself dinner for a change. What do you suggest?"

"We have some lovely pork loin chops. And our pork-and-leek sausages are on sale. Or perhaps you'd fancy a steak? Bruce is cutting up some filet mignons right now."

"I imagine those are pricey. Probably beyond my budget."

Gladys winked. "I'm sure we can give you a good deal. What do you say?"

"Okay," Penelope said, suddenly salivating at the thought of a nice juicy steak.

"Give me one of those filets," she said to Bruce. "The nice plump one there."

Bruce grunted and handed the meat to Gladys, who pulled a length of brown paper from the roller, wrapped up the filet, and tied it securely with a piece of twine. She was handing the tidy package to Penelope when the sleeve of her blouse slid up her arm, briefly revealing a large and angry oddly shaped purple bruise that was beginning to turn yellow.

"Gladys! What happened to your arm?"

Gladys hastily pulled down her sleeve. "Oh, that? It's nothing. Looks worse than it is." She glanced behind her. Bruce was glaring at her.

Gladys smiled again, only it looked strained this time. "I walked into a door on the way to the loo in the middle of the night. Silly me."

Penelope didn't press her—it was clear she didn't want to talk about it . . . or couldn't talk about it. Penelope strongly suspected Bruce had something to do with that nasty black-and-blue mark.

Penelope was about to leave when the door opened and Charlotte walked in. All three of them looked stunned to see her. She was wearing yoga pants, a baby blue cashmere sweater, and a Barbour jacket. Her hair was in a ponytail and she had no makeup on. She was still stunning.

Gladys began to flutter, her facial expression alternating between a welcoming smile and sheer astonishment. Penelope could have sworn she actually dipped into a small curtsy as Charlotte approached the counter. Gladys might have been complaining about Charlotte's unsuitability as a match for Worthington just the other day, but in Charlotte's presence, she dissolved into a fawning fan awed by the seemingly royal connection, however distant.

"Penelope," Charlotte said when she noticed her. "How

are you?" Charlotte glanced over her shoulder at Gladys. She lowered her voice. "Can I talk to you?"

Penelope was taken aback. "Sure."

"Let's go outside." Charlotte put her hand on Penelope's arm and led her to the door.

They stepped outside, leaving Gladys sputtering behind the counter.

"Have you found out anything yet?" Charlotte said as they stood in the shadow of the butcher shop awning. "Please tell me you have."

Penelope hated to disappoint her. She shook her head reluctantly. "No, not yet, I'm afraid."

Charlotte chewed on her bottom lip—an anxious gesture that surprised Penelope. Charlotte always projected such a calm and collected image—as if she were gliding through life on greased rollers.

"Please tell me you'll keep trying," Charlotte said, gripping Penelope's arm with a fierceness that surprised Penelope.

Penelope again wondered why Charlotte was so convinced the police were going to consider her a suspect. She'd barely known Regina and, as far as Penelope knew, the two had managed to get along well enough.

Regina had to have known something about Charlotte that was making Charlotte so nervous. But what? Charlotte obviously wasn't prepared to reveal any secrets to Penelope. Penelope would have to operate on the assumption that there was something—something that could have come between Charlotte and Worthington—something serious enough to make Charlotte believe she was a suspect in Regina's murder.

Charlotte fiddled with the zipper on her jacket, pulling it up and down.

"Detective Maguire came to Worthington House yesterday. He spent a long time talking to Arthur and then to me." Charlotte bit her bottom lip again. "He wouldn't let Arthur stay in the room—he said he wanted to talk to us separately." She looked down at her highly polished leather ankle boots. "I suppose he wanted to see if our stories matched." She gave a pained smile. "I've watched my share of *Law and Order*, and that's how they always do it."

Did Maguire actually suspect Charlotte or Worthington? Penelope wondered. Or was this simply the usual procedure and Charlotte was blowing it out of proportion? After all, Regina had been killed at Worthington House, so surely Maguire had plenty of questions that needed answers.

"I'm sure Detective Maguire is interviewing anyone connected with Regina or the fest," Penelope said.

Charlotte shook her head and her ponytail swished back and forth.

"It's not only that." She began pulling her zipper up and down again. "He told us they—the police—found the gun that killed Regina."

"Oh?"

Charlotte looked at Penelope, her eyes wide with fear. "He said the gun came from Arthur's collection. The killer took it from the gun safe in the basement. But the safe is always locked. Arthur keeps one key on his key chain and the other is in a drawer in a table in the drawing room."

"So someone must have stolen the key," Penelope said.

"Yes, but . . ." Charlotte paused. "Who would have known where to find it? Aside from Arthur, of course."

Penelope thought for a moment. "One of the servants,

perhaps? Would they have known where the keys were kept?"

Charlotte shrugged. "Probably. But what motive would they have had? I doubt any of them even knew Regina."

"Perhaps Regina caught them out in something? Stealing, perhaps?"

"They've all been with Arthur for ages. Besides, if they'd wanted to steal something, there would have been plenty of other opportunities. Why choose the day the fest was going on and people were coming and going from the cellar?"

Penelope had to admit that didn't make any sense.

On the other hand, she couldn't imagine either Charlotte or Worthington killing Regina. It had to have been someone else.

And she had rashly promised Charlotte that she would try to find out just who that was.

TEN

❧

Mabel was behind the counter, staring at a book in her hands with a quizzical expression, when Penelope returned to the Open Book. Penelope put her package of meat in the refrigerator in the stock room and joined her.

"What's that?" Penelope pointed to the book in Mabel's hands.

Mabel made a face. "It was sent to me by a local author who wants to have a book signing here."

"The cover is rather . . . odd," Penelope said. "Do you know the author?"

Mabel shook her head. "Not well, no. But I know who she is—she's the wife of a solicitor in town. He works long hours." Mabel held the book up. "I guess this is how she passes the time."

"What are you going to do?"

Mabel stuck the book under the counter. "Avoid the issue as long as possible." She grinned at Penelope.

"You'll have to deal with it eventually," Penelope said. She liked to tackle things head on herself—like a runaway train, her sister often said, since it meant Pen occasionally acted without thinking things through.

"Did you get your meat?" Mabel changed the subject.

"A lovely piece of filet mignon. A bit rich for my blood, but Gladys gave me a discount."

"What a treat," Mabel said.

"You know, I'm worried about Gladys." Penelope couldn't stop thinking about that angry bruise on Gladys's arm.

Mabel cocked her head. "Oh?"

"I don't think her husband treats her very well."

"He doesn't," Mabel said matter-of-factly. "He's a terrible bully and takes advantage of her. I think that's why she takes refuge in her romance novels. Books can transport you to another reality—one where earthly cares no longer exist—at least not while you're engrossed in the story. And then in romance, there's always the happily ever after ending. It's an escape for Gladys."

"I'm glad she has that comfort at least. But I'm worried that he's abusive. Gladys has a large bruise on her arm—it was a strange shape and now I realize it looked like fingerprints—it was still purple but beginning to turn yellow so she must have gotten it a couple of days ago."

"Did you ask Gladys about it?"

"Yes. She said she walked into a door in the middle of the night. She seemed very nervous and kept looking over her shoulder at her husband."

Now Mabel looked concerned. She frowned. "I didn't know that. Poor Gladys. It does sound as if Bruce has become abusive."

"What are we going to do? Gladys is terribly sweet and doesn't deserve to be treated like that. No one does."

"I'll see if I can have a word with her," Mabel said. "Perhaps she'll confide in me."

Penelope closed herself in the tiny room Mabel had set aside for her to use when she wasn't busy in the shop. She had her laptop open and her fingers on the keys, and for once the words were flowing. She was shocked when she looked at the clock and realized the entire afternoon had flown by. Perhaps England was working its magic after all.

The room was windowless, so she hadn't noticed the passage of time and was surprised to see that outside the windows of the Open Book it was dark and the streetlights had come on.

Figgy was slumped at a table in the tearoom, texting on her phone. Penelope plopped into the seat opposite her with a sigh.

Figgy looked up from her phone, peering at Penelope from under her bangs. "You look totally fagged out."

"I am," Penelope admitted. "I've never been able to figure out how sitting in a chair and writing can be so tiring." She blew out a breath and the lock of hair that had drifted onto her forehead momentarily went back into place. "Rescuing Annora wasn't easy, but I managed to do it. Fortunately I was able to plant a rusted iron bar that had come loose from one of the windows in the basement for her to make use of. I'm proud to say she wielded it expertly." Penelope grinned.

* * *

The bright red neon-lit Tesco sign was a brash modern intrusion amid all the quaint wooden signs that hung in front of Upper Chumley-on-Stoke's shops along the high street and broke the illusion of having stepped back into a century long past.

Penelope had decided that she would get a bottle of inexpensive red wine to go with her steak dinner. She felt she deserved a bit of a celebration having accomplished so much on her manuscript that afternoon.

Pen was turning into the car park behind Tesco when another car pulled in behind her. The driver appeared to be in a hurry—shooting into an empty parking space in the row next to Pen. The driver had barely cut the lights when she was already opening the door and getting out of the car.

She looked around her furtively as if she didn't want to be seen. She was passing under one of the lights in the car park when Pen realized it was Nora Blakely.

Her movements were peculiar—appearing cautious and almost stealthy. Penelope's curiosity was piqued. She shut her car door as quietly as possible and followed Nora at a discreet distance.

The smell of curry and exotic spices wafted from the takeaway next door and mingled with the odor of exhaust fumes as cars made their way down the high street.

By the time Pen reached the entrance of the store, Nora had disappeared somewhere inside. Penelope paused as the door whooshed shut behind her. She peered down each of the aisles and finally spotted a figure standing at the very back. She ducked down an aisle and quietly made her way to the rear of the store.

Nora was standing in front of a display of Highland Black Scotch whisky. She hesitated, her hand hovering in the air, then selected a bottle. She looked around her before adding it to her cart. She moved to a shelf of Russian Standard vodka, grabbed a bottle of that, and added it to her cart as well.

As Penelope watched, Nora picked out a bottle of gin and two bottles of wine.

She was turning to go when Penelope approached her.

"Oh!" Nora jumped. "I didn't expect to see you here," she said when she noticed Penelope standing next to her. She smiled anxiously. Her knuckles were white from clutching the handle of her shopping cart and her face was flushed.

She was clearly nervous and it was obvious she wasn't happy to run into someone she knew.

Penelope thought that made it quite clear—Nora and her husband weren't planning a party or simply restocking their liquor cabinet. Nora had obviously not given up drinking even though she had been seen going to an Alcoholics Anonymous meeting.

Penelope said good-bye to Nora, who scurried away, obviously relieved to move on, and stood in front of the display of wine scanning the price tags until she found something that would fit her budget. She picked up a bottle with a plain white generic Red Wine label and took it up to the cashier.

The clerk was an older woman with hair dyed an improbably bright red and a friendly smile. Her name tag read *Patricia Wright*.

"And how are you this evening, love?" she said as she slipped the bottle of wine into a paper bag. "You're the American lass that's working at the Open Book. You were at Worthington House when Regina was murdered, weren't you?"

Penelope nodded.

"What a shame it was," Patricia continued. "Such a lovely woman—so cultured. She shopped here a lot and even as busy as she was, she always had time for a bit of a natter." She handed Penelope the bottle of wine. "I suppose her daughter can go ahead with the wedding now that her mother is gone."

Penelope, who had been only half listening, having been thinking about Nora, perked up her ears. "Daughter?"

"Yes, dear. Victoria, she's called—after our great queen. Such a disappointment to her poor mother. Insists on calling herself Poppy. Can you imagine?"

"Really?" Penelope was grateful she didn't need to throw in more than a word or two here and there to keep Patricia talking.

"Yes. Regina had her heart set on her daughter marrying the Duke of Upper Chumley-on-Stoke. She said that Worthington had taken a real interest in her Victoria— asking after her regularly and even speaking to her at last year's fest. Regina had her hopes up, but then Victoria met this fellow Ronnie and became engaged to him instead. I'm sure he's a good lad and he's got a good job and all." She leaned closer to Penelope. "He works as a plumber and you know how much they charge. Highway robbery, if you ask me. Still, it very nearly broke her mother's heart."

"That's too bad." Penelope couldn't imagine why Regina thought there was a chance Worthington would marry her daughter.

Patricia nodded. "I must say it would have been nice if Worthington had taken up with a local lass. It would have been a bit of excitement for all of us."

"Charlotte is quite nice, actually."

Patricia's eyes goggled. "You know her?"

"Well, we've met," Penelope said.

Patricia frowned. "Still." She puffed out her cheeks. "I suppose Victoria can do what she wants now with no interference. Regina was completely set against the match and wouldn't even hear of attending the wedding and now she's dead." She frowned again. "It makes you wonder, doesn't it?" Patricia swiftly put her hand over her mouth. "I didn't mean anything by that. I shouldn't have said it. I've been watching too many of those murder mysteries on the BBC, I suspect." She laughed.

Penelope didn't know what to say. She made a noncommittal noise and finally managed to get away with her bottle of wine. It sounded as if Victoria had been in the same position that Figgy was in now.

But had Victoria actually done something about it?

G ood morning," Mabel said. She had a pencil stuck behind one ear and her glasses propped on her head. Her laptop was on the counter and her fingers were hovering over the keys.

Pen took off her coat and hung it on the coat-tree. "Need help with anything?"

"I'm finishing up the Open Book's monthly newsletter. It feels a bit thin. Do you have any suggestions?"

Penelope peered over Mabel's shoulder at the computer screen.

"How about something on books that deserve to be read more than once?"

Mabel's face lit up. "That sounds interesting. Go on."

"We could create a list and even do a display of the books in the shop. And perhaps we could ask people to respond with their own suggestions. You could print those in the next monthly newsletter."

Mabel had taken the pencil from behind her ear and was absentmindedly chewing on it.

"I like it," she said. She tapped the pencil against the desk. "I'd have to include *Pride and Prejudice*."

"Definitely," Pen said. "How about *The Stand* by Stephen King."

"I'll add that," Mabel said, her fingers flying over the computer keys.

They were finishing their list—they'd agreed to limit the number of books to twenty—when a customer walked in.

"Hello, hello," the woman said brightly. She was in her fifties and wearing pastel blue slacks with a matching sweatshirt appliqued with gingerbread men sporting pale blue bows.

Mabel did not appear pleased to see her. She put on a smile that looked positively painful.

"Felicity, how lovely to see you."

"Did you decide?" Felicity said, pushing a tangled curl of gray hair behind her ear. "When shall we do the book signing?" She clapped her hands together. "I've wanted to be a real writer since I was at school. And now my name is in print. I can't tell you what a thrill it is."

No wonder Mabel looked cornered, Penelope thought.

"Felicity, have I introduced you to the Open Book's writer in residence? Penelope Parish, this is Felicity Dickens."

"Like the famous author," Felicity cooed as she shook Penelope's hand. She looked at Penelope appraisingly. "So you're a writer, too?"

"Yes." Penelope hated talking about herself and particularly hated talking about her writing.

"Where can I get your books?" Felicity tilted her head.

"Here," Mabel said, rapping on the counter. "Or in any bookstore. Or online."

"Oh," Felicity said. "How wonderful." She tilted her head. "Have I heard of you?"

Mabel was beginning to look exasperated, but before either she or Penelope could answer, Felicity continued.

She turned to Mabel. "You do love my book, don't you? Have you decided about my book signing? What's a good day for you? I'm thinking a Saturday because that should draw more people."

Mabel gave another pained smile. "I haven't gotten to it yet, I'm afraid. I've been run off my feet here in the shop. Can you give me a few more days?"

Felicity was obviously disappointed but did her best to conceal it.

"Of course." She wagged a finger at Mabel. "But don't wait too long. You know it's going to be a wonderful event." She rummaged in her purse and pulled out a dog-eared planner. "Let me check something though. I did agree to join some women from the Women's Institute for a class in beekeeping." She looked up from her notebook. "Speaking of which, isn't it a shame about Nora Blakely? You do know Nora, don't you?"

"Yes," Mabel and Penelope chorused.

"You'd never guess, would you? Of course you never know about people. It's the quiet ones you have to worry about."

"I can't imagine why anyone would worry about Nora Blakely," Mabel said. "She seemed fine the last time I saw her."

"Maybe not worry exactly," Felicity said, smoothing down her sweatshirt. "But you do have to wonder how someone like that got involved with drink. She worked for my husband for years," Felicity said. "And we got to know her rather well."

"Alcoholism is a form of illness," Mabel said.

"Of course." Felicity said. She turned to Pen. "If you should ever need any legal advice—book contracts or the like—my husband is a solicitor here in Chumley. Dickens and Charles Solicitors, they're called. Quite fortuitous that he found Robert Charles to be his partner." Felicity laughed showing large horsey-looking teeth.

Felicity dropped her planner into her purse, snapped it shut, and hung it from the crook of her arm.

"I must be going—so much to do today. Don't forget about the book signing." She turned and wagged a finger at Mabel again before going out the door.

Mabel groaned and rolled her eyes. "What a nuisance that woman is."

T he bookstore was quiet, so Penelope decided to walk down the street to Francesca and Annabelle's Boutique. Her sister's birthday was coming up and she had seen a lovely scarf in the window that she thought Beryl would like.

The sun was out and she stopped for a moment outside the door of the Open Book to feel its warmth on her face. The leaves on the trees were in full color and beginning to turn brown around the edges. The slight chill in the air made her think of autumn back home when they were children—jumping into piles of leaves and shuffling through them as they collected in the gutters, carving pumpkins into grinning jack-o'-lanterns, and drinking warm cider and eating powdered sugar doughnuts.

The door to Pierre's Restaurant, the Open Book's nearest neighbor, was propped open and the heady scent of wine, garlic, and herbs drifted out.

Penelope was about to open the door to the boutique when she heard someone call her name. She looked up to see Detective Maguire coming down the sidewalk. He waved to her.

"Good morning," he said. Once again Penelope noticed the charming lilt to his voice.

"Good morning," Penelope replied. She hesitated. "Is there anything new in Regina Bosworth's murder case?" She suspected that Maguire would probably dodge the question.

He smiled. "Things are moving along."

He didn't say any more although he seemed inclined to linger. Penelope studied his face. She couldn't decipher what made him so appealing.

He seemed reluctant to leave but another shopper came along and Penelope had to move out of the way of the door to the boutique. He took that as his cue, said goodbye, and continued on down the sidewalk.

Francesca and Annabelle's stock could best be described as eclectic. There were the elegant silk scarves Penelope had admired in the window; tie-dyed T-shirts and tops; brightly colored plaid, polka-dotted, and pinstriped rain boots; a selection of sophisticated-looking cocktail dresses; and ordinary sweaters, trousers, and skirts.

A woman came from behind a rack of wool coats and Penelope realized it was Evelyn Maxwell-Lewis.

"Penelope," Evelyn said in her cultured tones.

She was not in her accustomed jodhpurs but rather dark gray wool trousers and a Shetland sweater. Her hair was in a low ponytail tied with a Hermès scarf.

"How lovely to see you," Evelyn said. "I enjoyed our writing group the other day." She tweaked the jacket on the mannequin next to her. "I was quite productive afterward and managed nearly ten pages in my manuscript."

"I'm glad to hear that."

"I was telling Charlotte about it last night. She and Arthur had me to dinner. I must say that woman is growing on me. Now, Regina couldn't abide her. Of course, Regina had the silly notion that she could engineer a match between Arthur and that daughter of hers. The woman had to have been absolutely delusional. Have you seen Victoria?" Evelyn didn't wait for an answer. "She's an attractive girl but terribly rough around the edges. Arthur and I had quite a good laugh over it when we went on a shoot together last week."

Evelyn began going through the coats on the rack. "Regina seemed quite convinced that she could put Charlotte out of the picture. Which makes you wonder, doesn't it?" She paused with her hand on a bright red belted wool coat and for the first time Penelope noticed a nasty, raised scar on the back of her hand. "Did Regina have something on Charlotte—something so damning that she was convinced it would cause Arthur to break off his engagement? I can't imagine what that might be. The man is positively besotted."

Penelope had had the same thought herself but she wasn't about to admit that to Evelyn.

ELEVEN

❧

I'm starved," Penelope said, putting the finishing touches on the display of bestsellers in the shop window. "I think I'll go out and get myself something to eat."

"Have you tried the Chumley Chippie yet?" Seeing Penelope's blank expression, Mabel continued. "The local fish-and-chips café across the street between the Knit Wit Shop and Pen and Ink Stationers. I highly recommend it. Their fish is always very fresh."

"That sounds good, then." Penelope took her coat from the coat-tree. "Can I get you anything?"

"No, thanks."

Penelope slipped on her coat, looked out the window—it wasn't raining so she didn't need her umbrella—and opened the door.

"Be sure to ask for the haddock," Mabel called after her. "And if they've run out of that, get the pollack or the plaice."

The Chumley Chippie was totally unpretentious if you ignored the fact that it was housed in a centuries-old medieval building. The wooden sign hanging out front was painted blue and in the shape of a fish. The interior, however, looked slightly more modern—as if it had been built in the nineteen fifties—assuming you could call that modern, which, in a town as old as Upper Chumley-on-Stoke, you probably could.

Inside, there was a long Formica counter edged in metal with several deep fryers sizzling and spitting behind it. An older man in a white jacket with stains down the front and a ring of frizzy white hair around his otherwise bald head stood behind the counter taking orders, shouting them over his shoulder to another fellow who was thin and gawky and had long black hair pulled into a ponytail and contained in a hairnet. Yet another fellow was manning the fryers, lifting baskets full of golden fried fish from the bubbling oil.

Penelope got in line behind a girl with purple hair that was long on top and shaved on the sides. She was studying the menu board hanging over the counter when someone tapped her on the shoulder.

Daphne Potter smiled at her. She was in her barmaid's uniform with an unbuttoned trench coat thrown over it. There was a small dark stain on the front near her right shoulder and one of the cuffs was frayed. She looked tired—her face drawn and her eyes puffy.

"You're working at the Open Book, aren't you?" Daphne said. "I'm Daphne Potter. I'm a barmaid at the Book and Bottle." Daphne looked down at her feet. "Do you mind if I ask you a question?"

Penelope shook her head.

"Have the police been around to talk to you? I heard you were there when Regina's body was found."

"Yes, Detective Maguire has spoken to me."

"Oh." Daphne fiddled with the belt of her coat. "They've questioned me and Gordon several times. Poor Gordon—he's so worried." She looked at Penelope. "They always suspect the husband, don't they? They do on those television shows and in the movies."

"I suppose it's normal to at least question those closest to the victim."

Daphne sniffed. "I think they have it in for me, too. Everyone thinks I'm after Gordon's money, but that's not true. He's been very kind to me and my sister. Layla spends most of her time in a wheelchair, you see, and only has me caring for her. I think Gordon feels sorry for me. At least he's never tried anything on, if you know what I mean."

He probably also finds you very attractive and enjoys looking at you, Penelope thought, glancing at Daphne's figure in her skimpy uniform, but she didn't say that.

"But Gordon said he did hear Worthington arguing with Regina the day of the fest."

"Did he tell Detective Maguire about it?"

"Yes. Maguire wrote it down on his notepad along with everything else."

"Do you know what they argued about?"

Just then the girl in front of Penelope moved away and the fellow taking orders stood patiently waiting to hear Penelope's.

"What will it be?"

"Fish and chips, please," Penelope said.

"Kind?" The fellow sounded impatient now.

"Oh. Haddock," Penelope said, remembering what Mabel had told her.

"We're out."

"Pollack then, please."

The fellow called out the order and then turned to Daphne with his eyebrows raised.

Penelope moved along and watched as the other fellow behind the counter selected a piece of fish from a warming oven and chips from another and pushed the paper plate across the counter.

"You'll want some malt vinegar and plenty of salt for that," Daphne said, coming up in back of her. "Are you eating here? The owner of the Book and Bottle doesn't like us bringing any food around, as he sells a ploughman's lunch and a steak-and-kidney pie himself. He doesn't want us giving his customers any ideas."

"I'll get us a table while you wait for your order," Penelope said.

There was a bottle of malt vinegar and a huge shaker of salt on the table along with a dispenser of paper napkins. The tabletop was scarred from age and use and the initials *J* and *C* were carved into the wood at one end. The red leatherette covering the booths was worn, too, and mended in spots with black electrical tape.

Daphne plopped into the seat opposite Penelope. "I'm right hungry, I'll tell you that. All I had for breakfast was a couple of Jaffa cakes." She put the folded newspaper she'd had tucked under her arm on the seat beside her. "I brought the *Times* along in case I had to sit by myself. I like to try my hand at the crossword puzzle. Some of the girls at the bar laugh at me, saying what do I think I'm trying to do—better myself?" She grabbed the bottle of malt vinegar and shook it liberally over her fish and chips.

Penelope was impressed. She had given the *Times* crossword puzzle a go herself and found it extremely difficult—the clues were word puzzles in and of themselves.

"You were saying that Regina and Worthington argued at the fest," Penelope said, after they'd begun eating. "Do you know what they argued about?"

Daphne shook her head. "I don't know. Something to do with the fest is what I told Gordon it probably was, but he wasn't convinced. He said Regina liked to poke her nose in where it didn't belong."

"What do you mean? Poking her nose into something to do with Worthington?"

Daphne speared a chip. "Yes. Or Charlotte. Gordon said you don't mess with royalty. They'll come after you right quick, and they've got the money to do it."

"Do you think Regina did something like that— something serious enough to get her killed?"

"That's what Gordon is afraid of."

Penelope came out of her writing "hole," as she liked to think of the little room at the Open Book where she had set up shop, and stretched her arms over her head. The afternoon had been productive. She'd found a way to incorporate the plot twist she'd thought up the other day and things were looking good. A change of scenery had been what she needed after all.

India was sitting in the café drinking a cup of tea— Earl Grey no doubt. In India's mind, English breakfast was for mornings, Earl Grey for afternoons, and Lapsang souchong for when one needed an indulgence. India was devoted to the idea of routine—routine leads to good habits, she liked to say.

She was chatting with Mabel and Figgy, who wasn't sitting but had both hands braced against the back of one of the chairs.

Penelope went over to the join them.

Figgy tapped Penelope on the arm. "It's teatime. I think we could do with a bit of a pick-me-up." She went off and quickly returned with a plate of shortbread cookies.

"I heard that our very own Pen and Ink Stationers will be doing the invitations for the Worthington wedding," India said, lifting her teacup to her lips. Penelope noticed that her hand shook slightly.

"Worthington has always been very good about patronizing the local shops whenever possible," Mabel said, selecting a cookie. "Not like some of the residents of that new development that was built on the outskirts of town."

"I wonder who will be on the guest list," India said. "Perhaps the queen herself will come. Worthington is a favorite of hers after all."

"I don't know." Figgy nibbled the edge of a cookie. "She is knocking on a bit." Her face brightened. "Perhaps Will or Harry will come. I think Prince Harry is quite adorable, don't you?"

"I'm disappointed in him for marrying that American actress," India said, her nose in the air. She turned to Penelope. "No offense meant to you, my dear, but there is such a thing as tradition, you know."

"I wonder whether the wedding will even be a traditional one," Mabel said. "The ceremony followed by the wedding breakfast." She turned to Penelope. "That's a bit of a misnomer, as it's more luncheon than breakfast. Then a gala in the evening with the men in black tie and the women in ball gowns." She laughed. "Oh, to be the proverbial fly on the wall."

"Where will they be married?" Penelope said. She found it hard to picture Charlotte walking down the aisle at St. Andrew's Church.

"There is a chapel at Worthington House," India said. "It's quite big and I doubt Worthington's guest list will be as vast as Prince William's was when he married Catherine Middleton."

"I wonder who's catering it," Figgy said. "And doing the wedding cake. I'm sure it will be splendid. I do hope we will see some pictures."

India finished the last of her tea. "I must be going, I'm afraid." She began to stand up but swayed alarmingly and put a hand on the table to steady herself.

"Are you okay?" Mabel's face creased with concern.

"Just a bit of a spell," India said, but her face was white, her breathing shallow and rapid, and beads of perspiration had formed on her forehead.

"You'd better sit down until it passes," Mabel said.

"But I must get home before the sun goes down. Those lanes are so dark at night and I'm afraid I might fall. There are no streetlights, you know."

"You walked?" Penelope said in disbelief. "I have my car. Let me drive you."

"I don't want to be a bother." India put a shaking hand to her throat.

"It's no bother at all," Penelope insisted.

She managed to overcome India's objections and eventually hustled her out of the Open Book to her car. She thought she heard India give a sigh of relief as she settled in the front passenger seat of the MINI.

They headed out of town and wound their way down

narrow country lanes. Penelope prayed they would not encounter an oncoming car lest that require her to back up into one of the lay-bys.

India's cottage was on the Worthington estate, but the estate was vast, and Worthington House itself was not even a speck in the distance by the time they reached it.

The cottage was not unlike the one Penelope was living in—charming and slightly larger but also slightly less well maintained. Wild roses were thick on the fence lining the stone path to the front door, their blooms now faded, and English ivy crawled up the stone façade. The lintel over the doorway was cracked and the front door could have used a coat of paint.

India fished her keys from her purse, her hands still shaking slightly, and opened the door. Penelope followed her inside. The foyer was dim, and India switched on a light.

A stone fireplace dominated one wall of the sitting room with a nearly threadbare armchair pulled up to it. Beams ran across the low ceiling and the windows were small and set deep in the stone walls.

A small, framed painting of a coat of arms along with several horticultural watercolors hung on the walls.

Penelope encouraged India to sit and when India swung her feet up onto the small ottoman pulled up close to the chair, she noticed that India had a hole in the bottom of her shoe.

"Would you like another cup of tea?"

Penelope hadn't been on British shores long before she'd caught on to the fact that a cup of tea was the Englishman's answer to everything—feeling sad, feeling happy, feeling sick—there was virtually no situation that didn't call for a good strong cup of tea laced with plenty of sugar.

India tried to refuse, saying she didn't want to be a bother, but Penelope wasn't having any of it. She marched out to the kitchen and began opening cupboards. The kettle was already sitting out on the ancient Aga, and she quickly found a collection of mugs—some commemorating historical events like the wedding of Charles and Diana and the queen's 1953 coronation. She chose one and set it out on the counter, then went in search of some tea.

She found a used Earl Grey tea bag in a small dish next to the sink. Ever frugal, India obviously reused them. Penelope couldn't find any others, so after boiling water and filling the mug, she plunked in the tea bag. It must have been used repeatedly because it barely colored the water.

Penelope opened the refrigerator in search of milk and found it nearly empty, save for a small carton of cream, two eggs, and some leftover beans in a plastic container.

The cupboards were equally bare. Penelope thought about the worn upholstery on India's furniture, the hole in her shoe, and the scarcity of food in her kitchen. She noticed that it was terribly cold in the cottage, too, as if the heat had been turned down very low or even turned off completely. She began to wonder if India's circumstances were even more straitened than they originally thought. She would have to talk to Mabel about it. Perhaps there was something that could be done. At the very least they ought to let Worthington know. He was India's relative after all, however distant the connection.

By the time Penelope returned to the sitting room, India had switched on the television. The television itself was so old that Penelope wouldn't have been surprised to see it in an exhibition in the Smithsonian.

She put the tea down on a table within reach of India's chair.

"What are you watching?"

India quickly switched off the television. "I'm sorry. That was rude of me." She smiled at Penelope. "I'm afraid I have a penchant for true crime and detective shows. Very silly of me, I admit. But lately I've been watching a program on cold cases: *Resurrected—Unsolved Crimes Then and Now*. Most interesting." India took a sip of her tea. "The latest episodes have been about a cold case up north where someone set fire to a rather stately home. It burned to the ground killing a young maid who was working there at the time. The family had all gone out for the evening and were spared.

"They investigated, of course, and there was conjecture at the time that the couple's fourteen-year-old daughter was the culprit but it was never proven. The girl was whisked away somewhere never to be heard from again."

"Do they have any new leads in the case?" Penelope said.

"They've just started investigating it again. There's a reporter following the story. I suppose we'll know more in future episodes."

Penelope wasn't sure how to broach the topic but decided to plunge ahead.

"Would you like me to do some grocery shopping for you? I didn't see much in the refrigerator."

"It's lovely of you to offer, but I'll be okay. I have a can of soup and tomorrow my check comes."

Penelope didn't press the issue. Perhaps she would talk to Mabel about it and get her advice.

TWELVE

❧

I was thinking about what Felicity Dickens told us when she was here," Pen said when she got back to the bookstore after escorting India home. "About Nora Blakely and how she worked for Felicity's husband. She used the past tense. I can't help but wonder if Nora still works there." She picked up a publisher's catalogue and began to flip through it.

Mabel tilted her head. "Why?"

"That entry in Regina's notebook about Nora and drink and work and the WI. What if she got fired for drinking on the job? That would certainly give Regina something to hold over her head."

"To what end, though?" Mabel peered over Pen's shoulder at the catalogue and pointed to a book. She tapped the page. "That's bound to become a big hit," she said.

Penelope paused with her hand on the catalogue. "What if Regina used the information to persuade Nora to fiddle with the votes for the election of the president of the Women's Institute? By all accounts, everyone was surprised when Regina won and several people have already said they didn't vote for her."

"I suppose that's possible," Mabel said. She went behind the counter and pulled out a box of McVitie's chocolate digestives. She held them out toward Penelope.

"No, thanks."

Mabel took a biscuit from the box and began to munch on it.

"Do you still have Felicity Dickens's book?" Pen said, closing the catalogue.

Mabel reached under the counter, pulled it out, and waved it in the air.

"I need an excuse to drop by Dickens and Charles Solicitors to see if Nora is there. What if I bring the book with me and ask Mr. Dickens to return it to his wife?" Penelope began pacing back and forth. "You can put a note in it saying that you've ordered your own copy or something."

Mabel handed the book to Pen. "It's all yours. I doubt it's improved any since it's been sitting under the counter."

It was almost dark and the streetlights had begun to wink on. The wind was sharp and tore at Penelope's coat as she walked down the street, Felicity's book tucked under her arm. Dickens and Charles, Solicitors were at the opposite end of the high street toward the Tesco. It was a brisk walk and several times Penelope was sorry she hadn't thought to take the car.

Finally she reached the two-story building that housed

Felicity's husband's law practice. It was two doors down from Kebabs and Curries and the faint scent of spices suggesting warm and exotic places drifted toward Pen on the wind.

A highly polished brass plate announcing Dickens and Charles, Solicitors was over the door at the top of the stairs leading to the second floor. Faint outlines were visible through the frosted glass on the top half of the door.

Pen hesitated briefly, then knocked.

"Come in," a feminine voice rang out.

Penelope turned the knob and opened the door.

The office was not luxurious. The anteroom was small and crowded with an old wooden desk, metal filing cabinets, and a coat-tree where several dark wool coats hung from the pegs. A tall, rotating fan on a stand was pushed into the corner. Penelope had no doubt it came in handy in the summer months—most of the buildings along Chumley's high street were not air-conditioned.

A woman sat behind the desk, which was covered from one end to the other with papers. A stack of file folders a foot high tottered on a table next to it.

The woman raised her eyebrows in inquiry, her lips set in a straight line, and the telephone receiver tucked between her shoulder and her ear. She was wearing a navy pinstriped suit and a polyester blouse with a floppy bow. Her light brown hair was coming out of the bun at the nape of her neck, giving her a somewhat frazzled appearance.

She had just hung up the phone when it rang again. She mouthed an apology at Pen and picked it up.

"Dickens and Charles, Solicitors," she said.

Pen gave her a bright smile, hoping to win the woman over to her side.

"I'm from the Open Book—the bookstore down the street," she said when the woman had finished the call. She motioned vaguely in the direction of the Open Book. "Mr. Dickens's wife, Felicity, left a copy of her book with Mabel Morris, the owner. I wanted to return it and hoped that Mr. Dickens would be willing to take it home with him."

The telephone rang a third time and the woman groaned and picked it up.

"Dickens and Charles, Solicitors," she barked into the receiver.

Her hands were shaking slightly and despite the chill in the room, a faint sheen of perspiration was visible on her brow. When the call was finished, she slammed the receiver into the cradle with considerable force.

"I'm sorry," she said, attempting to smooth down her hair. "Ever since Mr. Dickens's secretary left I've been stuck doing double duty." She blew out an exasperated breath that fluttered the bits of hair around her face. "I'm actually a paralegal." She swept a hand over her desk indicating the mess of papers. "But I've been pressed into service as the temporary secretary and receptionist."

"So Mr. Dickens is looking for a new secretary?" Pen said.

"Yes." The woman brightened. "You wouldn't be interested, would you?"

"No, I'm afraid not." Pen fiddled with the button on her coat. "What a shame his former secretary left him in the lurch like this. In the States, we have to give at least two weeks notice before quitting a job."

"Oh, she didn't quit," the woman said. She lowered her voice. "Mr. Dickens had to let Nora go."

Pen raised her eyebrows. "She was fired?"

The woman nodded. "I'm afraid she . . . drank."

"Oh, dear," Pen said. "How awful."

The woman sniffed "It was frightfully awful, I can tell you—falling asleep at her desk, knocking into things, making a dog's breakfast of the paperwork. Especially poor Mr. Ashworth's divorce."

"Oh?"

The woman sat up straighter and threw out her chest.

"I did my part. I had the paperwork all filled out right and proper and ready to go, but Nora was too busy faffing about to take them to be filed. Can you imagine? Mr. Ashworth didn't know he wasn't actually divorced until he was practically standing at the altar with his new bride. It created quite the stir as I'm sure you can imagine." She shook her head. "Poor Mr. Dickens was right brassed off about it. He sent her packing as soon as he heard—never mind that she'd worked for him for years. There was no room for mistakes like that, he said."

She'd certainly gotten an earful, Pen thought as she left Dickens and Charles Solicitors. It looked as if Nora had lost her job after all. Had Regina threatened to tell everyone that Nora had been fired? And had that been the leverage Regina had needed to convince Nora to lie about the results of the Women's Institute election?

Mrs. Danvers was waiting by the door when Penelope got home. She followed Penelope out to the kitchen where Penelope put her grocery bags on the counter and then bent to give Mrs. Danvers her due. Mrs. Danvers purred softly as Penelope scratched her under the chin.

The cat eventually became bored with Penelope's ministrations and wandered off to sit under the kitchen table and groom herself.

Penelope unpacked the contents of her grocery bags. She was planning what Figgy referred to as a "fry up" for dinner—fried eggs, fried bread, bangers, bacon, a grilled tomato, and some beans. She had decided to forgo kidneys, which were often part of a fry up. She wasn't ready to be that adventurous.

She got out a frying pan and started the bacon. She'd fry everything else in the rendered fat.

By the time she finished cooking her dinner, the poor Aga was splattered with grease, but Penelope had a plate of delicious-looking food.

She carried her meal out to the sitting room and flicked on the television. The eggs were perfect—the yolk, when she pierced it, ran satisfactorily, just the way she liked it.

Coronation Street was ending when Penelope's cell phone rang. She glanced at the number and groaned. It was her editor.

"Hello?"

"Darling, how are you?" Bettina's voice drawled over the telephone. "Everything awesome across the seas?"

"Yes, thanks. How about you?"

Bettina groaned. "Fine, except I spilled my chai crème Frappuccino all over my new Jason Wu this morning. I don't know which I minded more—losing my drink or ruining my dress. You know I can't start my day without my Frappuccino." She groaned.

Penelope rolled her eyes.

"Enough about me, darling. How is the book coming along?"

"I'm making progress," Penelope said and for once she was telling the truth.

"Sounds like England was just the shot in the arm you needed. We've got Alexis Monroe to do the cover again. And we've got buy-in from marketing and sales on the design. I think you were pleased with the results for *Lady of the Moors*."

"Yes, I was." Penelope stretched out her legs and propped them on the coffee table.

"Good. So glad to hear it." There was a slight pause and Bettina continued. "So we're on time, then, to meet our deadline?"

Penelope heard the distinct note of fear in her voice.

"Yes," she said, praying she wouldn't hit another block.

"Good, good," Bettina said in sultry tones. "They've become positively Simon Legree-ish around here about deadlines. Everyone is walking around scared to death."

"Sorry to hear that."

"All in a day's work, right, darling?" Bettina drawled. "I just wanted to give you a ring to see how things were going—and to put my mind at rest. Stress is so bad for one's skin, you know. I'll be off now and let you get back to that new bestseller you're working on."

Penelope's spirits sank as she hung up the telephone. The book was coming along but as to its being a bestseller, she had no idea. She told herself not to let the word spook her, but it hung over her like a cloud all evening and when she read over what she'd written earlier, she decided it was terrible and all of it had to go.

I'm worried about India," Penelope said the next morning as she, Mabel, and Figgy were packing up cartons of Charlotte Davenport's books.

Mabel paused and brushed a wisp of white hair out of her eyes.

"How is she? She did have that spell yesterday. It was quite worrisome."

"She was fine after a cup of tea." Penelope smiled. "The English are right—tea cures everything."

"I told you," Mabel said, bending over the cartons again.

"It's not that though. When I went to prepare the tea for her, I noticed that there was very little food in her cupboards." Penelope pictured the contents of India's refrigerator. "Actually, there was practically no food at all."

"Oh, dear," Mabel said. She paused, her hands on her hips. "That is alarming. I suppose that's why she felt faint yesterday—she's not eating enough."

"She said something about her check coming today. I offered to go grocery shopping for her but she said she would be fine."

"I noticed at your book group meeting that India had taken several cookies, wrapped them in a napkin, and put them in her purse." Mabel closed the carton flaps and ran packing tape along the top. "I imagine she was saving them for her tea. It does sound as if poor India is in rather dire financial straits."

"I thought we might mention something to Worthington." Penelope picked up one of the cartons. "Perhaps he can do something."

Mabel frowned. "I don't know. India is as prickly as a pear about things like that. She might be offended."

"Or she might starve," Penelope said a little louder than she intended.

Mabel put a hand on Penelope's arm. "I understand

your concern, but you have to understand people like India. Their pride is worth more than their life."

There had to be a way to help India without injuring her outsized pride, Penelope thought as she began carrying the cartons out to her car. She would have to think about it.

"Are you sure you can manage?" Mabel said, putting the last carton of books in Penelope's car.

"No problem," Penelope said. "I'm sure I can find someone at the other end to help me unload the boxes."

Charlotte Davenport was speaking at a meeting of the Women's Institute on romance in Regency times, which would be followed by a signing of her latest book *The Fire in My Bosom*. The Open Book was providing copies of her novel and Figgy had been hired to cater the event with tea, sandwiches, and pastries.

The talk was being held in a room at the Oakwood School for Girls just outside Chumley. Penelope drove down narrow, winding country lanes past green fields dotted with sheep and cows, until she saw a white sign with a gold crest and the words *Oakwood School for Girls* in discreet script. She had reached the vast estate that housed the girls' boarding school. The private drive that led to the school itself was nearly a quarter of a mile long, but at last Penelope could see an imposing stone building in the distance.

The campus was impressive, Penelope thought as she drove past numerous buildings in the Gothic Revival style of architecture. Finally, she pulled into the circular drive that wound around in front of the main building.

Figgy, in her white van with *Figgy's Tea and Catering* written on the side, pulled in in back of Penelope.

"This is quite the place, isn't it?" Penelope said when she and Figgy had gotten out of their respective vehicles.

"It reminds me of Pemberton Hall, where I went to school," Figgy said.

"Do you suppose we ought to ring?" Penelope said as they approached the main door.

Just then Maribel Northcott, the headmistress, opened the door and stepped outside.

"Welcome to the Oakwood School for Girls." She nodded toward Figgy's van and Penelope's car. "You'll need some help unloading, I should imagine. I'll ring for the porter."

She pulled a cell phone from the pocket of her tweed jacket and punched in some numbers.

"He'll be down shortly." She smiled. "Let's leave it to him, shall we? He'll get Tommy to help him."

She led them into an expansive foyer and down a corridor that smelled of must and lemon furniture polish to a room at the end of the hall. The elaborately carved double doors were open and they followed her inside.

"I thought we'd use the Jane Austen room. It should accommodate the event nicely."

The room was spacious with high ceilings, ornate crown molding, large floor-to-ceiling windows, and a crystal chandelier. A magnificent Oriental rug, its rich colors glowing like jewels, covered most of the dark wood floor.

Folding chairs had been set up in tidy rows, and two tables with white linen cloths were on either side of the room.

Maribel pointed to them. "I thought we'd set Miss Davenport's book signing up over there and have refreshments on the other table." She indicated the table on the other side. "That should keep things from getting too congested."

An older man in overalls came into the room, pushing a handcart stacked with boxes marked *The Open Book*. A younger man with red hair followed him in with a trolley stacked with Figgy's tea things.

"I'll let you get settled," Maribel said. "I imagine Miss Davenport should be here shortly. I don't want to miss her arrival." She clasped her hands together. "We'll soon be calling her the Duchess of Upper Chumley-on-Stoke."

Figgy got busy plugging in her electric teapots and setting out cups and saucers. The porter soon returned with the cart now loaded with trays of tea sandwiches and pastries, which she arranged on the table.

Penelope opened the cartons the porter had stacked for her and began organizing the books. She placed one on a stand at the front of the table and angled it just so. She stood back to regard the effect.

"Penelope," Charlotte called, striding across the room. "So lovely to see you." She put her hands on Penelope's shoulders and gave her an air kiss on both cheeks.

Penelope was enveloped in the scent of her flowery perfume.

She was wearing slim-fitting black pants, a white double-breasted blazer, and black suede high-heeled pumps. Her blond hair was gathered into a casual bun.

By now members of the Women's Institute were arriving, and soon the room was filled with the rise and fall of feminine voices. Charlotte mingled with the crowd, smiling and shaking hands. The women clustered around her, vying for her attention, in awe of having a near duchess in their midst.

Penelope had to laugh—these were the same women

who had probably been aghast when it was announced that Worthington would be marrying an American romance author. She had no doubt that the knives would come out again as soon as Charlotte was gone.

The women began moving toward the chairs, firmly shepherded by Shirley Townsend. Helen Hathaway separated herself from the crowd and made her way toward the lectern at the head of the room.

She took her place and tapped the microphone tentatively.

"Can you hear me?" Her voice boomed around the room. She looked startled and slightly horrified.

"Yes," the women chorused.

Helen's voice shook slightly as she welcomed everyone to the meeting of the Women's Institute. She unfolded a piece of paper and reached for the pair of half-glasses that hung from a chain around her neck. They became intertwined with the button on her cardigan and her strand of yellowing pearls, and everyone shifted in their seats in embarrassment as she attempted to untangle them. Finally she managed to free them and placed them on the end of her nose. She glanced down at the piece of paper and cleared her throat.

"The Women's Institute is very proud to present bestselling author Charlotte Davenport." She took off her glasses and let them fall to her chest. She stepped to the side and looked to the left where Charlotte was seated.

Charlotte moved toward the lectern, adjusting her jacket and putting a hand to her hair. Helen resumed her seat, an immense look of relief settling on her face. Charlotte smiled at the crowd. She didn't have any notes with her but began to speak eloquently and warmly to the audience. It was clear that within five minutes she had them in the palm of her hand.

Penelope was impressed. Writers by and large were introverts, and speaking in front of a crowd was generally not one of their best skills. Penelope had worked on her ability to give presentations, but it still didn't come naturally to her. Charlotte, on the other hand, was quite impressive—warm and friendly but authoritative at the same time.

Finally, the talk was over and there was the sound of chairs rattling as everyone stood up and headed toward Figgy's tea table. While the women were enjoying bites of cucumber sandwiches and nibbles of shortbread cookies washed down with cups of Darjeeling, Charlotte got set up for her book signing, retrieving a gold pen from her purse and settling in behind the table.

Penelope wandered among the women, saying hello to Helen who seemed quite cheerful now that her stint as master of ceremonies was over and talking to Shirley about *My Brother Michael*, which they were reading for Pen's other book group.

She had her back to a cluster of women gathered around a tall, rather severe-looking brunette who was holding court. Her voice was loud and commanding, and Penelope couldn't help but overhear the conversation.

"It would be a terrible scandal if it got out," the woman said in ringing tones. "That's why it's been kept under wraps and she's been allowed to quietly leave."

"What's this?" someone said. "I'm afraid I've been occupied caring for my mother who fell and broke her hip—poor thing—and haven't been attending meetings."

The two women began walking out of the room.

Were they talking about the Women's Institute? Penelope wanted to hear what they had to say. She began to follow them.

She noticed Helen bearing down on her but pretended not to see her and continued to follow the women out of the room and down the hall where the brunette pushed open the door to the ladies' room.

Penelope ducked in right behind them. She looked around. There was a long vanity with four armless chairs upholstered in black-and-white striped silk in front of it.

The women each went into a stall and Penelope hovered nearby, straining her ears to listen. She prayed no one else would come into the room because she had no explanation for hovering so close to the stalls.

The brunette's strident voice came clearly through the closed door. "I don't see how she thought she could get away with it. With money missing, it was bound to point a finger right at her—she was the treasurer, after all."

Could they be talking about Nora Blakely?

"As bold as brass," the other women sniffed.

One of the toilets flushed and any other words were drowned out.

Penelope quickly sat down at the vanity, took out her compact, which was at least ten years old and still contained almost the same amount of powder in it as when she'd bought it, and pretended to powder her nose.

The brunette began talking about her garden—black spots on her prize Queen of Sweden roses—and Penelope got up and quietly left the ladies' room.

She went back to the Jane Austen room and stopped by Figgy's tea table, where she helped herself to a curried egg salad sandwich. By now a line had formed in front of

Charlotte, and Penelope was glad to see they were selling a lot of books. Mabel would be pleased.

Helen was standing off by herself, sipping a cup of tea. Penelope joined her.

"Lovely event, isn't it?" Helen said. "It's such a privilege to meet Charlotte Davenport in person."

They made general conversation while Penelope tried to think of a way to bring up the topic on her mind—Nora Blakely and her supposed theft.

"I heard Nora Blakely has left the Women's Institute," Penelope said as casually as possible.

"Oh, dear. Have people been talking about it?" Helen clutched her eyeglass chain. "It's a terrible shame. I can't imagine what drove her to it—stealing money from the WI treasury like that."

"Was it a great deal of money?"

Helen whispered a sum in Penelope's ear. "That's not a fortune, mind you, but it was enough to be noticed."

Penelope excused herself and walked away. She was so busy thinking that she nearly bumped into a young woman, sending her teacup rattling precariously in its saucer. Penelope apologized and moved on.

The book signing line diminished slowly and people began to leave. Penelope packed up the few books remaining and put the carton by the door.

Figgy was cleaning up as well. "Pen," she said when Penelope reached her. "Do you want to take some sandwiches for your dinner? I'll save them for you."

"Thanks." Penelope began gathering up some of the teacups for Figgy and putting them in the bins Figgy had brought with her. "I overheard something very interesting," Penelope said.

"Oh? Something to do with Regina's murder?"

"Possibly. Apparently money went missing from the Women's Institute treasury. And Nora Blakely was the treasurer. It seems she was allowed to retire quietly."

Figgy whistled. "So Regina could have known about it and was blackmailing her? Because even if the Women's Institute let the matter drop quietly, which I gather they have, Regina could have easily spread the news throughout the entire town."

"Yes." Penelope brushed some crumbs off the tablecloth into the palm of her hand and tossed them in the trash can behind the table. "I think that's quite possible. Likely even."

Figgy turned to Penelope with a frown. "So Nora killed Regina to keep the story from spreading? Is that what you're thinking? It's hard to picture her doing that—she's so . . . so timid."

Penelope shrugged. "If I made Nora the villain in a book, I'm pretty sure my editor would shoot it down, but in real life you never know about people, do you?"

THIRTEEN

❧❧

I t looks like we sold a lot of books," Mabel said, removing the handful of volumes from the box Penelope had carried into the Open Book. "How was Charlotte's talk?"

"She did a wonderful job. They loved her."

Mabel laughed. "Unfortunately that doesn't mean they won't continue to gossip about her behind her back."

"I had the exact same thought." Penelope wrinkled her nose. "By the way"—she paused with a book in her hand—"did you get a chance to talk to Gladys?"

Mabel frowned. "I did. I tried to be delicate about it, but I believe the message was clear enough. Gladys wasn't inclined to confide in me, I'm afraid. I tried to leave the door open in case she wanted to talk about it in the future—or if she decided she wanted help getting away from the situation. Abuse often escalates. Let's hope Gladys has the smarts to get out before that happens." Mabel peered into the boxes. "Looks like that's it. We've got them all." She pinched the bridge of her nose. "Let's call it a day, shall we?"

Penelope switched the sign on the front door of the shop to Closed as the last customer left with a shopping bag full of the latest cozy mysteries. The streetlights were on and pedestrian traffic going by on the sidewalk outside the Open Book had slowed.

She put on her coat and gloves. "I'll be heading off now unless you need me for something?"

Mabel zipped the canvas bag with the day's bank deposit and tucked it into her tote bag. "Have a good evening. I'll see you tomorrow, then."

As Penelope walked to her car, she noticed that the small light left burning during the night at the Pig and Poke was on but that the Chumley Chippie was ablaze and still doing a brisk business with customers leaving with grease-stained bags containing their takeout fish-and-chips dinner.

The cleaning lady's used Citroën was parked outside Penelope's cottage when she got there, and the lights in the sitting room were on. Penelope hoped Ashlyn was nearly finished. She was normally gone by the time Penelope got home. Penelope was planning to work on her manuscript before dinner and wasn't fond of writing while the vacuum was running.

Ashlyn was perched on the sofa in the sitting room, a newspaper spread out on the table in front of her, when Penelope walked in. She jumped up when she heard the front door open, her pasty-white face coloring from her neck to the dark roots of her dyed blond hair.

"I—I wanted to show you something," she stammered, pointing to the newspaper.

At least she had gotten a fire going in the fireplace,

Penelope thought as she peeled off her gloves. The temperature had dipped considerably since the afternoon. She stood with her back to the flames and sighed as the warmth chased away the chill in her bones and eased the ache in her shoulders.

"What is it, Ashlyn?"

Mrs. Danvers slinked in from the kitchen, paused for a moment to take in the scene, then gracefully leapt onto the coffee table, sat right on top of the open newspaper, and clawed gently at the pages with her right paw.

"Shoo, shoo," Ashlyn said, waving her hand at the cat as if it were a fly.

Penelope noticed that her nails were bitten short and that one of her cuticles was bleeding slightly as if she had been chewing on it.

"I have to show you something," Ashlyn said after unseating Mrs. Danvers. "It's here in the paper." Her hand shook slightly as she held the paper up.

"What is it?"

Penelope took the copy of the *Daily Star* and glanced at the page. She gasped.

"Where did you get this?" She brandished the paper.

"I got it at the newsstand, didn't I?" Ashlyn said almost defensively. "I was right shook up when I saw that." She pointed to the paper. Her lower lip trembled. "She shouldn't have done it."

"What do you mean?"

Ashlyn shook her head. "Nothing. I didn't mean nothing."

Penelope looked at the article again—if you could call it an article—it was more pictorial than anything else. Under the bold headline *Page Two* were pictures of a young woman, her blond hair in a long braid, her makeup, despite thick false eyelashes, light enough to show off the freckles on her nose. She was wearing a thong bikini and in some of the photographs was topless.

Penelope had no trouble recognizing the woman—it was Charlotte Davenport.

Penelope managed to persuade Ashlyn to let her keep the copy of the *Daily Star*. She couldn't imagine how the paper had come in possession of those photographs. But she could easily imagine how upset Charlotte was going to be when she found out about it.

Mabel was nursing a cup of tea and leafing through a book catalogue when Penelope arrived at the Open Book.

Penelope had had a restless night thinking about a number of things from her manuscript to Charlotte Davenport to Regina's murder. She had decided that tea wasn't going to fit the bill that morning so she had stopped to pick up a coffee at the local wine bar—the Sour Grapes—that also served coffee and pastries in the morning.

Mabel glanced at the coffee cup in Penelope's hand.

"Rough night?"

"Sort of." Penelope fished the *Daily Star* out of her purse. She opened it to the Page Two feature. "Look at this."

Mabel slipped on her reading glasses and held the paper up to read it. She lowered it slowly, her mouth open in surprise.

"That's Charlotte Davenport."

"Yes. Apparently the *Daily Star* dug up an old issue of some men's magazine that Charlotte posed for eons ago and reprinted the photographs."

Figgy wandered over with a mug of tea in her hand. She gestured toward the newspaper and grinned. "Mabel, somehow I wouldn't have pegged you as a *Daily Star* reader."

Mabel made a face. "I'm not."

Figgy took a sip of her tea. "Our family's housekeeper was an avid reader of the *Daily Star*. I used to sneak a look whenever I could. Mother didn't approve. She said you can't believe everything a paper like that prints."

"I'm afraid this one comes with pictures," Mabel said, "and the camera doesn't lie." She handed the paper to Figgy and pointed to the Page Two feature.

"Bloody hell!" Figgy exclaimed. "That's Charlotte Davenport."

"What's this?" India had come in while they were talking. "A tea party?"

Figgy silently handed her the newspaper.

"Oh," was all India managed to say. "Poor Arthur." She handed the paper back to Figgy. "Do you think he's seen this?"

"Maybe he knows. Maybe Charlotte already told him about those pictures," Penelope said.

"I wonder why she posed for those photographs," Mabel said. "It's not like she was after a career in film or wanted to be on the telly and thought that was a good way to get noticed."

"I suppose poor Arthur will have to cancel the wedding," India said. "The people won't accept a duchess of Upper Chumley-on-Stoke who has posed for indecent pictures. This isn't America." She turned to Penelope. "No offense, my dear. But the British are a stodgy lot especially in provincial towns like Chumley and especially when it comes to the aristocracy."

"I certainly hope he doesn't cancel the wedding," Penelope said.

"Everyone has a past," Mabel said. "There's no reason to think Charlotte is any different. From what I've heard, Worthington has quite the past himself."

India grimaced. "He certainly does."

Penelope suddenly remembered her conversation with Ashlyn and the one thing Ashlyn had said that had struck her as odd at the time.

"You know, Ashlyn said something rather strange when she showed me the newspaper. She said, 'She shouldn't have done it.'"

"What do you suppose she meant?" Figgy said.

"Did she mean Charlotte?" Mabel said. "That Charlotte shouldn't have posed for those pictures?"

"I don't think so." Penelope frowned. "It didn't sound that way at the time."

"I wonder how the *Daily Star* found those pictures. They were taken almost twenty years ago." Figgy fingered the gold stud in her nose.

Mabel raised her eyebrows. "I can't help but wonder if someone sent a copy of the magazine to the paper. The *Daily Star* is known to pay for stories like this."

Penelope thought of Ashlyn's words again—"She shouldn't have done it." Was it possible that Ashlyn knew—or suspected—how the paper had gotten hold of those pictures? It didn't seem likely—Ashlyn was rather proud of the fact that she'd never been to London or anywhere else for that matter. She was perfectly content in Upper Chumley-on-Stoke, she'd told Penelope, and she couldn't understand why people wanted to travel— *traipsing around to all sorts of strange places* was how she had put it.

Penelope couldn't imagine her or her friends, who held similar views according to Ashlyn, knowing enough to contact the *Daily Star* and offer to sell them twenty-year-old pictures of Charlotte Davenport.

Penelope was collecting books for a display of Gothic novels she was putting together when she noticed Katie Poole, Charlotte's assistant, standing near the front desk, scanning the store as if she was looking for someone.

"You're Katie, right?" Penelope said to her. "Can I help you with something?"

"Yes," Katie gushed, sounding grateful. "I wanted to talk to you if you have a minute."

Penelope stacked the books she was carrying on the counter. "Why don't we sit down? Would you like a cup of tea?"

"I'd prefer coffee if you have it," Katie said as they took seats at a vacant table in the tea shop.

"Would you like a plate of cookies with that?" Figgy said when she came to take their order.

Penelope nodded.

Katie was quiet until Figgy walked away. She glanced at her cell phone, which she'd put out on the table.

"I have a favor to ask you." Katie bit her lower lip.

"Yes?"

"I'd love it if you would come and talk to Charlotte. She hasn't . . . been herself lately."

"What's wrong?"

"I don't know. But she's crying all the time and Charlotte never cries. She's the most upbeat person I've ever known. And she hasn't been writing either. She said she's blocked, but I don't believe it. She's always managed to do her daily pages even when she learned her mother had cancer."

Penelope was surprised—obviously Katie hadn't yet seen the photographs in the *Daily Star.* Or was there something more that was upsetting Charlotte?

"Ever since the fest when she talked to that woman . . ."

"Oh? Who?"

"I don't know her name, but she made Charlotte cry. Charlotte won't say what's wrong. I don't think even Arthur knows."

Two women at an adjoining table had stopped talking and were leaning in their direction. Penelope lowered her voice.

"Did you see what the woman looked like?"

"No, but I think she was the woman in charge of the fest. I'm pretty sure I recognized her voice. Charlotte had already met with her plenty of times, but this was the first time I heard her crying. It must have been something the woman said."

Regina. It must have been Regina who had been talking to Charlotte. But what had she said that had made Charlotte cry?

Penelope agreed to talk to Charlotte and promised Katie that she wouldn't tell Charlotte about their talk. She was dreading it, though. What could she possibly do to help? What if Charlotte expected to hear that she'd uncovered some clues in Regina's murder? Penelope had a lot of ideas swirling around in her head—including the idea that Charlotte now had an even stronger reason to want to murder Regina herself. Not that she believed for a minute that Charlotte was a murderer. But someone was certainly trying to make her appear to be the likeliest suspect.

The Open Book was quiet, so Penelope slipped on her coat, said good-bye to Mabel, and headed out to Worthington House.

She parked her car, squared her shoulders, and determinedly marched up to the front door. It was opened by a stone-faced butler.

"Is Miss Davenport expecting you?" he said, reaching for a telephone on a table by the door.

"No, she's not."

"Who shall I say is calling, miss?"

Penelope gave him her name and waited while he talked to someone on the other end of the line. Finally he replaced the receiver in the cradle and bowed slightly.

"This way, miss."

They arrived at Charlotte's study and the butler knocked on the door before opening it with a flourish.

Charlotte was behind her desk, staring glumly at the far wall. She gave a tired smile when she saw Penelope. She looked as if she hadn't slept well for days—dark circles formed half-moons under her eyes and her shoulders sagged. She appeared to have lost weight, too—her black-and-white tweed dress and matching jacket looked big on her—a surprise since Charlotte's clothes were usually impeccably tailored.

She got up from behind her desk and motioned Penelope to a chair. She glanced at her watch.

"I'm sorry, but we've got a luncheon for the American ambassador to attend in an hour, but I did want to see you.

I could use some support." She gave a wry smile. "I suppose you've seen the pictures?"

Penelope was tempted to deny it but didn't.

"I was young and foolish." Charlotte sighed wistfully. "And I needed money for college. I was a good student and already knew I wanted to become a writer, but attending college wasn't something most girls who grow up in trailers in Kentucky get to do. But I was determined. The magazine offered me money—to me it seemed like a magnificent sum—but now it seems almost laughable. But it was easy money—a lot easier than pressing clothes at the dry cleaner in the heat and humidity of a Kentucky summer, which would have been my only other option."

"Do you have any idea how the newspaper got hold of the magazine with those photographs?"

Charlotte held her hands out palms up. "I don't. The magazine is twenty years old. I can't imagine anyone saving a copy of it. Why would they?"

"A collector maybe?"

"I suppose that's possible. But, then, why send it to the newspaper? Why wouldn't they keep it?" Charlotte shook her head. "Someone did this to hurt me, I'm convinced." She twisted her engagement ring around and around on her finger and the diamond flashed rainbows in the light. "Someone wants to tear Arthur and me apart. And they went looking for a way to do it."

Penelope's first thought was that *the lady doth protest too much*. Something about Charlotte's insistence that she didn't know how the newspaper got the magazine didn't ring quite true.

Charlotte jumped to her feet and began pacing the room.

"People have been against me from the very beginning.

One"—she counted the items off on her fingers—"I'm an American and they object to that. Two, I write romance novels—Regency-era bodice rippers, critics have called them. I'd like to think they are slightly more than that, but that's neither here nor there. Three, everyone"—she turned and pointed a finger at Penelope—"*everyone* thought Arthur would or should pick them or their daughter to be his wife."

Penelope hesitated. "Do you think there's any chance that Regina Bosworth sent the newspaper those pictures?"

Charlotte stopped her pacing. Her face turned white.

Penelope had promised Katie that she wouldn't say anything, but she needed to get at the truth.

"Your assistant said that she heard you talking with Regina at the fest and that you were crying. And that you've been crying ever since. Was she trying to blackmail you?"

Charlotte crumpled before Penelope's eyes. She collapsed into a chair, buried her face in her hands, and began to cry quietly.

"She did. It was awful. She said if I didn't leave Arthur, she would send that magazine with those old pictures to that rag the *Daily Star*." She looked up at Penelope. Her face was tearstained. She lifted her chin. "I told her to go right ahead—Arthur knows all about them and doesn't blame me. He understands why I had to do it. He loves me." She struck her chest with her fist. She began to cry again. "But for everyone else to see them." She waved a hand around the room. "It's so embarrassing. It's a nightmare. I can't begin to imagine what the rest of Arthur's family is going to think."

Penelope managed to calm Charlotte down before she left. But as she followed the butler back to the front door, she thought about the one question she hadn't had the nerve to ask Charlotte.

Did she kill Regina?

So that gives both Charlotte and Worthington a motive for killing Regina," Figgy said after Penelope had told her and Mabel about her conversation with Charlotte.

Penelope, Figgy, and Mabel were sitting at a booth in the back of the Book and Bottle.

All the seats at the bar were taken and men were standing two deep, nursing tankards of lager, some in overalls and others in jeans and sweaters or khaki pants and casual shirts.

It was after five o'clock on a Saturday night and the crowd was getting warmed up for the night ahead. Voices were rising and many were enthusiastically cheering the heated soccer match on the television between Manchester United and Liverpool.

Figgy ripped open a packet of salt-and-vinegar crisps and another of bacon-flavored fries, which Penelope was surprised to see looked more like chips or, she corrected herself, crisps.

Daphne was behind the bar, pulling pints and fetching plates of sausage rolls and pork pies from the kitchen for those after heartier fare.

"If Worthington already knew about those pictures, what motive would Charlotte have had for killing Regina?" Figgy leaned her elbows on the table and popped a salt-and-vinegar crisp into her mouth.

"Worthington might be willing to overlook Charlotte's

past, but that doesn't mean the rest of the family will."
Mabel took a sip of her cider.

"And I suppose Worthington might have done it for the same reason," Figgy said. "After all, the queen could still try to persuade Worthington that the marriage is a mistake."

"But either Regina did send them the magazine," Penelope said, reaching for a crisp, "or someone else did after her death." She frowned. "If we assume that Regina went to Charlotte at the fest with her threats of blackmail—that's when her assistant heard her crying—then Regina wouldn't have sent the magazine off yet. She'd be waiting to see what Charlotte would say and if Charlotte would give in to her demands. And then not long afterward, Regina was found dead. When would she have had time to post the magazine to the *Daily Star* I wonder?"

"If that's the case, then maybe it wasn't Regina who was blackmailing Charlotte," Figgy said. She held up the last bacon-flavored fry. "Anyone?"

Penelope and Mabel both shook their heads.

Figgy popped the fry into her mouth. "But who else would want to break up Charlotte and Worthington?"

Mabel laughed. "Every female under forty in Upper Chumley-on-Stoke and every mother with a daughter, that's all. Regina herself was entertaining dreams of pairing her daughter, Victoria, with Worthington."

Penelope wrinkled her nose. "Wouldn't that be an awfully weak motive for murder?"

"It seems like it, doesn't it?" Mabel wiped a spot of condensation on the table with her napkin. "But people have committed murder for far less."

Figgy giggled. "This is like playing that game where you have to guess who did it—was it the butler in the library with a candlestick?"

"I remember that," Penelope said.

"We have nearly as many suspects." Mabel pulled a tissue from her purse and dabbed her nose. "We have Charlotte and Worthington. Then there's Nora Blakely, poor thing."

Penelope looked over to the bar where Daphne was busy pulling a pint. She lowered her voice. "And don't forget Daphne."

"And Gordon," Figgy added.

Mabel smiled. "We know the murder weapon and the location at least, so no need to guess those. All we need to figure out is who did it." Mabel's expression abruptly changed. "Of course Cluedo—I think you call it Clue in America—was a game and this isn't. A real person is dead." She shivered. "I do hope the police find out who did it."

FOURTEEN

❧

Penelope opened the door of the Book and Bottle and was tempted to duck back inside when she felt the sharp edge of the wind that had picked up while they were in the pub.

She wrapped her scarf around her neck and pulled her gloves from her coat pocket.

"Come over for a drink," Figgy said as they stood in a pool of light thrown by one of the streetlamps. "I know we just had a drink, but I'm sure you can handle a small glass of wine. Besides, I have some lovely Stilton with mango you have to try." Figgy shivered and turned her collar up. "Derek is coming over. He might be bringing a friend of his," she added casually. "We'll be quite a jolly little party."

"Sure," Penelope said, as they began to walk toward Figgy's apartment. She should go back to her cottage and work, but she was in no hurry to face her manuscript.

Outside activities were supposed to stimulate the imagination, weren't they?

Figgy lived above Pierre's Restaurant in what Penelope had heard the British call a bedsit and which would be called a studio apartment in the United States.

The brisk walk to Figgy's apartment—Figgy walked the way she did everything else—fast—warmed Penelope, and by the time they arrived she had loosened her scarf and unbuttoned her coat. A narrow set of stairs led to the second floor and they could hear noise and commotion from Pierre's—pots banging and raised voices—through the wall.

Figgy's apartment might have been small, but she had made the most of the space with clever décor that utilized it perfectly. She had a Murphy bed on the far wall that left room for a sofa, armchair, and small dining table. An alcove off to one side held a sink, stove, refrigerator, and microwave.

Figgy's quirky personality was evident in her choice of posters—dizzying op art pieces by Bridget Riley, the graffiti paintings of Jean-Michel Basquiat, and a Matisse drawing that indicated the breadth of her interest in art.

"What's this?" Penelope said, pointing to a small piece on the wall. It didn't look to be a poster but rather an original drawing.

Figgy flushed. "That's mine. I'm afraid I'm something of an artist manqué."

"It's very good," Penelope said, examining it more closely. "Are you still making art?"

Figgy looked away, out the small window at the other end of the room.

"No. There didn't seem to be any point to it. I wanted

to go to art college but my parents insisted on my reading history at Coventry." She made a wry face. "And now I'm running a tea shop."

"I never thought I could write a novel," Penelope said. "I thought I was only fit to study the work of others."

Once again, Penelope thought how amazing it was that she'd been able to produce not just a book, but one that hit the bestseller lists. Now if only she could do it again.

She squeezed Figgy's arm. "You should give it a go. Nothing ventured, nothing gained, as my grandmother used to say."

"That's what Derek keeps telling me," Figgy said. She sighed. "Maybe . . . someday."

Penelope sniffed the air. "What's that delicious smell?"

"Nothing I'm cooking, I'm afraid. It's coming from Pierre's downstairs. It's tantalizing, isn't it? Living here, I'm constantly hungry. But I can offer you a chilled glass of pinot grigio if you'd like." Figgy headed toward the refrigerator.

She was arranging some cheese and crackers on a plate when the doorbell rang.

"That must be Derek and his friend." She opened the door. "Oh."

Derek, who was standing in the doorway, was quite obviously alone.

"I thought your friend was coming," Figgy said, as he kissed her on the cheek.

"I'm sorry. Richard couldn't make it. His boss called a last-minute meeting. He said to send his regrets."

Penelope had met Derek once or twice before but was again struck by how attractive he was. It wasn't so much a function of his features, which were fine but not out of the ordinary, but rather something about him—something almost magical. She supposed it was what people meant when they talked about charisma.

Figgy poured Derek a glass of wine and carried the cheese plate to the table in front of the sofa.

"Have you heard from your parents? When are they coming?" Derek turned to Penelope. "Figgy isn't convinced that I can win her parents over." He gave a cheesy smile.

Figgy gulped her wine and began to cough. "That's not true," she sputtered.

"Easy there." Derek patted her on the back.

Finally Figgy caught her breath. "Soon. They haven't said exactly when yet."

Derek ran his hands through his hair. It was dark with a slight wave. He was dressed in a suit that looked as if it had been tailored on Savile Row although he had loosened his tie and unbuttoned his collar.

"How was your day?" Figgy said, handing him a cracker with cheese.

Derek blew out a puff of air. "Okay. Busy." He munched on the cracker. He smiled at Penelope. "How are you enjoying England?"

"It's lovely although it's turned out to be more exciting than I expected."

"Oh?" Derek said, raising his eyebrows.

"I've never been this close to a murder before; I've only written about them. It's both horrifying and thrilling at the same time."

"Have the police arrested anyone yet?" Derek reached for his wineglass. "I'm afraid I haven't had time to read more than the business section of the newspaper."

"No, not yet," Penelope said. "Unless they're keeping it under wraps."

"One of my clients was talking about it." Derek stretched his legs out under the table. "News like that doesn't usually reach the London papers—unless it's something sensational—but our client lives here in Chumley. Do you know him—Sir Bertram Maxwell-Lewis?"

Penelope reached for a cracker. "That must be Lady Evelyn Maxwell-Lewis's husband. She's in my writing group."

Derek pulled on the knot in his tie and loosened it further. "He said he doesn't pay much attention to the goings on in Chumley—he spends so much of his time in London—but his wife knew the murder victim and has been following the story."

"The victim—Regina Bosworth—was somewhat notorious," Figgy said dryly. "She made it a point to know everyone who was anyone. There's no way she would have missed making the acquaintance of Lady Maxwell-Lewis. She was positively potty about titles."

Derek reached for the bottle of wine and offered it to Figgy and Penelope. "Maxwell-Lewis was quite vocal about her. His wife had complained to him about her more than once. This Bosworth woman was trying to get Lady Maxwell-Lewis to convince Sir Bertram to put Bosworth up for a knighthood." Derek held up the empty bottle of wine "Shall I go fetch another one? I can run down to the Tesco."

Figgy jumped up. "No need." She smiled. "I have another one in the refrigerator."

"Maxwell-Lewis was knighted for the work his company did in the development of some new vaccine," Derek said. "I've forgotten exactly what it's for. All very technical, and frankly I couldn't make heads or tails of it. I barely scraped together an O level in science."

"Regina certainly had a lot of nerve," Figgy said, returning with a new bottle of wine. "I wouldn't dream of asking someone to do that for me." She handed it to Derek along with the corkscrew. "I don't suppose Sir Bertram Maxwell-Lewis had any intention of even considering it."

"But what if Regina had some information to use as leverage over Evelyn?" Penelope said, holding out her glass for a refill. "That's what she tried to do to Charlotte Davenport. She collected people's secrets and then used them against them to get what she wanted."

Derek looked shocked. "You mean like blackmail? I'm pretty sure the Maxwell-Lewises are above reproach."

"Oh, trust Regina to ferret out something," Figgy said, licking a bit of cheese off her finger. "Everyone has a skeleton in their closet no matter how trivial."

S unday the skies were overcast and there was a powerful wind that shook the leaves from the trees and whistled down the chimney of Penelope's cottage.

Penelope had invited Figgy for an early supper—or tea, as Figgy would probably call it. Mrs. Danvers followed Penelope back and forth between the kitchen and the sitting room, where Penelope was setting out plates, silverware, and napkins on the coffee table. She had been to the Jolly Good Grub gourmet shop for some cheeses—a blue-veined Stilton, an English cheddar with leeks, some chicken liver pâté, a loaf of crusty bread, some olives and a container of giardiniera salad.

They were planning to watch *Imitation of Life* on

television—the original one with Claudette Colbert. It was a favorite of Penelope's and Figgy had never seen it.

Penelope was throwing another log on the fire when the front door opened.

"Hello?" Figgy called from the foyer. "Should you be leaving the front door unlocked when there's a murderer on the loose?"

Her hair, even as short as it was, had been tossed by the wind, and her cheeks and the end of her nose were pink, giving her the look of a rather tipsy elf.

"Mrs. Danvers would protect me," Penelope said. "Right, Mrs. Danvers?"

Mrs. Danvers gave Penelope an incredulous look that clearly said *every man or woman for themselves* and then strutted off to bat at a leaf that had blown in when Figgy opened the front door.

"That fire looks heavenly," Figgy said, standing in front of it and holding out her hands. "I nearly blew away out there. I half expected to find myself suddenly transported to Kansas. Something nasty is brewing, I'm afraid." She unbuttoned her coat and tossed it on a chair.

"That looks delicious," she said, pointing to the spread on the table, "and I'm starved." She held out a paper bag. "I've brought us some plonk to go with it."

Penelope raised an eyebrow as Figgy pulled the bottle of red wine from the bag.

"Plonk is cheap wine—usually red," Figgy explained. "It's vintage yesterday but I've had Dark Forest Estate before and it's relatively decent."

She plopped onto the sofa and helped herself to an olive.

Penelope turned on the television—there was a bit of static at first from the storm, no doubt—but finally it cleared and they settled in to watch the movie.

Penelope dabbed at her eyes and noticed Figgy doing the same as the final credits rolled.

"Aren't we a bunch of old softies," Penelope said, laughing.

Figgy smiled, but the smile didn't reach her eyes.

"Is something wrong?" Penelope said.

"That was so sad." Figgy sighed and slumped down farther in her chair. "For some reason it made me think of me and Derek. I don't know what to do." She turned to Penelope. Tears trembled on her lower lashes. "I told you my parents are planning to set a date to come and visit and they expect to meet Derek." She balled up the paper napkin in her hands. "Derek and I nearly had a fight about it last night after you left. He's convinced I'm embarrassed by him—because he's Pakistani—but it's not that. I'm not worried about my father—he's a bit of an absentminded professor—he's an anthropologist and has traveled all over and studied different cultures. But my mother is a different story. She's a snob, I'm afraid, and she's already disappointed that I'm not engaged to Arthur Worthington by now. How is she going to react to my dating Derek? But I love him, and I think he's going to propose." She sighed. "I'm darned if I do and darned if I don't."

"What do you mean?"

"If I do introduce him to my parents, I run the risk of them offending him, and if he blames me—which I hope he wouldn't, but who knows—then it will end our relationship. If I don't introduce him, and he finds out they were here visiting . . . he's going to think that's proof that I am embarrassed by him." She looked at Penelope, her eyes wide. "And I'm not. I'm proud of what Derek has accomplished. He's successful in his field, he does volunteer work, he helps old ladies cross the street."

At that last, Figgy began to laugh and her face cleared. She was always in such buoyant good spirits that Penelope was surprised her funk had lasted as long as it had.

"You know how charming Derek is. I'm sure he will work his magic on them and bring them around." Penelope smiled reassuringly.

Figgy raised her chin. "I guess my parents are just going to have to deal with it."

D o you know where they publish the *Daily Star*?" Penelope said the next morning as she and Mabel were discussing which books to order from the winter sales catalogue.

"Birmingham, I believe. Why?"

"I'm wondering if the paper knows who sent that magazine with the pictures of Charlotte Davenport."

"I doubt the person will have enclosed a calling card."

"If they expected to get paid . . ."

"True."

"Still, I think I will give them a call."

Penelope ducked into her writing room and jiggled the mouse on her computer. The screen sprang to life. She went to her favorite search engine and typed in *Daily Star, Birmingham, UK*. She hit enter and the paper's website popped up. Pen scribbled the telephone number down on a piece of scrap paper, reached for her cell phone, and dialed.

She was about to hang up when someone finally answered.

"Daily Star," they said brusquely.

Pen cleared her throat nervously. "Can I speak to Graham

Peterson, please?" she said, asking for the reporter named in
the story's byline.

Penelope was put on hold. She examined her cuticles
while she waited. She really ought to start putting cream
on them. Beryl was constantly telling her that a lady had
a duty to take care of her hands. The problem was, Penelope didn't consider herself a lady—at least not in the
sense that Beryl meant.

Finally her call was picked up and someone growled
something indistinguishable into the receiver. Penelope
thought the person said *Graham speaking*, or something
like it, but she wasn't sure.

"Are you the reporter who broke that story on Charlotte Davenport posing for those pictures?" Pen said.

"Are you a lawyer? Because if you are, then you need
to call the legal department. And if you're from another
paper, all I can say is that I'm not giving up my sources."
And he banged the telephone down.

Penelope sat and stared at her cell phone for a minute.
The reporter had asked if she was a lawyer. A plan began
percolating in her mind. The old cliché was true after
all—there was definitely more than one way to skin a cat.

M abel turned a page in the catalogue and pointed to
one of the covers. "Look. It's Charlotte Davenport's new book. "'*The Regency Rogue*, the sequel to *The
Fire in My Bosom*,'" Mabel read from the catalogue. "'A
tempting and tempestuous tale of treachery, lust, and
love.' Looks like it will be out on September fifth." Mabel
made a face. "That should hit the bestseller lists for sure."

"If Charlotte finishes it. This whole affair had been interfering with her writing, she said."

"She's a professional. She'll do it." Mabel closed the catalogue.

"I'm thinking of going to Birmingham," Pen said.

Mabel looked at her with lowered brows. "Why do I think you're up to something?"

Penelope threw her hands into the air. "I'm not. I'm just following up on something."

"I suppose you should see a bit more of England while you're here," Mabel said with a twinkle in her eye. "Birmingham has several museums and some very interesting architecture. The Winterbourne House and garden should still be lovely at this time of year with all the leaves turning. You could spend the day." She put the catalogue on a shelf under the counter. She glanced at her watch. "There's a train from the Chumley station in an hour that will take you directly to Birmingham."

And thus it was that Penelope found herself on the eleven fourteen train steaming its way north toward the city of Birmingham, the second-largest city in England. She had the address of the newspaper on a piece of paper in her purse and a list of places that Mabel thought she ought to see along with recommendations from Figgy for some pubs for lunch and a tea shop where she could get a cuppa before boarding the train back to Chumley.

Figgy had offered to drive Penelope to the station—it wasn't far but if Penelope had tried to walk she might have missed the train. Even though Figgy was well ac-

quainted with driving on the other side of the street—
having done it all her life, unlike Penelope—it was still a
hair-raising ride since she viewed speed limits and stop
signs as mere suggestions, which she would either take or
not according to her whim; and her shifting was slightly
erratic depending on how much attention she was paying
to the car and how much she was focused on her conversation with Penelope.

Penelope breathed a sigh of relief when they pulled in
front of the Upper Chumley-on-Stoke station, which was
a small brick Victorian building with one platform—
trains running north and those running south switched
tracks before entering the station. A large clock with ro-
man numerals hung from a stanchion right outside and
was permanently stuck at six o'clock—although whether
that was six in the morning or six at night, no one knew
or could remember.

Penelope waved good-bye to Figgy and went inside to
buy her ticket. The man behind the counter was older with
a luxurious gray mustache and the bearing of a retired
army colonel. Penelope handed over several pound notes
and her ticket was returned with brisk efficiency.

She had half expected the train to be like some of those
she'd seen in televised versions of Agatha Christie's Miss
Marple series, but when it came chugging down the tracks,
Penelope was surprised to see that it was quite modern.

The carriage was quite full—mostly men and women
in suits heading north from London on business—but
there were still plenty of seats scattered here and there,
and Penelope managed to find one next to a window.

The doors were about to close when two women got
on, laughing as they dashed across the threshold. Penelope thought she recognized them from the Women's In-

stitute meeting where Charlotte had spoken. They took seats in back of her just as the train began its slow crawl out of the Chumley station.

The train quickly picked up speed and Penelope gazed out the window at the scenery going past. The town was soon behind them, replaced by green fields rocketing by on either side of the train.

What was she doing? Penelope wondered. Was she off on a fool's errand? Why couldn't she leave well enough alone and let the police investigate Regina's murder? Curse her infernal curiosity anyway! She thought again of how her father had often said that her middle name was trouble. The word repeated itself in her head in time to the chugging of the train . . . *trouble . . . trouble . . . trouble.*

Her thoughts were interrupted when one of the women behind her raised her voice, and a name—Nora Blakely—caught Penelope's attention.

"She promised him she would stop," one of the women said. She had a breathy, rather high-pitched voice.

"Yes. I heard he really put his foot down that time—gave her an ultimatum, he did."

Was this about Nora's drinking? Penelope wondered.

"Poor thing. Once the drink gets hold of you, it's hard to get away from it."

"No, it's not easy. But she was causing him no end of trouble. He had to do something."

"So now they're getting a divorce?"

"I don't know. But Harriet told me he said if she didn't stop drinking, he was going to leave her."

"I heard she lost her job because of her drinking."

"Yes. Harriet said she didn't tell him—just pretended to go to work every day as usual. Who knows where she spent her time."

"But wouldn't he expect to see her paycheck or the money deposited into their account? My husband pays all the bills and he knows where every penny comes from and where it goes. He knows if I so much as buy a Curly Wurly bar for fifty p."

The train pulled into the next station and the women's conversation was cut off. But Penelope was left wondering—had Regina threatened to tell Nora's husband about her relapse if Nora didn't lie about the Women's Institute votes in Regina's favor?

Poor Nora was certainly being squeezed—she had lost her job and was suspected of taking money from the Women's Institute treasury plus she'd most likely fiddled the votes to help Regina become president—was it any wonder that the woman might have snapped?

The New Street train station in Birmingham couldn't have been more different than Upper Chumley-on-Stoke's solid Victorian edifice. It was a cavernous space with a soaring ceiling of glass panels positioned between steel ribs and boasted an extensive and rather exclusive shopping center.

Birmingham was a bustling city compared to sleepy Chumley—far more crowded and with a considerably faster pace. Penelope felt a bit like someone coming out of the dark and emerging into the light. It took her a few minutes to get her sea legs as she left the station and joined the crowd on the sidewalk outside. She had to laugh at herself—it hadn't been that long since she'd been living in New York City and she was already settling into being a small-town girl.

A line of taxis idled outside the station. They filled up and took off one by one as people exited the train station. Penelope waited her turn and opened the door to the next taxi that pulled up.

"Hello, love," the driver said.

He was wearing a black-and-white checked cap and had a forest of gray hair sprouting from his rather large and protruding ears. The inside of the cab was clean but worn and smelled of cherry tobacco.

"Where are you off to on this bright sunny day?"

Penelope gave him the address of the *Daily Star*.

"Ah, so you're a reporter, are you?"

"No." Penelope reached out a hand to brace herself as the cabbie went around a sharp bend. "I'm just running an errand."

"You're American, aren't you?" the cabbie said, turning around to look at Penelope. "I can tell by your accent."

"Yes," Penelope admitted somewhat reluctantly.

"Never been," the cabbie said, leaning on his horn when someone cut in front of him. "Great big place, it is. Wouldn't know where to start."

The cabbie flicked on his turn signal. "Is this your first trip to Birmingham?"

"Yes."

"You'll want to visit Cadbury World and see how the chocolates are made. The missus can't get enough of their Double Decker bars."

Penelope hadn't thought of Cadbury in years. The chocolate cream-filled eggs had been a favorite and there had always been at least one in her Easter basket every year.

"Then there's the Tolkien Trail—it's a bit north of here. If you have time, you won't want to miss that. Did you know the author lived in Birmingham?"

"No, I didn't."

Penelope glanced out the window. They were leaving the shops behind and were entering a more industrial area. The cabbie turned a corner and pulled up in front of a no-nonsense-looking redbrick building with a large sign on the front that read *Daily Star Publications*.

"There you go, miss. It's been lovely getting to know you."

Penelope handed over the fare and got out. She stared up at the building. Here goes nothing, she thought.

The lobby was spare and utilitarian and smelled vaguely of ink and newsprint. A receptionist sat behind an old-fashioned metal desk, typing on a computer and fielding telephone calls. Penelope approached him and cleared her throat.

"Yes?" He pulled out his earbuds and tilted his head inquiringly.

He was wearing a lavender shirt with ruffles down the front and dark red pants, and had a thin gold bracelet around his rather bony left wrist. He ran a hand through his bright yellow hair.

"How can I help you, darling? Ronald Penrose at your service."

"I have an appointment with Graham Peterson." Pen tried to keep her voice from squeaking. Thankfully, Ronald couldn't tell her palms were sweating.

"Third floor. His name's on the door." Ronald pointed behind him. "Elevator is over there."

Penelope thanked him and headed toward the bank of elevators. She noticed that her hand was shaking as she pushed the button for the third floor. Courage, she told herself.

The elevator arrived on the third floor and noise washed over Pen as soon as the doors opened.

Row upon row of desks filled the open space with men and women seated behind them, staring intently at their computer screens, typing furiously or leaning toward their neighbor, chatting.

At the back of the room desks were partitioned by chest-high cubicle walls. Rodney had said Graham's name was on the door so Pen headed toward them. There weren't any doors per se, but labels with names on them were affixed to the fronts. Penelope went down the row until she found the one marked *Graham Peterson*.

Peterson was at his desk, the sleeves of his sweater pushed up and a pair of glasses perched on top of his head.

He looked up. "Can I help you?" He studied Penelope. "Are you a lawyer?" He shook his head. "I knew your sort would be around eventually." He motioned toward the chair in front of his desk. "Have a seat."

Penelope perched on the chair, which wobbled slightly. She planted both feet on the floor hoping to steady it.

She cleared her throat several times and then began to cough.

When she didn't immediately stop coughing, Peterson began to look alarmed.

"Let me get you some water." He sprang from his chair, sending it spinning, and sprinted from the cubicle.

Penelope immediately stopped coughing. She waited a beat and then moved to Peterson's desk. She began to rifle through the array of papers spread across it, glancing over her shoulder every couple of seconds.

She heard a noise outside the cubicle and froze, her hand on a stack of files. A woman in a tan corduroy skirt walked past, her head bent over a piece of paper in her hand.

Penelope let her breath out in a whoosh and continued searching. She glanced behind her again and then pulled another stack of papers and folders closer and began to go through them. She caught a glimpse of the corner of a manila envelope and pulled it out.

It was the right size for mailing a magazine like the one that had printed Charlotte's pictures. It was addressed to the *Daily Star*. She peered inside. It was empty but the postmark on the front was clear enough—it had been sent from Upper Chumley-on-Stoke.

Penelope tucked the envelope back into the pile of papers and walked out the entrance of Peterson's cubicle. With any luck, she could make it to the elevator before he came back.

She was almost there when Peterson came around the corner, holding a cup of water. Penelope's shoulder collided with his arm, and the water spilled all down the front of Peterson's sweater.

"Hey," he shouted as Penelope continued running.

She jabbed the button for the elevator repeatedly and jumped on as soon as the doors opened. Peterson stared at her openmouthed as the doors closed and she disappeared from view.

She flew past Ronald Wright's desk and didn't pause for breath until she was out of the building and several blocks away.

FIFTEEN

❧

"I hear Worthington is suing," Figgy said.

The Open Book was preparing for business. Mabel was organizing the money in the cash register and Figgy and Penelope were standing around the counter, enjoying some of the fresh cottage loaf—a round loaf of bread with a smaller round on top—that Figgy had made that morning.

"That's not surprising," Mabel said, straightening a stack of twenty-pound notes. "Remember the French magazine that printed those topless photos of the Duchess of Cambridge when she was in Provence on vacation? They lost in court and were ordered to pay a tidy sum."

Figgy snorted. "And how much did they make on that issue? Millions of pounds I should imagine. It probably more than made up for the inconvenience of being sued."

"Did you enjoy your day in Birmingham?" Mabel said. "I hope you got to see Winterbourne House."

"I did. And I made it to the Birmingham Museum. I saw the exhibit of Anglo-Saxon gold—the Staffordshire Hoard—which was stunning."

Mabel looked at Penelope, one eyebrow raised. "So that's why you went to Birmingham? To see the Staffordshire Hoard?"

Pen felt her face flush. "Not exactly," she finally admitted. "I went to the *Daily Star*."

"And?" Mabel said, both eyebrows raised now.

"I met with Graham Peterson."

"The reporter who printed those pictures of Charlotte?"

"Yes." Penelope cracked her knuckles. "The magazine with those pictures was sent from Upper Chumley-on-Stoke."

"He told you that?" Mabel's voice was incredulous.

"Not exactly."

"Penelope Parish," Mabel said sternly.

"The envelope happened to be on his desk." Pen looked at her feet.

"And you happened to see it," Mabel said.

"Yes."

Mabel sighed. "I'm not even going to ask. I really don't want to know."

"But no name or return address?" Figgy sounded disappointed.

"I'm afraid not."

Mabel stroked her chin. "That does tell us something, though, doesn't it? Apparently the person who sent the magazine wasn't looking to get paid for the story. They obviously had some other motive altogether."

"What?" Figgy cut herself another piece of bread and slathered on some butter.

"Revenge?" Penelope said.

"Or, as we originally thought, the person was black-mailing Charlotte." Mabel closed the cash register drawer. "She didn't pay up—whether that was with money or something else—so the blackmailer, presumably Regina, carried through with the threat."

P enelope spent most of the morning working on her manuscript and preparing for her writer's group, which was meeting after lunch. She was marking up pages for each of the members and was horrified to see how much red ink there was on the paper. Was she being too hard on what was, after all, a group of amateur writers?

Did she really know enough about writing herself? A wave of self-doubt threatened to engulf her. She'd only had one book published and perhaps the fact that it had hit the bestseller list was a fluke and not because of any real talent on her part.

She was working herself into a frenzy for nothing, Penelope told herself. She tried doing some of the diaphragmatic breathing she'd learned from an opera singer she'd once dated for a few months. It worked surprisingly well. Slowly, her pulse returned to normal and she felt herself growing calmer.

Once she was feeling herself again, Penelope gathered all her papers together in a folder and brought everything to the table where the group was to meet.

Someone had left a newspaper behind. Penelope picked it up planning to discard it when a headline caught her eye: Future Duchess Caught in Nude Pix and Murder Scandal.

Penelope sank into the nearest chair and began to read. It was a London paper, and it erroneously referred to Chumley as Lower Chumley-on-Stoke, but the truly horrifying part was the insinuation of a link between Charlotte Davenport and the murder of Regina Bosworth. The reporter seemed to believe it wasn't a far reach to think that a woman who had once posed nude would be involved in a local murder.

Penelope was aghast. Poor Charlotte—she must be beside herself. She quickly stuffed the newspaper into the recycling bin as if that would somehow bury the story and took a seat at the table to wait.

Evelyn Maxwell-Lewis was the first to arrive, breezing in in her usual confident manner. She wasn't wearing jodhpurs this time but rather the English country gentlewoman's uniform of a well-worn Barbour jacket, plaid wool skirt, cashmere twin set, and pearls.

"So what did you think?" she said in her gruff voice, dropping into a chair at the table. "You've read my pages, I assume."

Penelope swallowed hard. She had read them and frankly hadn't known quite what to make of them.

Evelyn didn't wait for an answer. "Shocking business about Charlotte Davenport, don't you think? I was never quite on board with the match, mind you. I feared she wouldn't understand our ways, but nude pictures! That is something I never expected."

Penelope opened her mouth, but before she could say anything, Evelyn continued.

"I had breakfast with Arthur this morning to discuss the annual October pheasant shoot. I always look forward to it, and it's a wonderful day spent outdoors."

Doing what? Penelope couldn't help but think. Shooting innocent birds?

"Apparently Arthur knew about the pictures already and of course he hoped they wouldn't come out. But when he saw that article in the London paper this morning, he was positively livid. Hinting that Charlotte was somehow linked to Regina's murder just because they lived in the same town." Evelyn made a hissing sound.

"Arthur blames himself that he can't give Charlotte an alibi, since he was off seeing to things and Charlotte was closeted in her office writing one of those books she writes." Evelyn pulled a monogrammed linen handkerchief from her purse and blew her nose. "Mind you, I wouldn't be in the least bit disappointed if the wedding didn't come off. I'm sure Charlotte is a nice gel but one doesn't know a thing about her background and whether or not she really would make a suitable wife for the Duke of Upper Chumley-on-Stoke."

She took a breath. "I honestly feared he would have a stroke when he saw that ghastly paper, but then, while Arthur isn't in the first bloom of youth, he is in excellent shape. The nerve of that newspaper. How dare they?"

Twilight had settled over Upper Chumley-on-Stoke by the time Penelope left the Open Book. The skies were clear and blanketed by stars. It was colder than it had been earlier, and a brisk wind was swirling leaves along the gutter like miniature tornadoes.

Penelope had walked to work and was now headed home, hurrying down the sidewalk and pulling her collar closer around her neck.

She had turned her head to look at the display of chocolates—one of her weaknesses—in the Sweet Tooth shop window when she ran smack into a body—a male body judging by its relative size and heft.

"Oh," Penelope said, flustered. "I'm so sorry. I was thinking and I wasn't looking where I was going."

"We do have a habit of running into each other, don't we?" It was Maguire bundled up in a worn sheepskin jacket and tartan wool scarf. "No harm done. I don't think I'm even bruised." He smiled. "It's turning cold. Would you fancy a glass of wine to warm you up?"

"Oh," Penelope said for the second time. "Yes, why not." That didn't sound very enthusiastic so she added, "That would be lovely."

They were two doors down from the wine bar and Maguire gestured toward it.

"Is the Sour Grapes okay with you?"

"Certainly."

Maguire opened the door and followed Penelope inside.

The proprietor of the Sour Grapes was the cousin of the man who owned the Book and Bottle and when he'd opened the bar, he had decided it didn't make sense to compete with the pub but rather to offer something more upscale to appeal to the tourists who flooded Chumley during the nicer weather.

The Sour Grapes had pretentions toward being hip and modern, mixing hanging brass fixtures and sleek furniture with the original beamed ceiling, but since the décor hadn't been changed for nearly twenty years, it looked more like an aging woman trying to look younger by wearing a miniskirt and crop top. Despite its pretentions, it was really more pub than trendy wine bar.

It was quiet inside with two men with leather brief-cases by their sides sitting at the long, granite-topped bar and two smart-looking young women chattering animatedly at one of the tables.

Penelope took off her coat and hung it from a metal hook on the nearby wall. Maguire pulled out Penelope's chair and she found she was pleased by the chivalrous gesture. Miles usually flung himself into his own seat and left her to fend for herself.

Maguire ordered a lager and Penelope the house red. There was a moment of awkward silence before Maguire began to talk.

"How is the book coming along? You did say you were writing one, right?"

Penelope was pleased that he'd remembered. "Yes. At least I'm trying to," she said, thinking of the last scene she'd written. She still wasn't satisfied with it.

"Writers, artists, and musicians have a special place in the heart of an Irishman." He smiled and thumped his chest with his fist.

A waiter in a black vest, stiffly starched white shirt, and bow tie arrived and slid their drinks in front of them along with a plate of olives.

Maguire gestured toward the dish. "Looks like Chumley is going continental on us." He took a sip of his lager. "What did you leave behind in the States? Family?"

Expectations? Penelope thought.

Penelope took a deep breath. "My sister lives in Connecticut in a perfect house with her perfect husband. She's the pretty one," Penelope said, looking for a laugh.

Maguire obliged. "Isn't there a proverb about beauty being in the eye of the beholder?" He smiled at her warmly.

Penelope shifted in her chair. She wasn't used to being

the center of attention and she suddenly felt as awkward as a teenager.

"My parents are divorced. My mother is what we call a snowbird in the States. She spends summers in Connecticut and winters in Palm Beach. My father has an apartment in the city—New York City," Penelope clarified, "and a house in Amagansett along with a blond trophy wife."

"Is that all? One sister?" He shook his head. "Hard to imagine. I have five siblings—two brothers and three sisters. Your typical big Irish family." He was quiet for a moment, running his finger around the rim of his glass. "Is there anyone special back home?"

Penelope didn't try to—and didn't want to—analyze the look in his eyes.

Was Miles special? Reluctantly she had come to the conclusion that he wasn't. She'd barely given him a thought since leaving New York. In this case, clearly out of sight, out of mind was more accurate than absence makes the heart grow fonder.

Maguire looked down at his beer as if he'd read her answer in her lack of response.

Penelope didn't know why, but she didn't want him to get the wrong impression. That thought made her uncomfortable but she decided to leave analyzing it until later.

Instead, she said, "No, not really. No one all that special."

Maguire's face began to light up, but he quickly changed his expression to one of mild interest.

"How are you getting on in England? Finding it quite different, are you?"

"More different than I thought and at the same time, less different," Penelope said hoping that didn't make her sound ridiculous. She poked at her cocktail napkin, picking little pieces off and rolling the paper between her fingers. "The languages are distinct despite the fact that we're all speaking English. I am catching on, though. But people and their feelings and emotions are universal, don't you think?"

Maguire nodded.

Penelope realized she was becoming more and more relaxed—and it wasn't because of the wine. It was Maguire's calm, steady demeanor that was having that effect on her. She'd even stopped jiggling her foot—a nervous habit that always drove Miles crazy—and was feeling at ease.

"What about you?" Penelope said. "Your accent is . . . Irish?"

"Yes. Born and raised in Dromod, a small town—population barely five hundred—in County Leitrim. It's on the River Shannon in the Border Region of Northern Ireland. County Leitrim has a wee bit of coastline along the Atlantic Ocean." He chose an olive from the dish and popped it into his mouth. "My parents ran a pub. It's long, hard work. I wanted something better for myself, so I came to England."

"Why Upper Chumley-on-Stoke?" Penelope said.

"You go where the job is and where you're sent." He pinched the bridge of his nose. "I started out in Leeds and . . . now I'm here. Quite the change." He gave a small smile.

Penelope had the feeling there was more of a story behind his transfer than he was willing to admit, but she didn't want to pry.

"At least you have a murder to solve," Penelope said. She immediately felt ashamed—a murder wasn't something to celebrate.

"True," Maguire said, giving another small smile.

"I didn't mean—" she began.

Maguire waved a hand. "Of course not." He smiled, a more genuine smile this time.

Penelope decided that she might as well be in for a penny, in for a pound, as the expression went.

"Have you discovered anything new? New leads? New suspects?" She didn't really expect an answer.

"This case has us running around in circles. They're talking about bringing in the top guns from London if we don't come up with a solution soon." He ran a hand over his face. "At least we've been able to clear Worthington himself. That made the governor happy. It's a bit dicey when it comes to the nobility. Obviously they can't get away with murder—at least not in this day and age—but they still have to be handled with the proverbial kid gloves."

"So Worthington has an alibi?" Penelope said as casually as possible.

Maguire took a sip of his lager and licked the foam off his upper lip. He leveled a look at Penelope, one eyebrow raised, then gave a knowing smile.

"Yes, and it checks out, too. He was with his groundskeeper all morning until someone went to get him after the body was found. The coroner puts time of death within an hour of the discovery—lividity was minimal and the blood hadn't completely congealed." He looked at Penelope. "I'm sorry. That's a bit graphic. I forget—I've become used to it, I'm afraid."

Penelope waved a hand and put on a stoic face. "That's okay. I'm fine." She forced herself to stop picturing congealing blood, which was a little like the old parlor game of trying not to think of pink elephants after being told not to.

They continued to talk, the conversation moving to less morbid topics, and Penelope was disappointed when she finished her glass of wine and saw that Maguire was draining the last bit of his lager.

"I've enjoyed this," Maguire said, standing up.

"Me, too," Penelope said.

The stood smiling at each other somewhat awkwardly until Penelope finally began to move toward the door.

Penelope had a bit of a lift in her step as she left the Sour Grapes, and she didn't want to think about the reason for that right away either or it would mean admitting she'd thoroughly enjoyed her conversation with Maguire—he was easygoing and there was a calmness and steadiness about him that was relaxing.

The faint scent of meat roasting combined with pungent and exotic spices wafted on the air as Penelope got closer to her cottage. It was coming from Kebabs and Curries, the takeaway place on the edge of town. Her stomach began to rumble and she decided she would treat herself to a takeout meal.

She studied the menu while she waited in line, finally deciding on the lamb tikka masala. The delicious aromas tantalized her and her mouth was watering as she carried the bag out of the shop.

Mrs. Danvers was not amused when Penelope arrived home. She sniffed disdainfully at the Kebabs and Curries bag and then went to stare pointedly at her own empty dish.

Penelope took her coat off, threw it on a chair, and hastened to open a can of Mrs. Danvers's favorite cat food—turkey and chicken casserole from an upscale and overpriced brand. She spooned a portion of it into Mrs. Danvers's dish and stood back.

Mrs. Danvers walked over to her dish, her tail high in the air and swishing back and forth like a metronome. She sniffed the dish, turned around, and looked accusingly at Penelope.

"What?" Penelope said. "It's your favorite."

Mrs. Danvers blinked slowly, her tail moving back and forth in a furious rhythm. After staring at Penelope for several more minutes, she got up and stalked off to groom herself in the corner of the kitchen.

Penelope set a place for herself at the kitchen table and dished out her tikka masala. Her thoughts kept returning to her drink with Maguire, ricocheting back and forth between the feelings the meeting had stirred up and the information Maguire had shared.

They now had one less suspect with Worthington out of the running. Poor Charlotte—this would focus more attention on her. Penelope hoped the newspapers wouldn't renew their vicious attacks. The news cycle was short and with any luck the story of her nude pictures would soon disappear from their pages and be forgotten.

They didn't appear to be any closer to a solution than they were the day Regina was found murdered in Worthington's basement. Even the police appeared to be stumped. She wasn't being much help to poor Charlotte. She thought about the possible suspects that she, Figgy, and Mabel had identified. She would like to know if Daphne had been anywhere near the fest around the time of the murder. The Book and Bottle had had a booth, but Penelope didn't remember seeing her there. Of course it had been crowded and she had been distracted by thoughts of her upcoming talk.

Daphne had plenty of motives—with Regina out of the way, it wouldn't take her long to bring Gordon to his knees so to speak with a proposal. Her life at the moment was fairly grim and full of drudgery—working hard behind the bar at the Book and Bottle and spending her free time caring for her disabled sister. It wouldn't be a stretch to think that she might have decided murder would be a good way out of her situation.

Penelope needed to find out where Daphne had been that day. But how?

She finished her dinner—putting half of it in the refrigerator for another night—and was about to turn on her laptop when her cell phone rang.

She glanced at the caller ID—it was Miles.

"You're up late," she said when she answered.

"It's earlier here. Have you forgotten?" Miles said, sounding testy.

"Of course. You're right."

Their conversation continued at a desultory pace until it wound down to a prolonged silence.

Miles finally said, "I miss you."

Penelope replied with "I miss you, too."

Detective Maguire suddenly came to mind with his craggy face and blue eyes and Penelope hastily banished the thought saying "I miss you" again, only with a little more fervor this time.

"Good morning, love," Gladys said when Penelope walked into the Pig in a Poke. "What can I do for you today?"

She put the book she'd been reading down on the counter—a romance, Penelope thought, judging by the cover where a bare-chested man in knee breeches and tall boots had his arm around a woman with long blond curls and a bouffant gown with a neckline so low she was tee-tering on the verge of a wardrobe malfunction.

"I thought I'd get one of your Cornish pasties to take to work for my lunch," Penelope said.

"You won't be sorry," Gladys said with a twinkle in her eye.

Penelope glanced at Gladys's arm. The bruise had now faded to a kaleidoscope of greens and yellows. Gladys must have noticed her looking at it because she hastily pulled down her sleeve so that only the very edge of the bruise showed.

Behind her Bruce grunted as he butterflied a chicken, raising his cleaver over his head and bringing it down with a swift and practiced motion. Suddenly Penelope no-ticed the smell in the shop—animal blood and raw meat—and her head swam momentarily.

"Are you okay, love?" Gladys said, her brow puckering in concern. "Gone a bit faint, have you?"

"I'm fine." Penelope smiled reassuringly.

Gladys was busy wrapping the pasty in a glassine sheet. "You'll want to give this about forty-five minutes in the oven—until it's good and golden brown. But be care-ful." She shook a finger at Penelope. "It will steam when you cut it open. Don't go burning yourself, now."

"Bake?" Penelope said.

"Yes, love. You'll have to pop it into the oven to cook it."

Penelope felt deflated. "Can't I just put it in the micro-wave at the store?"

A horrified look came over Gladys's face. "A micro-wave?" she said as if Penelope had suggested some futuristic nuclear device.

"I'll tell you what. You let me know when you want your

lunch, and I'll pop this in our oven for you, okay? Then you can nip over and pick it up, and it will be all nice and hot."

"Thanks." Penelope fished her wallet out of her purse. "Your pasties were such a hit at the fest—I was sorry I didn't get a chance to try one."

"That they were." Gladys beamed.

"I saw the Book and Bottle had a booth at the fest as well. I suppose Daphne was working the counter."

Gladys frowned. "You know, I don't remember seeing Daphne there come to think of it."

"Bruce," Gladys called over her shoulder. "Did you see that young lass Daphne from the Book and Bottle at the fest?"

"I couldn't have, could I? I had to keep my head down and serve the customers what with you being taken faint and all," Bruce grumbled.

Penelope glanced at Bruce, who was scowling at his wife. No wonder Gladys lost herself in romance novels, Penelope thought. She had to escape somehow.

"Perhaps Daphne's sister had one of her spells," Gladys said, leaning both hands on the counter. "It wouldn't be the first time Daphne had to rush Layla to hospital."

Penelope thanked Gladys and turned to leave.

"Don't forget to ring me and we'll have the pasty all nice and ready for you," Gladys called after her.

Penelope stood on the sidewalk for a moment and then determinedly headed in the direction of the Book and Bottle after ringing Mabel from her cell phone to tell her she'd be a bit late.

There was no reason Daphne's boss should give her any information, but Penelope figured there was no harm in trying. At the worst, he'd put her down as a snoop and a busybody. Or he'd blame it on her being American—

that seemed to be an explanation readily accepted by the residents of Chumley.

The Book and Bottle was closed for business, but Penelope could hear a vacuum running behind the locked door. She rapped on the door several times and then stood back. The vacuum cleaner was switched off and a man opened the door. He had a mop in his hands.

Penelope recognized him from her visits to the pub. She assumed he was the owner.

"Sorry, miss, we're closed." He leaned on the mop. "And if you're here to sell me something, I don't need it. I've got my regular suppliers—I've been doing business with them since I took over the pub from my father—and I have no intention of changing."

"I'm not selling anything. I just wanted to ask you a question."

He scowled. "You might as well come in, then." He held the door for her.

He was wearing a worn plaid flannel shirt, jeans with patches on the knees, and a pair of mud-spattered black Wellingtons.

He gestured to them. "Pardon the boots. Been cleaning up a mess in the gents. Broken pipe sent water spraying everywhere." He sighed. "It's always something. Know what I mean?"

The interior of the pub looked different with all the lights on. The shabbiness of some of the upholstery was apparent along with the smoke stains on the walls although now smoking was no longer allowed. A woman was behind the bar, swabbing it down with soap and water. She looked up briefly when Penelope walked in, glanced at her boss, then went back to what she was doing.

"The name is Daniel Barber, by the way."

"Penelope Parish." Penelope took a deep breath. "You had a booth at the fest," she began.

"Yes." A wary look came over Barber's face. "So did a lot of people."

"Was Daphne Potter at the booth that day?"

Now Barber's expression turned angry. "No, she wasn't. She was supposed to be but at the last minute she claimed she had to take her sister to hospital and couldn't work. I ended up manning the booth myself and pulling pints all day when I was supposed to take the missus to Ipswich to see her mother who had been taken into care after breaking her hip." He scowled. "The wife wasn't half angry that I had to work. She said what's the point of being the boss when you end up doing all the work yourself?"

"So Daphne didn't show up at all?"

Barber shook his head. "Nope."

Had Daphne really been at the hospital? Penelope wondered as she left the Book and Bottle. Or had she snuck into the fest and murdered Regina?

Penelope still needed to mail off the scarf she'd bought her sister for her birthday. Mabel had scrounged up an appropriately sized box for the present, which Penelope had managed to wrap after much wrangling with the Scotch tape. It looked a bit sad, she thought—she never could get the paper on straight or tie the ribbon without getting her finger caught. She sighed. It was the best she could do. Beryl was a perfectionist—her gifts always looked as if they'd been professionally wrapped—but at least Penelope was confident she would like what was inside.

It was quiet in the Open Book—a handful of people were browsing the shelves and one person was sitting in the corner with a laptop nursing a container of coffee—so she decided to make a quick run to the post office.

The weather was milder than it had been for a few days, and Penelope was able to leave her coat open and her scarf trailing untied from her neck. As she passed shop after shop, she tried to avoid thinking about the fact that she was secretly hoping to run into Maguire again and she had to squash a feeling of disappointment when she arrived at the post office without seeing him.

Penelope found it quite charming that the post office was actually a small counter inside the Sweet Tooth. The downside of the location was having to traverse all the aisles of delectable candy and chocolate without succumbing to temptation. She passed a bin filled with colorful Swedish fish that brought back memories of buying bags of them in the grocery store and then smuggling them into the movie theater, giggling wildly with her friends as they scooted past the ticket taker and declared themselves home free.

A short line had formed in front of the one clerk who was doling out stamps and weighing packages. Penelope helped herself to a chocolate sample set out on a plate nearby. Waiting in a line at a post office inside a candy store certainly had its compensations.

She never did mind waiting in lines—it gave her the opportunity to think without anyone—with raised eyebrows—asking her what she was doing (nothing, according to them) or being made to feel guilty for "not joining in." Some of her best plot ideas had come to her while standing in a line, which was very productive for a writer but not something many other people would understand.

The woman in front of Penelope moved slightly to the left, shifting her brown trilby, and Penelope was able to catch a glimpse of the postmistress. She was surprised to recognize Victoria Bosworth, Regina's daughter. She wasn't a pretty woman but Penelope supposed she was the sort who might be called handsome. She had strong features and marked brows that were like straight lines over her brown eyes.

Her dark hair was cut in a short bob and she wore no makeup. Her movements, as she stamped the woman's packages, were swift and efficient.

Finally the customer's mail was all weighed, stamped, and transferred to a bin on the counter behind Victoria and it was Penelope's turn. She put her package on the counter. Victoria glanced at the label.

"You must be the American who's working at the Open Book."

If you want to hide, don't try to do it in a small English village, Penelope thought.

"Yes," she said. "You're Regina's daughter, aren't you? I'm very sorry for your loss."

The platitude sounded inadequate, but Penelope didn't know what else to say.

Victoria briefly ducked her head. "Thanks." She put Penelope's package on the scale and watched as the needle registered the weight. "That will be five pounds, please."

Penelope got out her wallet and removed a five-pound note. As she handed it to Victoria, she noticed Victoria was wearing a ring with a small diamond on her left hand.

"Are you engaged? Your ring is lovely."

Victoria looked pleased. "Yes. Ronnie asked me on my birthday a month ago." She frowned. "My mother wasn't terribly pleased—she's never approved of Ronnie—but he's a good man and we're happy." She leaned her elbows on the counter. "My mother was seriously hoping that Worthington would take an interest in me. Can you imagine?" She rolled her eyes. "No, I'm perfectly content with my Ronnie. We haven't set a date yet but are planning a spring wedding. Nothing fancy, mind you, just a few friends to celebrate with us."

Victoria certainly seemed like the chatty type, Penelope thought. That surprised her—she'd read so much about the famous English reserve but everyone she'd met so far had been warm and friendly. She wondered if she dared introduce the subject of the magazine mailed to the *Daily Star.* Perhaps Victoria knew something about it.

"You didn't happen to mail a package to the *Daily Star* in Birmingham, did you?"

"Not for a customer, no." Victoria frowned. "But I did mail a package for my mother to that address. It was sitting on her desk so I picked it up and brought it with me to post."

"Do you know what was in it?"

Victoria shook her head. "No. I figured it wasn't any of my business. I just brought it to work with me, weighed it, put a stamp on it, and tossed it in the bin to be collected with the rest of the mail."

That solved one riddle, Penelope thought as she left the Sweet Tooth. Victoria had been the one to mail the package to the *Daily Star,* which undoubtedly contained the magazine with Charlotte's pictures. It would be too much of a coincidence to think that two people in Chumley had mailed something to the newspaper around the same time.

But she had to wonder—did Victoria really not know what she was sending off?

SIXTEEN

❦

"So Victoria is the one who mailed that magazine to the *Daily Star*," Mabel said when Penelope returned to the Open Book. "That solves that. But what I'd like to know is how did Regina get hold of that magazine in the first place? She'd hardly have bought *Men's Fancy* for herself."

"Maybe it was Gordon's?" Penelope said, helping herself to one of the shortbread cookies Figgy had left for them on a plate on the counter.

"Possibly. But I can't see Regina allowing Gordon to read something like that. The poor man was bullied half to death. Plus, the magazine was nearly twenty years old. Surely Regina would have rooted it out and gotten rid of it shortly after their marriage. And if not then, certainly by now." Mabel ran a hand through her unruly white hair. "Poor Gordon. Apparently he wasn't even allowed to go into his own bureau drawers—Regina put his clothes away for him so he wouldn't disturb her elaborate folding method. He wouldn't have been able to hide something like that magazine at home."

"Then maybe he kept it at work." Penelope finished the last bite of her cookie.

"But why bring it home with him, then? He had to know Regina would find it eventually." Mabel drummed her fingers against her chin. "No, I think Regina came by it some other way." She shrugged. "We may never know."

"By the way, have you had a chance to speak to Worthington about India's situation?" Penelope brushed some crumbs from her top. "I can't stop worrying about her."

"Yes, I did. He was quite grateful. He said he didn't realize she was struggling to quite that extent. He's looking for a way to make things easier for her without offending her. India can be quite prickly. She views herself as part of the aristocracy and that means keeping up appearances at all cost."

The bell over the door tinkled and the door opened. "Hello," India called out.

Penelope and Mabel jumped apart as if they had been caught doing something wrong and Mabel's greeting to India was a bit more effusive than usual to cover her embarrassment.

India was wearing the plaid skirt and twin set Penelope had seen her wearing previously, only this time she noticed the wear at the hem of the skirt and the neatly darned spot on the cardigan.

"I've been enjoying that biography of Churchill by Andrew Roberts you recommended," India said. "I'm so grateful you found me that used copy." She joined Penelope and Mabel at the counter. "What a man!" She sighed. "They don't seem to make them like that anymore, do they?"

"Oh, to be fair, I suppose there are a few here and there," Mabel said.

India glanced at the cookies on the counter. She quickly snaked out a hand, plunked one from the plate, and slipped it into her purse.

Penelope supposed she was saving it for her tea later, but it brought back all her worries about India's situation. She hoped Worthington really did plan to do something.

"There's soon going to be quite a bit of excitement in our little corner of the world," India said.

Mabel raised an eyebrow. "Regina's murder wasn't exciting enough?"

"You're quite right, of course. That was exciting in a rather horrid way. A bit of excitement we could have lived without." A small frown appeared between India's brows. "Certainly Regina's murder wasn't something one expected to happen in Upper Chumley-on-Stoke."

"You haven't told us what this new excitement is going to be," Penelope said, reaching a hand out for another cookie. She realized her breakfast that morning had been a cup of English breakfast tea and she hadn't had any lunch yet even though it was after noon already. No wonder her stomach was growling.

India fingered the ancient yellowing pearls around her neck. "This is rather embarrassing"—she gave a forced laugh—"but I have to admit to watching that BBC show *Resurrected—Unsolved Crimes Then and Now.* It's my guilty pleasure, I'm afraid." She clasped her hands together and sighed.

"I've watched that show," Mabel said. "The reporters try to track down the solution to old crimes."

India beamed. "Yes. And one of those reporters is coming here, to Upper Chumley-on-Stoke." Her face turned slightly pink.

Mabel looked confused. "I didn't realize there were

any unsolved crimes in Upper Chumley-on-Stoke." She picked up the last cookie from the plate and took a bite. "Of course I haven't lived here forever, so maybe it was before my time?"

India pursed her lips. "The crime didn't necessarily take place here." She pointed out the window to the high street. "The reporter could be following a clue that has led them to Chumley."

Penelope shivered. "Does that mean we might have a criminal living right here in Chumley? Someone who got away with murder and was never arrested for it? Other than whoever killed Regina, of course."

"That's exactly it," India said somewhat breathlessly. "It could be anyone. A neighbor or a clerk at the Tesco or the hygienist at your dentist's office."

"Let's just hope it's not the dentist." Mabel laughed.

"That does sound exciting, though," Penelope said. "Do you think the reporter will be able to flush the person out?"

India tapped her index finger to her head. "They're smart. They've caught a number of people so far, including one man who murdered his tennis partner twenty years ago."

"Maybe they'll figure out who murdered Regina," Penelope said.

It was nearly two o'clock by the time Penelope ran across the street to the Pig in a Poke to pick up her Cornish pasty.

"We'd just about given up on you, love," Gladys said as she wrapped the steaming-hot savory pasty in a piece of butcher paper. "But I've saved one for you." She handed

Penelope the pasty in a white paper bag that had the out-line of a pig on the front in black ink. "Mind, that's hot now. Be careful you don't burn yourself."

"Don't worry," Penelope said handing over the money.

She held the paper bag close as she left the shop. The warmth felt good. She'd dashed out of the Open Book without bothering with her coat and it was quite brisk out.

She walked past Brown's Hardware and glanced at the display of rakes in the front window and the paper leaves of different colors that were taped to the glass.

It would be safer to cross the street in front of the Crown Jewels—the local jeweler—where there was a pe-destrian crossing. There wasn't much traffic on the high street at this hour, but people came whipping around the corner terribly fast and Penelope had already witnessed a near accident in front of the newsstand when a gentleman in a tomato-red Triumph Spitfire had nearly hit an elderly lady crossing the street at a turtle-like pace.

Penelope stopped to look in the window of the Crown Jewels. She wasn't particularly attracted to jewelry for its own sake although she did cherish the few pieces she had that had special meaning to her—the small gold cross from her godmother when she made her Confirmation at Calvary Episcopal Church, the silver ring she'd bought herself when she backpacked through Ireland, and the thin gold chain her first boyfriend had given her for Christmas the year they were dating.

The display in the Crown Jewels window was interest-ing, however, as it was an exhibit of antique silver snuff-boxes made in Sheffield, England, in the late eighteenth century.

Penelope sensed someone passing close by her and turned around. It was Lady Evelyn Maxwell-Lewis.

"They're quite lovely, aren't they?" Evelyn said, standing next to Penelope and pointing to the display in the window. "These were made in Sheffield, but by the early nineteenth century, the silver industry started to blossom in Birmingham. Box makers like Samuel Pemberton began producing oblong containers decorated with purely British images like castles and abbeys."

A movement in the shop must have caught Evelyn's eye.

"Look," she exclaimed. "Isn't that Daphne Potter with Regina's husband, Gordon?"

Penelope peered through the glass. "Yes, it is."

Daphne was standing at the counter with Gordon Bosworth. She appeared to be trying on gold bracelets. Penelope watched while Gordon fastened one with gold links around her wrist and Daphne held her hand up to admire it.

"Good heavens," Evelyn exclaimed.

Penelope felt slightly self-conscious lingering in front of the window, but she wanted to see what was going to happen.

"I can hardly believe my eyes," Evelyn said, squinting through the glass. "Does that woman have no shame?"

"Do you suppose Daphne is helping Gordon pick out a present for Victoria? Perhaps it's for her birthday or a wedding present?"

They waited and watched, but Daphne didn't take the bracelet off. Instead, Gordon handed over a credit card and waited while the clerk rang up the sale. Daphne smiled at Gordon and leaned over and gave him a chaste kiss on the cheek.

"The nerve of that woman," Evelyn exclaimed. "With Regina hardly cold in her grave. Not that I gave a jot for

Regina, troublemaker that she was, but one must have a sense of propriety after all. You'd think Gordon would know better, but then I think his background is—how shall I put this—rather common."

Evelyn lifted her chin. "I still have to see Mr. Witherspoon about restringing a necklace. It's been in the family for several generations, and it needs a bit of repair." Evelyn moved away from the window and began walking toward the door of the Crown Jewels. "Ta-ta," she waved to Penelope. "I'll see you at our writing group meeting next week. I've made quite a bit of progress on my manuscript. I think you'll be pleased."

Penelope moved away from the window as well, looked up and down the street, and crossed over to the other side. She hoped Daphne hadn't seen her and Evelyn. She didn't think so. Besides, so what? They'd been looking at the display of snuffboxes in the window. There was nothing wrong with that.

But it looked as if their original assessment of Daphne and Gordon's relationship was wrong. Daphne wasn't simply tolerating Gordon's attentions, she was actively enjoying them.

Penelope stared woefully at the contents of her closet. Derek was taking her, Figgy, and Mabel out for dinner at Pierre's to celebrate Figgy's birthday, and she wanted to wear something other than her usual leggings and a sweater. Her closet, however, did not yield anything particularly special, not even after she had gone through everything on the rod twice.

Suddenly she remembered a paisley pashmina shawl a

college friend had brought her after spending a semester in India. She couldn't imagine why she'd thought to bring it with her. She dug through her bureau and pulled it out. She would wear black trousers, a black sweater, and drape the colorful shawl around her shoulders.

Penelope put on the black trousers from her pantsuit and a black turtleneck sweater, and arranged the shawl just so. She looked in the mirror. She thought even her sister, Beryl, would approve of the outfit—smart and sophisticated but without being fussy. Penelope just didn't do fussy.

Mrs. Danvers snaked in and out between Penelope's legs and Penelope suspected the cat was trying to transfer as much of her fur as possible to her pants.

She bent down and scratched Mrs. Danvers's back. Mrs. Danvers immediately retreated to the farthest corner of the room and sat with her back to Penelope.

Penelope retrieved her coat from the foyer closet and slipped it on. She'd decided she would walk to Pierre's, which was next to the Open Book, so not that far. Mabel, Figgy, and Derek would be meeting her at the restaurant.

Penelope ran into Mabel just as Mabel was about to open the door to Pierre's. They went inside together where the warm air was a welcome change from the brisk nighttime temperatures. The restaurant was redolent with the scent of garlic, herbs, and butter. Penelope's mouth began to water almost immediately.

Derek and Figgy were already seated at a table. A bottle of champagne sat next to them in a bucket filled with ice, and champagne flutes were set out at every place. Derek jumped up when he saw Penelope and Mabel. He kissed them both on each cheek and then pulled out their chairs.

Penelope noticed that Figgy was glowing. Her face was slightly pink, and she couldn't stop smiling.

"I wonder what Derek got Figgy for her birthday," Mabel whispered to Penelope. "She seems terribly pleased about something."

A waiter appeared, retrieved the bottle of champagne from the ice, wrapped a white cloth around the bottom, and filled each of the glasses. He then disappeared as silently as he had arrived.

Derek stood up and held his glass aloft. Penelope supposed he was going to make a birthday toast, and she reached for her own glass.

Derek cleared his throat. "I would like to wish my beautiful fiancée a happy birthday," he began. "And to announce that she has accepted my proposal of marriage and agreed to be not just my wife, but my life mate and my soul mate."

Penelope and Mabel gasped, then quickly raised their glasses.

"Happy birthday to Figgy and congratulations to you both," Mabel said. "What splendid news."

They clinked glasses all around.

Figgy held out her hand, which Penelope realized she had been keeping hidden under the table, and wiggled her fingers. A diamond ring sparkled on the third finger of her left hand.

"It's beautiful," Penelope said, holding Figgy's hand as she examined the ring.

"Derek had it made especially for me at the Crown Jewels here in town," Figgy said with a proud smile. "It's an antique setting that's come back in style again."

"It's perfect," Penelope said, and she meant it. The ring

was so Figgy—elegant and yet still different enough to stand out.

"This is a wonderful occasion," Mabel said, taking a sip of her champagne. "I'm happy for you both."

Penelope was happy for them, too. It was obvious they were in love. They were different and yet they complemented each other. Derek was in finance—a fairly conservative field—and was quite successful, but he had an unconventional side to him as well. Figgy appeared to be a total free spirit, but she managed to successfully run a business.

There was only one problem—Figgy's extremely conservative mother. Penelope wasn't going to bring that up, though—this was a night for celebrating—Figgy and Derek would have to deal with that later.

The waiter appeared again to take their order. Penelope was torn—there were so many delicious choices—cassoulet, osso buco, lamb Provençal, roast duck with cherry-rosemary sauce.

She finally decided on the cassoulet and handed the waiter her menu.

A party of three was being seated at a table near them. Penelope looked up and saw that one of the guests was in a wheelchair. She also recognized Daphne and Gordon.

"Is that Daphne's sister?" she said to Mabel.

Mabel turned around and looked. "Yes, that's Layla. How nice of Gordon to take them out to dinner—and to such a lovely restaurant. I know Layla isn't able to get out much."

Mabel turned back to Penelope, Figgy, and Derek. "Have you set a date for the wedding yet?" She laughed. "I suppose it's early days yet—you've only just gotten engaged."

"No," Figgy said. "We haven't even told our families

yet." Her expression clouded. "But I don't want to think about that right now. I want to live in the moment." She beamed at Derek.

The waiter brought their appetizers—Penelope had chosen a bowl of butternut squash bisque. It had a swirl of crème fraîche on top and was dotted with toasted pecans.

"Do you smell something funny?" Derek said, putting down his fork. He sat up and sniffed.

"Just the smell of yummy food," Penelope said, tilting her bowl and finishing up the last spoonsful of her soup.

"I don't smell anything either," Mabel said.

"It smells like something burning." Derek half rose from his chair.

"Oh no," Figgy said. "Let's hope the chef hasn't burned our dinner. I'm really looking forward to having their coq au vin."

Derek sat down again. He laughed. "I suppose that does happen occasionally even in the best of restaurants."

The waiter approached their table, a tray balanced on the palm of his hand. He put it down in back of them and began placing their meals in front of them.

"Did you notice a funny smell?" Derek asked as the waiter set a plate in front of Figgy. "Like something burning?"

"*Non*," the waiter said in a strong French accent.

He finished serving the table and quickly disappeared.

"I don't think he appreciated your telling him you thought something was burning," Figgy said with a mischievous smile. "He's probably run to tell the chef and who knows what they'll put in our dessert."

They all laughed.

Just then there was a commotion at the back of the dining room and people began to turn in that direction.

A busboy came through the swinging door to the kitchen. His eyes were wild and staring like a spooked horse and his hair was disheveled. He opened his mouth but at first nothing came out.

"Fire," he finally blurted out. "Everyone get out."

The room, which had been fairly hushed, was suddenly filled with the sounds of chairs scraping back and people's raised and panicked voices.

"No need to be alarmed," Derek said, throwing his napkin down on the table. "We're near enough to the door and it seems as if the fire is quite small and contained in the kitchen." He pulled out Figgy's chair and took her hand in his. "Let's go," he said, smiling at her.

"We'd best hurry," Mabel said. "I should imagine these old buildings would go up like tinder boxes if the fire got out of hand. I do hope the fire doesn't spread. Figgy's apartment is right above."

Meanwhile, sirens sounded outside and soon they saw rotating flashing red lights through the window.

"Our coats . . ." Figgy said, hesitating in front of the curtained alcove where the patrons' coats were hung.

"I don't think we should try to retrieve them," Derek said, shepherding them toward the door. "We might be in the way."

Mabel stopped suddenly. "I wonder if Daphne and Gordon need any help with Daphne's sister," she said, turning around to check. She gasped and pointed behind her.

Layla was on her feet, her wheelchair abandoned at the dining table. She was pushing her way through the crowd, a look of panic on her face.

"What?" Penelope exclaimed. She exchanged a glance with Mabel. "But how . . ."

"Something very fishy is going on here," Mabel said. "And it's not the sole meunière Derek ordered for dinner."

One or two couples began walking toward their cars parked along the high street, but everyone else huddled around the front door of Pierre's, undecided as to what to do, their breaths making frosty clouds in the air. Penelope wrapped her shawl around her more tightly, glad that she had thought to wear it.

Mabel was sensibly dressed as always in a warm purple heather sweater and gray wool slacks. Figgy, however, was shivering in her sleeveless black jumpsuit and strappy sandals and had her arms wrapped around herself to try to stay warm.

"You must be freezing." Derek whipped off his suit jacket and draped it around Figgy's shoulders.

"I don't see Layla anywhere, do you?" Mabel said to Penelope, twisting around to look in back of her.

"I don't either," Penelope said, "but there's Gordon and Daphne."

"Oh, my," Mabel said. "Gordon doesn't look too happy."

Gordon's face was beet red, and it wasn't from the cold. Daphne appeared as if she was about to cry.

"It looks like Daphne and her sister were putting one over on poor Gordon. It's pretty clear that Layla doesn't need that wheelchair and probably never did. But they managed to get a car and who knows what else out of Gordon. He's not going to take kindly to being made a fool of," Mabel said.

"Is it possible that Layla fooled Daphne as well? Maybe she didn't know."

"Hard to believe she wasn't in on it," Mabel said. "Layla was bound to slip up at one point or another and the jig would have been up."

"I wonder if Regina knew or found out somehow," Penelope said.

Mabel raised an eyebrow. "I wouldn't be surprised in the least if she did. And that gives Daphne another reason to want to get rid of Regina. The whole house of cards would have come tumbling down—no chance of marrying Gordon and not even the chance he'd continue with his gifts, which I am sure have made Daphne's life quite a bit easier."

Penelope looked over at Daphne and Gordon again. They were standing next to each other in stony silence.

A thought suddenly occurred to Penelope. If Daphne's sister wasn't really disabled, then Daphne would have had no reason to take her sister to the hospital the day of the fest—which meant she didn't have an alibi after all.

SEVENTEEN

❧❦

Penelope rolled over, opened one eye, glanced at her alarm clock, and sighed. She had another half hour before she had to get up. She burrowed deeper under the down comforter and closed her eyes.

A noise woke her moments later. Something banging. It took her several long seconds to realize someone was knocking on her front door.

Reluctantly, she threw back the covers and got out of bed. She didn't bother with a robe—in fact she didn't even own one—she'd slept in her usual outfit of an old pair of sweatpants she'd had since college and a long-sleeved T-shirt with a hole under the arm and *Cornell University* written on the front. She'd borrowed it from a guy she'd dated so long ago she didn't remember his name and had forgotten to give it back.

Mrs. Danvers accompanied Penelope down the stairs, meowing her displeasure at having been woken so early.

She wove in and out between Penelope's legs, but fortunately Penelope had by now perfected the art—if you could call it that—of not tripping over the cat.

Penelope crossed the foyer and pulled open the front door.

It was pelting rain outside and nearly as dark as dusk due to the heavy cloud cover. Ashlyn was huddled on the doorstep, sheltering from the weather under the small overhang.

"Ashlyn! Today's not your day." Penelope rubbed her eyes. "Besides, it's so early."

"I'm sorry," Ashlyn said, stepping into Penelope's foyer. "I didn't mean to wake you, but I need to talk to you, and I have to be at Mrs. Turner's by seven thirty or she'll raise an unholy fuss. She has a fit if I'm even five minutes late."

"Come in," Penelope said. "You can put your coat on the coat-tree."

Ashlyn took off her raincoat, which was soaked in the back where the water dripping off Penelope's roof had run down it.

They went into the sitting room and Ashlyn perched on the edge of the sofa. She was clearly in some sort of distress—her eyes were red rimmed as if she'd been crying and she was twisting the button on her shirt so energetically that Penelope was afraid it was going to pop right off at any minute.

"Would you like a cup of tea?" Penelope hesitated by the kitchen door.

"That would be brilliant." Ashlyn gave a weak smile.

"I'll be right back."

Penelope filled the kettle with water and plugged it in. She'd gone full-on English and had purchased an electric teakettle. According to Figgy, the water boiled faster and the kettle had an auto shutoff feature, which appealed to Penelope.

The kettle whistled, Penelope rinsed out a mug with hot water, dropped in an Irish breakfast tea bag, and poured the water.

"Here you are," she said, putting the mug down in front of Ashlyn. Penelope sat in the armchair nearest the fireplace.

"I'm sorry to bother you like this," Ashlyn said. "I don't know who else to talk to." She made an attempt at a smile. "People in this town will talk—know what I mean? But you're not from here and you're a writer so you must be smart," she said in a rush. "You'll know what to do."

"Do you want to tell me what the problem is?"

Ashlyn sniffed and nodded her head. She cradled the mug in her hand. "I told her not to do it. I didn't know they were going to sue."

"Who was going to sue?"

"The duke, who else? Haven't you seen the paper?" She sniffed again. "Everyone is talking about it."

Penelope felt like she was having one of those dreams where nothing made sense although you kept trying and trying to put the pieces together.

"Who did you tell not to do it?"

"My sister, Gracelyn. I told her she shouldn't have done it."

"What did she do?" Penelope tucked her feet up under her. She was wearing socks, but there was a draft coming from the fireplace.

"She found it, didn't she? That filthy magazine that had the pictures of Miss Davenport."

Penelope sat up a bit straighter. This was an unexpected turn of events.

"How did your sister find that magazine? Where was it?"

"Gracelyn works as a maid at Worthington House. She used to clean for Mrs. Bosworth and Mrs. Bosworth got her that job. The duke pays well and Gracelyn doesn't want to lose her position so I told her that in that case she was a ninny to have done it."

Penelope still wasn't clear about what the hapless Gracelyn had done. Fortunately Ashlyn continued with her story.

"Mrs. Bosworth got Gracelyn that job so that Gracelyn could fill her in on things—you know, what was going on at Worthington House and all. Mrs. Bosworth was that interested. So when Gracelyn found that magazine her first thought was to show it to Mrs. Bosworth."

Penelope wondered how Gracelyn had "found" the magazine. It sounded more as if she'd been snooping where she shouldn't have.

"What happened then?" Penelope asked although she could guess.

"Mrs. Bosworth told her to leave it with her—that she'd handle it—that Gracelyn might even get some money for it. Gracelyn was that excited—she's been saving for ages to go on holiday to Majorca with a bunch of her pals from school."

Ashlyn took a sip of her tea and looked up at Penelope with what Penelope thought of as puppy dog eyes.

"Do you think Gracelyn will get in trouble? The magazine wasn't hers and she took it."

"I don't know," Penelope admitted. "I hope not."

*   *   *

Despite her umbrella, the hem of Penelope's raincoat was soaked when she arrived at the Open Book.

"Good heavens, Pen," Mabel said. "You're soaked. Did you walk?"

"Yes," Penelope said, shaking out her umbrella. "I decided it was safer, given my tendency to drive on the wrong side of the street."

"Very wise," Mabel said. "I'm surprised you decided to come out in this weather."

"My book group wanted to reschedule for today since several of them can't make it next week. They should be here in about fifteen minutes. Meanwhile, I'll go see if Figgy needs any help. Sometimes I think they just come for the food," Pen said over her shoulder.

Figgy already had a table set up with teacups, saucers, and small plates.

"What's on the menu today?" Penelope said.

She noticed that Figgy's eyes had a faraway dreamy look to them.

"I've made shortbread cookies and some fairy cakes. I'm afraid I made a proper mess of the Victoria sponge cake. I'm still a bit overwhelmed by Derek's proposal." She glanced at the diamond ring on her finger, then waved her hand toward Penelope. "It's positively smashing, isn't it?"

"Yes, it is," Penelope said. "It was quite an evening what with the fire and all."

Figgy giggled. "Yes. And in the end the inconvenience was worth it since the meal was free. Derek wasn't half-pleased by that. Of course we never did get to the main course, but I have to say the fish and chips from the Chumley Chippie tasted delicious. We were all quite peckish by then."

"What about your apartment?" Penelope said.

"It just needed a good airing out," Figgy said. "Derek let me stay at his place."

"Apparently the fire damage was minimal—I heard it was caused by a grease fire in the kitchen that briefly got out of control—and Pierre's should reopen soon. I noticed they posted a sign in the window," Penelope said.

Meanwhile, Mabel had joined them.

"That was quite the miracle we saw last night," she said dryly. "Poor disabled Layla Potter rising from her wheelchair and walking out of the restaurant!"

"Running, actually," Figgy said. "She couldn't get out of there fast enough."

"That's certainly put paid to her claim of being disabled," Mabel said.

"Oi! Where is everyone?" Gladys came around the corner, her hair frizzing around her head in a halo and her face its customary red. "Thank goodness the rain seems to have stopped for the moment. It was coming down cats and dogs earlier." She plopped into a chair with a sigh. "Bruce is none too pleased at having to handle the shop by himself, although it was empty when I left. He'll be grumbling all afternoon when I get back."

"Yoo-hoo," a voice called out and India appeared.

Laurence Brimble was right behind her. "Cheerio," he said, smoothing his mustache with his index finger.

They were taking seats when Violet Thatcher rushed in, unbuttoning her coat as she walked.

"What frightful weather," she said as she sat down, her skeletal hands resting on the arms of the chair. "And of course Robert would need the car. Reverend Paine over in

St. Ann's parish is on vacation and Robert has been filling in for him while doing his own job as well. He had an appointment to counsel a couple about to be married. I do hope his work doesn't go unappreciated."

"It looks as if this is it," Penelope said a few moments later when everyone was settled.

India leaned toward Brimble. "How are you enjoying retirement, Laurence? It's been a year now, hasn't it? Everything going well?"

Brimble smoothed his mustache again. Penelope suspected he did it when he was nervous.

"Yes, quite. Splendid, actually. Although I do miss the chaps in the office. But there are compensations." He gave a small smile and glanced around. "This book group for instance."

"Where did you work?" Penelope said, realizing that it would be better to allow some conversation at the beginning of the meeting rather than during the discussion, which inevitably happened.

"Bosworth's Uniforms," Brimble said. "I was in the accounting department."

"That's Gordon Bosworth's business," India said. "Didn't Layla Potter work there?"

"Ah, yes," Brimble said, clearing his throat and settling back in his chair as if he had a long and complicated story to tell. "Quite a tragedy. It cost the company a lot of money, I can tell you that."

"I remember that," Violet said. "Robert has offered up prayers for the poor thing every Sunday since."

"What happened?" Penelope said.

"An accident with some of the machinery," Brimble said. "I don't know the details, but Miss Potter claimed to be permanently disabled. The HSE found the factory to be at fault—something to do with defective equipment." Brimble cleared his throat. "Of course, Gordon Bosworth is an honorable man. I happen to know he's done right by Miss Potter, taking money out of his own pocket to pay for her care above and beyond what the company's insurance paid her."

Penelope's ears perked up. "You say Miss Potter *claimed* to be disabled?"

Brimble looked slightly alarmed. "We were not able to prove anything," he said. "But the company's director of safety never did find anything amiss with the machinery." He lowered his voice. "Frankly, I think the fault lay with Miss Potter. A coworker said he smelled alcohol on her breath that morning."

Penelope was about to tell him about the previous evening and Layla's bolting from her wheelchair, but Mabel caught her eye and shook her head.

Penelope decided it was time to get the book discussion underway. She cleared her throat.

"Let's talk about *Rebecca*. Why do you think the author chose not to reveal the name of the main character and what effect did that create?"

O h, there you are," Mabel said later that afternoon when she found Penelope kneeling on the floor next to a bookshelf she was rearranging. She smiled. "There's a woman here who would like you to sign her copy of *Lady of the Moors*."

Penelope felt her face color. She still wasn't used to having people ask her to sign books. Perhaps when her second book came out—and hopefully it would—she would feel a little less like an imposter.

Penelope followed Mabel to the front of the store where a woman was waiting, clutching a copy of *Lady of the Moors* to her chest. She was wearing a bright yellow raincoat, matching floppy-brimmed rain hat, and yellow rubber boots with ducks on them.

"You're Penelope Parish?" she said with a slight note of disbelief in her voice.

Penelope wished she'd taken more time with her hair that morning and had chosen her outfit more carefully. But writers were meant to look slightly eccentric, weren't they?

"I'd love it if you would sign this," the woman gushed, handing Penelope the book and a pen.

"Certainly. I'd be glad to."

Penelope took the book over to the front counter and opened it to the title page. She signed it with a flourish and drew a line under her name.

"Thank you so much," the woman said as she slipped the book into her shopping bag. "Wait till I tell Hazel I got you to sign my book. She just loved it, too."

The woman stood grinning at Penelope for several seconds before finally turning to leave. Penelope breathed a sigh of relief.

The shop had been busy earlier, but traffic had slowed as the afternoon wore on. Mabel was flipping through a catalogue so Penelope thought she would try to get some writing done.

As she was heading back to her writing room she noticed someone sitting at a table with a stack of books in front of her. Penelope paused when she realized it was Daphne.

Daphne was wearing a pair of jeans, a cable-knit sweater, and had a scarf tied loosely around her neck. Her hair was in a loose bun and she wasn't wearing her usual makeup. Penelope was surprised to see she looked much younger.

Daphne sniffed and pressed a balled-up tissue to her eyes. She'd been crying and her nose and eyes were red.

Penelope decided she would bring her a mug of tea. Figgy's kettle was always at the ready. Penelope poured two mugs, added a good dose of sugar, and carried them over to the table where Daphne was sitting.

"I thought you might be able to use a cup of tea," Penelope said, putting the mug in front of Daphne. "It's that sort of day."

Daphne looked up, surprised.

"Thank you," she said, then burst into tears.

"Go on, drink your tea," Penelope said. "It's supposed to cure everything."

Daphne gave a wan smile but she picked up the mug and took a sip.

"Thanks," she said again.

Penelope looked at the stack of books by Daphne's elbow and was surprised to see that they were all business books. What had prompted Daphne to choose those?

"Is something wrong?" Penelope said after a few moments. "Anything I can do?"

Daphne laughed. "Everything's wrong."

"Do you want to tell me about it?"

"I don't know where to begin." Daphne stared morosely into her tea. "I didn't know about Layla, honest." She gripped the mug so tightly her knuckles turned white. "All this time I've wasted taking care of her . . ." She buried her face in her hands.

Finally Daphne looked up. "And now Gordon is furious with me. He won't believe that I didn't know Layla was faking her disability to get money from him. He thinks I was in on it. And that I've only been . . . kind to him in order to get at his money.

"But that's not true," Daphne cried. "I care for Gordon." She smiled. "Okay, not in exactly the way he'd like, I admit. But I felt sorry for him. His wife was so critical and so cold. He couldn't even be comfortable in his own home."

Penelope nodded and took a sip of her tea.

"I know people thought I wanted to marry him. That if Regina was dead it would clear the way for me. But believe me, that was never my intention." She smiled briefly. "I happen to be seeing someone as a matter of fact." She quickly picked up her mug of tea and held it to her face as if she wanted to hide behind it.

"That's great," Penelope said.

Daphne frowned. "The police have been around again. Detective Maguire was very kind—but he still asked me a lot of questions that made it obvious I was a suspect in Regina's murder."

"Everything should be fine if you have an alibi . . ." Penelope said.

"I'm afraid I threw a spanner in the works the first time he interviewed me. I lied and told him I had taken my sister to hospital that day. I could hardly turn around now and admit the truth."

"I think it would be the best if you did tell him the truth," Penelope said. "I don't think they will hold it against you. And it would clear your name. I assume you were somewhere else?"

"Yes." Daphne ducked her head. "I didn't want to tell anyone in case I would jinx it." She ran her finger around the rim of her mug. "I was in Chelmsford for the day." She gave Penelope an earnest look. "You're going to think I've gone mad, but I had this plan. Believe it or not, I don't want to spend the rest of my life wearing a ridiculous skimpy uniform and working as a barmaid."

Penelope smiled.

"I was meeting up with a woman who owns a small consignment shop in Chelmsford. She sells upscale women's clothing and accessories. The shop is darling. All done in that shabby-chic style." Daphne got a dreamy look in her eyes. "The owner's mother is quite elderly and recently fell and broke her hip. The woman—her name is Amanda—is going home to Wales to care for her mother and is selling the shop." Daphne blushed slightly. "I wanted to buy it from her. Gordon offered to help me out with a loan.

"I know what you're thinking," Daphne hastened to add. "But I used to work in a shop like that in my teens. I even got promoted to assistant manager, so I do know a little bit about it."

"Is that why you're looking at those books?" Penelope gestured toward the stack of volumes by Daphne's elbow.

Daphne nodded. "Obviously with Gordon mad at me, I'm going to have to go to the bank for a loan." She tapped the pile of books. "So I'll have to write a business plan." She frowned. "Of course, it's a long shot that the bank will lend me money, but I won't know till I try, will I?" She lifted her chin.

"That's true," Penelope said. She thought back to when she'd applied for the writer-in-residence position at the Open Book. She'd done it as a bit of a lark never suspecting she'd actually be chosen.

Daphne shut the book she'd been thumbing through. "I

think I'll go speak to Detective Maguire. I'm not going to be able to rest until I do." She picked up the book.

"You found something?" Penelope said, indicating the volume in Daphne's hand.

Daphne held it up. The title was *How to Write a Business Plan in Ten Easy Steps*. "It's perfect," she said.

"Good luck," Penelope called after her as Daphne headed toward the front counter.

Mabel had left the Open Book early for a dental appointment so Penelope manned the front desk for the last hour. They had one customer who had come in looking for Charlotte Davenport's *The Fire in My Bosom*. Penelope found the book for her and noticed that it was their second-to-last copy. She made a mental note to tell Mabel to order some more.

"It's quite a thrill having the author right here in town," the woman said as she got out her wallet. "And marrying our dear duke no less."

Penelope mumbled something appropriate.

The woman's eyes clouded. "I dabble in astrology a bit and it doesn't look auspicious for a match between a Libra and a Capricorn. Libras can be too sensitive for a domineering Capricorn. But it does seem as if Miss Davenport and the duke are an exception." She beamed. "I am sure they will be deliriously happy." She clapped her hands together. "And then there will be the excitement of little Worthingtons to look forward to."

Penelope smiled and handed the woman her book.

She was the last customer of the day. Penelope closed

out the register and straightened the store, putting away books that had been left out on tables and repositioning chairs that had been moved around.

"I'm off," Figgy yelled. She had already turned off the lights in the tearoom. "I'm picking up some kebabs and Derek is coming over for dinner."

"Good night," Penelope said. "Have fun."

A hush fell over the shop with Figgy's departure. Penelope stood for a moment and savored the silence. She inhaled the scent of books that mingled with the faint aromas of tea leaves and vanilla coming from Figgy's tea shop. She felt a sense of contentment wash over her that she hadn't felt in a very long time. For once she wasn't stressing about trying to live up to someone else's expectations. Obviously, taking the writer-in-residence position, no matter how crazy her friends had thought it was, had been the right decision.

Penelope was locking the front door to the shop when she noticed a man had stopped on the sidewalk and was taking pictures of the façade of the Open Book. He was wearing a rather shabby tan raincoat, had a spot on his tie, and was quite desperately in need of a haircut.

He approached Penelope. "Do you work here?"

"Yes, I do. But I'm sorry, we're closed."

The man ran a hand through his thick thatch of sandy hair. "That's fine. I don't want to come in." He held out his hand. "I'm Noah Spencer. I'm a producer with the BBC— a show called *Resurrected—Unsolved Crimes Then and Now.* Have you heard of it?"

Penelope nodded. "Yes, but I have to admit I haven't seen it."

He smiled. "That's okay. Actually, I've got a favor to ask of you." He glanced at his watch. "Look, can I buy you a glass of wine? I saw a place nearby—Sour Grapes I think it's called."

"Why not?"

Penelope walked beside him as they headed down the street. He wasn't tall—perhaps three or four inches shorter than Penelope—and she judged him to be in his forties. He told her a bit about the show he was producing.

"One of our customers told me about it. She's a huge fan."

Noah smiled and held the door to the Sour Grapes open for Penelope.

The bar was beginning to fill up with commuters who had just gotten off the train from London and were looking to unwind before going home, as well as office workers who worked locally in lawyers', stockbrokers', and estate agents' offices.

A small table in the corner was free, a young couple having just finished their drinks and gotten up.

"Here we go," Noah said, holding out a chair for Penelope.

By now Penelope was quite curious as to what this was all about. India had said that the BBC was sending a reporter to Upper Chumley-on-Stoke, but Penelope hadn't expected to actually run into one.

"We're investigating a cold case from nineteen eighty-one," Noah said after they had placed their order. "Have you heard about it?"

"Very little," Penelope said, reaching for the glass of wine the waiter had set on the table. She tried to remember what India had told them. "It was up north somewhere, wasn't it?"

"Yes. Northampton. A fire that killed a young maid and burned Hadleigh House to the ground. They lost some priceless paintings and antiques, but fortunately the family was out when it happened—except for the fourteen-year-old daughter. She managed to escape. At the time, it was suspected that the daughter had set the fire. She was known for being willful and prone to violent outbursts. But she disappeared from view and the parents became reclusive—moving to the Isle of Jura off the coast of Scotland. Whether the girl went with them or not, no one ever knew."

"So what brings you to Upper Chumley-on-Stoke, then?"

Noah fingered the edge of his coaster. "We had an anonymous tip that the daughter was here—in Upper Chumley-on-Stoke—living under an assumed name." He gave a wry smile. "Not much to go on, I know. But I've been tasked with trying to track her down as well as find some locations where we can shoot and capture the essence of the town."

Penelope was confused.

"What does this have to do with the Open Book, though?"

"We'd like to set up shop in front of your store. The façade is marvelously picturesque with its traditional half-timbering and gabled roof and exactly the sort of thing we're looking for. It would mean taking over a bit of the sidewalk and possibly delaying people who want to come into or out of the shop. I can assure you we'd do our best not to make complete nuisances of ourselves."

"Oh," Penelope said. "I'm afraid you're talking to the wrong person. The owner, Mabel Morris, is the one you would have to ask."

Noah appeared momentarily disappointed but then smiled.

"All is not lost. This has been most enjoyable." He swallowed the last of his glass of pinot noir. "Can you tell me how I can get in touch with this Mabel Morris? Will she be on hand in the shop tomorrow?"

"Yes." Penelope dug a card with the Open Book's telephone number on it from her purse and handed it to Noah. "You can reach her anytime after nine o'clock."

"Thank you." Noah pocketed the card. "And if you learn anything that might prove useful to our investigation, could you let me know?"

"Of course, "Penelope said as she got up to leave.

She hoped Mabel would agree to let them film in front of the shop. It would be good advertising for the Open Book and ought to prove interesting as well.

EIGHTEEN

❧

They want to film in front of the Open Book?" Mabel said the next day when Penelope told her about her conversation with Noah Spencer. "I don't see why not. How exciting. And wonderful exposure for the store."

"He said he would call you this morning," Penelope said, picking a currant out of the Chelsea bun she'd bought at Icing on the Cake on her way to work.

"India will be right chuffed to hear that her favorite show will be filming here." Mabel leaned her elbows on the counter. "It really is an intriguing story—a young girl suspected of arson—and I suppose you could say murder, too, since someone died in the fire—disappearing afterward. Suspected of the crime but never charged or proven either, for that matter."

"I wonder where she went." Penelope licked some sugar off her fingers. "She could be with her parents, I suppose. Which wouldn't be much of a mystery at all."

"I don't know." Mabel frowned. "If the parents knew she'd set the fire, wouldn't they want to do something about it? Even if they'd shielded her from the law at the time, they must have realized she needed help. She had to have been mentally unwell."

"Hopefully they took her to a competent psychiatrist," Penelope said, crumpling up the piece of glassine from her bun and tossing it into the trash can.

"I wonder," Mabel said, and paused. "I know what I might have done in those circumstances—have the girl placed in a mental hospital where she wouldn't be a danger to anyone and might get the help she needed." Mabel tapped her lip with her index finger. "They might even have made a deal with the police so that the girl got locked up in a psychiatric facility instead of being locked up at Holloway women's prison."

Mabel shuddered. "Frankly, I wouldn't care to be locked up in either, but a hospital would be far better than prison I should imagine."

Penelope felt a shiver go down her spine. "The thought of being locked up anywhere is horrible."

Penelope was in her writing room, plugging away on her manuscript. It was going quite well—Annora had sussed out another clue as to the location of the hidden chest she had set out to find. She wished that her own detective work was going as well. She felt as if she were going down one blind alley after another when something suddenly occurred to her. She couldn't imagine why she hadn't thought of it sooner.

She grabbed her purse and rummaged around until she found her phone. She flipped through the photographs. There it was—Compton Lane, Northampton.

Why had Regina written down that address? What did it mean? It might not mean anything at all but so far everything in the notebook had panned out one way or another. Besides, Hadleigh House was in Northampton—there was bound to be a connection.

Penelope supposed there was only one way to find out—she'd have to go to Northampton and see for herself.

Thus it was that Penelope found herself on the train again—only to Northampton this time—later that morning. She leaned her head against the window and dozed lightly as the train rattled north and awoke with a jolt when she sensed the train slowing down as it pulled into Northampton station.

She retrieved her handbag—more oversized tote bag than dainty clutch—and followed the other passengers off the train.

She was in a bit of daze as she stood on the sidewalk outside the station looking for a taxi. She was going to check out the address in Regina's notebook and then she planned to head to the Northamptonshire Central Library where they ought to have an archive of the *Northampton Chronicle & Echo*, the local daily newspaper. She hoped to find some articles about the house fire that might add to her research.

A taxi pulled up to the curb and Penelope slid into the backseat. The car was spotlessly clean with an air freshener stuck discreetly to one of the doors. The driver was an older woman with close-cropped, iron-gray hair and dangling beaded earrings. She was wearing a denim jacket that had been rubbed thin in spots, and her hands on the steering wheel were large and mannish with blunt nails.

"I'm going to Compton Lane, please," Penelope said as she pulled the door closed.

The woman swiveled around. "American?"

"Yes."

"Visiting someone?"

"Not exactly. I'm doing some research actually."

"Off we go, then," the cabbie said, putting the car in gear and pulling away from the curb.

Ten minutes later they turned down a road with a sign announcing that it was Compton Lane. Tall, dense trees lined either side of the road. Traffic noise had retreated into the distance and Pen could hear birds singing and the rat-a-tat-tat of a woodpecker.

"It's terribly quiet, isn't it?" she said.

The cabbie swiveled around. "I suppose the quiet is good for them."

Good for them? Who were they? Where were they going?

Finally they came to a driveway and headed down it. The drive wound around until they came to a clearing with a large, forbidding-looking building in the center. A discreet plaque next to the front entrance read *Arbor View*.

"What is this place?" Penelope said.

The cabbie turned around and looked at her. "You don't know? It's a psychiatric facility. My old auntie used to work here as a cleaner."

"Do you think she would know something about the Hadleigh House fire?"

"Now that was a terrible scandal. Burned to the ground it was and the poor maid killed."

"Did they ever find out how the fire started?"

The cabbie shook her head. "No, but they suspected the daughter, although they couldn't prove it. Auntie told me that shortly after the fire, a young girl was brought in to Arbor View late at night. It was all very secret and hush-hush, but Auntie suspected it was the daughter and they were hiding her away until the furor died down."

"Does your aunt know what happened to the girl? The BBC is doing a segment on it for their show *Resurrected—Unsolved Crimes Then and Now.*"

"You're with the BBC then? Do you know why they canceled *Birds of a Feather*? A wonderful show it was—Auntie and I used to watch it while having our tea. It always made us laugh. Of course, ITV picked it up and we were that disappointed when they canceled it as well."

Penelope certainly wasn't with the BBC, but she decided that it served her purposes to let that slide.

"Auntie could tell you more about the Hadleigh House fire, I'm sure. Would you like to meet her? It would liven her day no end, I can tell you that."

Penelope couldn't believe her luck. "Yes, I'd love to meet her. Is she home now?"

The cabbie's aunt lived in a council flat not far away and in minutes they were pulling up to a utilitarian-looking brick building with white trim.

"Auntie has the ground floor apartment since she can't do the stairs anymore," the cabbie said as she opened Penelope's door.

The woman who answered the door was bent over a cane and had sparse white hair that revealed glimpses of her freckled scalp. Her blue eyes were sharp, though, and Penelope hoped that her memory was as well.

"Aunt Josie, this is . . ." The cabbie turned to Penelope.

"Penelope Parish." She held out her hand and the woman grasped it. Her fingers were cold to the touch.

"Penelope is with the BBC," the cabbie said. She turned toward Penelope. "I'm Bernadette, by the way." She showed them into a small sitting room.

Penelope felt another twinge of conscience over allowing the lie that she worked for the television network to continue, but she managed to quash it.

The sitting room was stuffed with furniture that looked as if it had once belonged in a larger space, and nearly every surface was covered with a crocheted doily.

"I'll put the kettle on, shall I?" Bernadette said as she bustled off.

Josie lowered herself onto a royal-blue velvet sofa and leaned her cane against the coffee table in front of it.

"This is a treat," she said, beaming at Penelope. "Bernadette and I watch all of your shows. We loved *Birds of a Feather* and were so disappointed to hear that even ITV had canceled it. Bernadette would get a takeaway curry for us and we'd have our tea while we watched the show."

Bernadette bustled into the room with a tray of tea things.

"Here we go," she said cheerfully as she filled teacups and handed them around.

"Penelope is doing a story about the Hadleigh House fire," Bernadette said. "It's going to be on that true crime show." She glanced at Penelope with her eyebrows raised.

"*Resurrected—Unsolved Crimes Then and Now,*" Penelope said, feeling that twinge of conscience again.

"Are you going to be on the telly, dear?" Josie said, peering at Penelope. "I don't think I've seen you before."

Penelope smiled. "I'm strictly behind-the-scenes, I'm afraid."

"I told Penelope you worked at Arbor View," Bernadette said, stirring a third spoonful of sugar into her tea. The delicate teacup looked out of place in her large hands.

Josie smiled, settled back in her seat, and folded her hands in her lap. "Yes, I started there as a young girl and eventually became head cleaner. We moved here to Northampton for Jeremy's job—he got a position at the Timkin Roller Bearing Factory—and I wanted something to do. We never had any children and I couldn't see staying home all day watching soap operas on the telly like some of them. I stayed at Arbor View until I retired. Jeremy was gone by then. I didn't need all that space we had in our house, so that's when I moved here to Cardigan Close."

"I think Penelope would like to hear about the Hadleigh House fire," Bernadette said. "You once said they brought a young girl in who you thought might be the daughter suspected of setting the fire. Do you remember?"

"Yes, I remember. Of course, I do. It was very late at night. A stormy night—rain coming down in sheets and the wind so fierce it rattled the windows. I was working late that night. Several of the girls had come down with the flu—it swept through the place like wildfire—so the rest of us pitched in where we could. I was mopping the floors when the door opened and they brought in this poor young girl. They tracked in all manner of mud and leaves and I had to mop the floor all over again."

"What can you tell me about the girl?" Penelope said.

"Not much, I'm afraid. She looked as if she had been sedated. I've seen that often enough to recognize it." Josie's eyes took on a faraway look. "One of her hands was bandaged, I do remember that. We all wondered if she had been burned in the fire." Josie smiled. "Always assuming it was the same young woman."

Josie picked up her teacup and it rattled in the saucer. Bernadette half rose from her seat, but Josie motioned for her to stay put.

"I can manage, dear," she said. "The girl was quite tall. I remember noticing that she was taller than one of the men who had accompanied her. And what you'd call big-boned, I believe. She looked like a strong, strapping country girl." Josie laughed. "Funny because you always think of those aristocratic lasses as being dainty will-o'-the-wisps."

"Did she stay long?" Penelope said, putting down her teacup.

"It was a number of years later when I went to mop her room and found it empty. I don't know if she left or she was moved somewhere else. I imagine she would have been close to eighteen years old by then."

"Do you happen to know her name?" Penelope said hopefully.

"No, but I did hear one of the nurses calling her Georgie once," Josie said.

Penelope was tired by the time she boarded the return train to Upper Chumley-on-Stoke. She'd managed a visit to the Church of the Holy Sepulchre, where she'd marveled at the remains of the Norman window in the nave. She'd also gone to Althorp, which had been deeply moving. She was only six years old when the Princess of Wales had been killed in the car accident, but she remembered watching the footage on television of Diana's life and had imagined herself as a princess, marching around the house wearing a plastic crown that said *Happy Birthday* on it, which she'd gotten at her sixth birthday party.

Penelope once again dozed off on the train, this time dreaming about a burning house and a girl named Georgie who was inexplicably fleeing the fire in a ball gown and a diamond- and pearl-encrusted crown.

She shook herself awake as they neared Chumley and gathered her things together. A number of people got off with her and they all filed into the station waiting room making it seem crowded.

Penelope thought she saw a familiar face in the crowd and when she looked again, she realized it was Evelyn Maxwell-Lewis. She appeared to be waiting for someone. She noticed Penelope, gave a small smile, and then glanced at the arrivals board, which was modern and electric and looked out of place in the old station. Evelyn frowned, looked at Penelope again, and then turned away when someone called her name.

For some reason, the encounter gave Penelope an uneasy feeling. She couldn't figure out why but she soon forgot it as she found her car in the car park and headed home.

Mrs. Danvers was by the door when Penelope opened it but then stalked off in high dudgeon to sulk under the coffee table, her long tail swishing back and forth.

Penelope hung up her coat and kicked off her shoes. She was pleased to see that Ashlyn had swept the grate and laid a new fire. Penelope lit the kindling and stood back and watched as the flames leapt up and licked the logs placed on top.

She was heading toward the kitchen to see what she might be able to rustle up for dinner when she remembered she'd turned the ringer off on her cell phone when she'd toured the Holy Sepulchre. She was tempted to leave it till later but found herself picking up her purse and retrieving the phone without even thinking about it. No wonder people complained that millennials were too attached to their electronic devices.

She had a missed a call from Miles and there was a voice mail waiting. Penelope sighed, tapped the voice mail icon, and put the phone to her ear.

There was a lot of background noise—people talking, glasses rattling—was Miles in a bar? Penelope wondered. Finally, Miles's voice came on. The gist of the message was that he was in London on business and would be driving down to Chumley the following day to see Penelope.

Penelope groaned and put her phone down on the table. She should have been thrilled that Miles was coming to see her, but the feelings she was experiencing were just the opposite. Why now? Why did he have to spring this on her like this?

She'd barely given him a thought since arriving in England and had actually been slightly relieved that the writer-in-residence position had allowed her to put their relationship on hold. And now he would be here and she'd have to deal with things. She'd have to be a full-fledged grown-up and tell him it was over. It was only fair she let him go so that he could be snatched up by some Isla or Binky or Tinsley. Penelope had no doubt that they were just biding their time and waiting patiently for Miles and Penelope to break up in order to pounce.

Miles had told her to make a dinner reservation at the best restaurant in town. The Chumley Chippie flashed through Penelope's mind and she had to stifle a laugh. Unfortunately Pierre's was still closed for repairs. She'd take him to the Book and Bottle, Penelope decided. It was authentic—the layers of grime on the walls and floor had been built up over more than a century—unlike so many of the flashy upstart pubs in London whose purpose was to attract businessmen with expense accounts and which the Brits thumbed their noses at.

Besides, Worthington was supposedly a patron. If it was good enough for royalty, surely it should be good enough for Miles.

Penelope put the thought of Miles out of her mind and went into the kitchen where she poked her head in the refrigerator. She had a wedge of Stilton and one of cheddar along with some crusty bread and the remains of some red wine. It would make a perfectly adequate dinner, she decided.

She put everything on a tray and carried it into the sitting room by the fire. She put the tray on the coffee table, sat down, and reached for her laptop. She ought to get a little writing done while she was at it.

Penelope nibbled on a crust of bread spread with some Stilton and put her fingers on her laptop keys. She managed a paragraph or two before her mind began wandering to what she'd learned during her trip to Northampton.

Josie had said she thought the girl brought into the psychiatric hospital after the fire had been named Georgie. Why did that name ring a bell? Penelope couldn't put her finger on it, but she was convinced it was important.

NINETEEN

❧

Penelope had planned to spend the morning writing but had barely completed a paragraph before she became distracted—looking through magazines and newspapers she'd set aside to be recycled, gazing out the window, watching as Mr. Patel was pulled down the street by his French bulldog and heading out to the kitchen to make a second cup of tea. When she found herself, sponge in hand, cleaning the kitchen sink, she realized there were too many distractions around for her to get any writing done.

She would head to the Open Book where her writing room presented her with four walls—the paintings hung on them had already been thoroughly examined—and no curtains to be straightened, windows to look out of, or sinks to be cleaned.

She grabbed her coat and laptop and was soon walking briskly down the high street.

"What brings you in so early on a Saturday?" Mabel said when Penelope entered the shop.

"I must get some writing done," Penelope said, as she pulled off her gloves and blew on her cold hands. "There are too many distractions around the cottage, I'm afraid."

"Can you spare a minute for a chin wag?" Mabel said. "Figgy's got the tea going. You look like you could use a cup to warm you up."

"Yes, certainly," Penelope said.

Figgy bustled over with the tea cart, the wheels giving an ungodly screech as she neared the front desk.

Mabel pointed at it. "That could do with a bit of oiling I should think."

Figgy poured the tea and handed around the mugs. Penelope held hers up and let the warm steam bathe her face.

"How did your trip go yesterday?" Mabel said. "Did you enjoy Northampton?"

Penelope helped herself to one of Figgy's Chelsea buns. She'd already had her breakfast, but they looked too delicious to pass up. Not for the first time, she thanked her ability to eat without gaining weight.

"Althorp was lovely and I'm so glad I was able to visit it. The Holy Sepulchre as well."

"Was this sightseeing or were you chasing a clue?" Figgy said, picking a crumb off her bun and licking it off her finger.

"A little of both. I was tracking down an address Regina had penned in her notebook. It turned out to be a psychiatric hospital. By great good fortune, the cabbie who drove me there had an aunt who used to work there."

Penelope explained about Bernadette the cabbie and her aunt and the story her aunt had told about the young girl being brought to Arbor View.

"She said she thought she heard a nurse call the girl Georgie. That name rings a bell for some reason, but I can't put my finger on it."

"It does ring a bell," Mabel said, stroking her chin. "Although I suppose we've all known a Georgie at one time or another. Hopefully it will come to one of us sooner or later."

"I'd better get to work," Penelope said, tucking her laptop under her arm.

"Off with you, then," Mabel said, making a shooing motion.

Penelope took her mug of tea and the last bit of her bun into her writing room and shut the door. Time to get down to business, she told herself.

She opened up her laptop and began to work. Her writing room was like a cocoon, cushioning her from the noise in the Open Book but without making her feel isolated. The scene she was working on flowed along nicely and soon Penelope was wrapped up in Annora's world as the real world slowly retreated.

Penelope stopped suddenly in the middle of a sentence, her fingers frozen on the keys. She grabbed her purse, rummaged through it, pulled out her cell phone, and thumbed through the photos she'd taken of Regina's notebook.

There it was—the telephone number she'd noticed earlier. It had never occurred to Penelope until now to call the number and see who answered. It might turn out to be Regina's doctor or the library or the local plumber, but then why would she have written it in this particular notebook?

Looking at her phone reminded her of Miles's voice message and a wave of near nausea swept over her. She pushed the thought aside and punched in the number Regina had jotted down.

It rang several times and Penelope was about to give up when someone finally said hello in a breathless voice.

"Who is this?" Penelope said.

"I think you must have the wrong—"

"No, sorry," Penelope said. "I wrote this number down and now I can't seem to remember why. I'm hoping you can help me." She tried to put a smile in her voice.

"Oh, I understand. That's happened to me more than once. This is Noah Spencer of the BBC. Do we know each other?"

"Oh," Penelope said, slightly disappointed. She didn't know what she'd been expecting. A great revelation? That was highly unlikely. "This is Penelope Parish," she said finally. "We spoke the other day."

"Yes, Penelope. Of course. From the Open Book."

"I . . . I wondered if you'd been able to get in touch with Mabel, the proprietor here. And . . . and if there was anything else I could do to help."

It was a flimsy excuse, and Penelope felt her face getting hot. She hoped Noah didn't think she was coming on to him or anything.

"Yes, I did. We've worked everything out. With any luck we'll be filming soon. Assuming I come up with a story, of course."

"Well, good luck," Penelope said. She hung up quickly.

That was that, she thought. Time to get back to work. Her fingers were hovering over the keys when she had a thought that nearly catapulted her from her chair.

Regina had noted Noah's phone number in her notebook full of cryptic notes about the incriminating information she had collected on some of the residents of

Upper Chumley-on-Stoke. It wasn't a huge leap to assume that Regina had somehow figured out the mystery woman Noah had tracked to Chumley for his program on cold cases. Had she been planning to call him with the information if the woman didn't cough up whatever it was Regina wanted from her?

And if that woman had discovered that Regina knew her secret, it wouldn't be surprising at all if she was the one who had murdered Regina to keep her quiet.

All Penelope had to do was to figure out who that was.

As soon as Penelope had finished her words for the day—she'd set herself a quota in hopes of reaching her deadline—she closed her laptop and went in search of Mabel.

Mabel was ringing up some customers. Penelope busied herself rearranging one of the displays while she waited.

Finally Mabel was free and Penelope joined her at the counter.

"You look like you have some sort of news," Mabel said, raising an eyebrow. "Hope it's good."

"Do you remember when I showed you Regina's notebook and we noticed that a telephone number was one of the entries?"

Mabel nodded.

"I called the number. It belongs to Noah Spencer, the BBC producer who is here for that cold case show."

"How interesting," Mabel said, fingering the amulet that hung from her neck on a leather cord. "Regina must have found the girl who had set that fire—although of course she'd be a middle-aged woman by now. Did you ask Noah if she'd phoned him with a tip that led him here?"

"I didn't think to." Penelope bit her lip. "I was so surprised when he answered the telephone. I don't know what I was expecting."

Penelope had her phone in her pocket. She dug it out and thumbed through the photographs again. They'd already decoded some of the clues. The one about D and money most certainly had to do with Daphne. Regina must have figured out that Daphne's sister wasn't disabled as she'd claimed. And *N = Work = WI/Drink* was clearly referring to Nora Blakely. And of course there was the entry about Mabel, but Penelope couldn't see any connection at all to Regina's murder.

"Excuse me," a woman said, gently tapping Penelope on the arm. "Can you tell me where the mysteries are?"

Penelope shoved her phone back in her pocket, smiled at the woman, and said, "This way."

Penelope's phone dinged, indicating she had a message. She showed the customer to the mystery section and once the woman assured Penelope that she didn't need any more help—she was simply browsing, she said—Penelope pulled her phone from her pocket. The message was from Miles saying he was picking her up at six o'clock and had she made dinner reservations? Penelope laughed. You certainly didn't need reservations at the Book and Bottle. Miles was in for a surprise in more ways than one.

I t was late afternoon when the door to the Open Book opened and a man walked in. Penelope looked up from the book display she was arranging and was surprised to see it was Noah Spencer.

His eyes looked as wild as his windblown hair as he looked around the shop. He obviously spied Penelope because he began walking in her direction. His hands were clenched and his expression was serious.

He stalked past the counter where Mabel looked at him, surprised, then at Penelope. She raised her eyebrows.

"Hello," Penelope said when he reached her. "I hope you're enjoying your stay in Chumley."

Noah nodded tersely. "I came to tell you that I won't be filming here at the Open Book."

"Oh?" Penelope was disappointed. Everyone had been looking forward to it. "Is there a reason why?"

Noah looked around quickly, then leaned closer to Penelope.

"It's not worth it. I've filmed dozens of these episodes and this has never happened to me before." He ran his hands through his hair.

"What happened?" Penelope said.

"My life has been threatened," Noah said. His eyes had taken on an even wilder look.

Penelope gasped. "What . . . how?"

"I received this note." Noah pulled a crumpled piece of paper from the pocket of his raincoat with shaking hands and waved it in front of Penelope. "It demanded I stop investigating the Hadleigh House fire cold case or there would be dire consequences—to me!" He stabbed his chest with his thumb.

He thrust the note at Penelope. She opened it up and smoothed it out. The letters were neatly cut from a magazine and pasted on the paper. They threatened Noah with death if he didn't drop the investigation.

"Where did you find the note?" Penelope said.

"It was pushed under my door at Primrose Cottage—the bed-and-breakfast where I'm staying." Noah shook his head. "And then"—Noah drew a deep shuddering breath as Penelope handed the note back to him—"someone tried to run me off the road! I originally put the note down to some practical jokester—it wouldn't be the first time since I've been producing these shows—but then when someone tried to ram my car as I was driving down the dual carriageway toward the high street . . ." He raised a shaking hand to his throat. "I nearly ended up crushed next to a concrete embankment."

"But don't you want to know—"

Noah was already shaking his head. "It's not worth it. I told the police about it, but I won't feel safe until I've put a good distance between myself and Upper Chumley-on-Stoke. I talked to my boss and she agrees. There are plenty of other cold cases out there to investigate. This one's simply not worth getting killed over."

It was almost closing time when a thought occurred to Penelope. The more she mulled it over, the more it made sense. She just had to check one thing.

"Excuse me," she said to Mabel who was talking to a sales representative from Bloomsbury. "I have to run an errand before the shops close. Do you mind locking up on your own?"

"Go," Mabel said, shooing Penelope away. "I'll be fine."

Penelope yanked her coat off the coat-tree and slipped into it. She didn't bother to button it—she was only going across the street to the Crown Jewels.

A stream of cars was going down the high street but finally there was a break in the traffic and Pen was able to dash across to the other side.

A man carrying a brown paper bag was coming out of Brown's Hardware and she could see Gladys behind the window of the Pig in a Poke leaning on the counter, talking to a customer.

The display in the window of the Crown Jewels had been changed to gold watches set out on black-velvet-covered stands as if they were tempting dishes being offered at a buffet.

Penelope opened the door and was pleased to find the store empty. An elderly gentleman stood behind the counter, his snowy white hair combed back from his high forehead and his mustache waxed to perfection. He had a loupe in his eye and was examining a stone pinched between the blades of a pair of tweezers.

When he saw Penelope, he put the stone in a box and slid it under the counter.

"May I help you, miss?" he said as he glided toward her.

Pen took a deep breath. "Yes. I'm Lady Maxwell-Lewis's assistant. She's asked me to find out if the repairs to her gold necklace are complete. She'd like to pick it up tomorrow—she's having a dinner party and plans to wear the piece."

The jeweler frowned. "Gold necklace? I don't recall that we have a gold necklace from Lady Maxwell-Lewis. Let me see." He pulled a leather book out from under the counter. The pages were edged in gilt and the cover was worn at the corners.

He flipped through it, found the page he wanted, and ran his finger down the column of names. His face brightened.

"You must mean her pearl necklace," he said, tapping the page. "She brought it in to be restrung. We had to replace a pearl—apparently the strand broke and one was lost. Fortunately the set was knotted or she might have lost them all." He smiled again. "We should be able to have it ready for her by tomorrow afternoon if that will do?"

"That will do perfectly," Pen said.

She thanked the jeweler and turned to leave. She felt a sense of excitement as she left the shop. India had found a pearl on the floor of Worthington's basement the day Regina was murdered and Evelyn had taken a pearl necklace to the jeweler to be restrung. Had the necklace broken while Evelyn was in the basement with Regina?

Perhaps there had been a struggle and Regina had grabbed Evelyn's necklace and tugged until it broke?

On the other hand, Evelyn was a frequent guest at Worthington House. She went shooting with Worthington and his guns were kept in the basement. It was quite possible her necklace had broken weeks ago and she'd only just now gotten around to having it repaired.

Pen was tempted to tell Mabel about her find and get her opinion, but then she decided to keep it to herself. It might mean something . . . but then again, it might mean nothing at all.

Mrs. Danvers was not in evidence when Penelope opened the door to her cottage later that afternoon. No doubt she was sulking about having been left alone all day. Penelope checked the cat's bowls just to be sure—there was still plenty of food and water so that was not the cause of Mrs. Danvers's pout. Penelope supposed she had gone out the cat door and into the back garden—although calling the small patch of grass a garden was a bit of an exaggeration.

Penelope thought about Noah Spencer as she climbed the stairs to the second floor. She shuddered when she thought of what had happened to him. Getting the threatening note would have been frightening enough but then to be nearly run off the road . . . She didn't blame him for deciding to cancel the investigation.

Penelope had a thought that suddenly froze her in her tracks—one hand on the banister and her right foot hovering in the air above the second-to-last step. What if the person Noah had been pursuing discovered that Penelope had been to Northampton asking questions? She shivered. Would she become a target as well?

She pushed the thought from her mind—she was being overly melodramatic—and once again stood in front of her closet. One of these days she really had to make time to visit Francesca and Annabelle's Boutique to expand her wardrobe. She sighed. Miles already knew what she looked like and how she dressed so there was really no need to fret. Besides, no one at the Book and Bottle would care either.

Penelope pulled on a pair of black leggings and a royal-blue sweater that Miles once told her brought out the color of her eyes. Then she settled down to wait.

Promptly at six o'clock the door knocker sounded. Penelope had to hand it to Miles—he was always on time. It was one of his better qualities.

Penelope plastered a smile on her face and opened the door.

"Hey," Miles said, giving Penelope a kiss on the cheek. "How have you been?"

He was impeccably dressed as always in a perfectly tailored navy blazer with gold buttons that had his initials on them, gray slacks, and an open-necked shirt. His Gucci loafers were polished to a high shine and his yellow socks added a pop of color. Even the Duke of Windsor would have been impressed, Penelope thought.

She led him into the sitting room where she'd gotten a fire going. She had two glasses and an open bottle of wine on the table—a Tesco special that had been well rated despite its affordable price tag. Miles was something of a connoisseur, regularly ordering ridiculously expensive bottles of Château Lafite Rothschild when they went out, but Penelope could hardly afford to do that.

Miles took a seat on the sofa and smiled at Penelope. He seemed slightly nervous. She felt a bit awkward, too—as if they were strangers on a first date.

Mrs. Danvers still hadn't returned by the time they finished their glass of wine and had their coats on ready to leave for the pub. She must have found something fascinating to stalk in the garden and Penelope wondered what animal carcass she would find on the mat by the back door when she got home.

Miles's rented Jaguar was at the curb. He held the door for Penelope, then sprinted around to the driver's side and got behind the wheel.

"Where to?" he said, as he turned the key in the ignition.

"Unfortunately, Chumley's one fancy restaurant, Pierre's, is closed for renovation following a fire. I thought we would go to an authentic British pub."

Miles raised an eyebrow and scowled.

"The Book and Bottle is a favorite of the Duke of Upper Chumley-on-Stoke."

"Really?" Miles said, pulling away from the curb. His expression lightened.

Now Penelope was feeling nervous as well. When should she broach the topic of taking a break with Miles? After she'd knocked back a good, stiff drink? Over the entrée? Or should she wait until they'd ordered dessert? If she put it off too long, she might lose her nerve. Now she wished she had texted him while he was still in the States. That would have been easier than telling him face-to-face.

But Parishes aren't cowards, Penelope's grandmother also said. Penelope lifted her chin. She could do this. Think positively, she told herself.

Miles's lip curled slightly when they opened the door to the Book and Bottle and were suddenly awash in the smell of spilled beer, fried food, and stale cigarette smoke.

"The duke comes here?" he said in tones of disbelief.

"He certainly does. As a matter of fact, he's standing at the bar right this minute." Penelope pointed to Worthington, who was leaning on the bar with one hand and holding a mug of lager in the other. He was wearing jeans and a cashmere sweater with the sleeves pushed up. He was the very picture of casual elegance.

The pub was crowded. It was Saturday night and the locals were out for a drink and a chance to catch up with friends, play a game or two of darts, and try their luck at one of the fruit machines. The commuters who lived in the new subdivisions were amusing themselves by "slumming" at the local pub instead of heading into London to some new and trendy spot.

"Looks like we'll have to wait for a table," Penelope said, looking around.

"Can't we go somewhere else?" Miles's voice was plaintive.

"There's the Chumley Chippie or Kebabs and Curries," Penelope said, trying to keep the laughter out of her voice.

Miles shuddered. "Let's wait."

"I'll fetch us a drink. What would you like?" Penelope said.

"A martini. Extra dry," Miles said. "Make that a dirty martini."

Penelope almost asked whether he wanted it shaken or stirred but bit her lip and managed to restrain herself.

She maneuvered her way through the crowd and insinuated herself between two people standing at the bar. Daphne was bustling about delivering drinks and pulling pints with incredible speed. Her expression was grim.

"Hey, Daphne," one of the patrons called out. "Give us a smile, there's a good girl."

Daphne curled her lips up briefly, then resumed her previous expression.

Penelope carried Miles's martini and her cider back to where Miles was standing. His expression was now one of bemusement.

"You're right," he said as he took a sip of his drink. "This place is authentic all right."

A table finally opened up and although it was crammed into a corner, they took it.

Miles twisted around in his seat. "Where's the waiter?"

"You have to go up to the bar to order and to pick up your food," Penelope said smoothly. She pointed to a blackboard hanging on the wall. "There's the menu." She adjusted her glasses as she read the selections. "I've heard the Welsh rarebit is very good here as well as the bangers and mash. Then there's the steak-and-kidney pie."

Miles sighed. "I guess I'll have the Welsh rarebit."

"I'll pop over to the bar with our order," Penelope said, starting to get up.

"I'll do it," Miles said. "What are you having?"

"The bangers and mash for me, please."

Penelope watched as Miles made his way through the crowd to the bar. She wasn't surprised when she noticed him squeezing into a spot next to Worthington. Nor was she surprised when several minutes later, the two men were chatting companionably.

Penelope began to think again about how she was going to break the news to Miles that she didn't think they were going to work out as a couple. She finally decided she'd tell him as soon as they began eating. Perhaps he'd be distracted by his Welsh rarebit. Not that she expected him to make a scene—making a scene simply wasn't comme il faut in Miles's playbook.

Miles returned with their meals along with two glasses of wine. He drained his martini but instead of picking up his knife and fork, began fiddling with the salt and pepper shakers.

Penelope was starving, so she immediately started in on her bangers and mash.

"Penelope," Miles said in a tone that made Penelope look up abruptly. "I've got something to tell you."

Penelope's mouth was full, so she just tilted her head to indicate she was listening and that he should go on.

"It's been difficult having you so far away like this."

Penelope was still chewing, so she nodded her head.

"It hasn't been easy for me." Miles looked off into the distance. "I have to attend any number of functions every week and it's expected that I'll have someone by my side."

He wasn't going to tell her he wanted her to come home, was he? Penelope took another bite of her sausage, reasoning that if she had food in her mouth she couldn't blurt out anything that she would regret later.

Miles gave a crooked smile. "There was a charity dinner at the Met and the firm had taken a table. Paxton suggested I take his sister. It seemed like a good idea at the time, so I gave her a call and convinced her to do me a favor and go with me."

Penelope knew Miles well enough to realize that Miles undoubtedly thought he was doing her a favor and not the other way around.

Miles cut a piece of his toast but didn't pick it up.

"We ended up having a great time. She's a wonderful gal—plays tennis, sails, and recently finished her third triathlon. Came out near the top, too. And it turns out she went to Dartmouth and knows my cousin Carter." He spread out his hands. "Small world and all that."

"She sounds wonderful," Penelope said.

"That's just it. It turns out that Sloan and I are perfect for each other." He shook his head as if he couldn't believe his good fortune. "That's what I'm trying to tell you." He looked up but off to the side, not directly at Penelope. "Sloan and I have fallen in love." He reached for Penelope's hands and grasped them. "I'm sorry. I never meant for this to happen."

The forkful of mashed potatoes Penelope had just eaten stuck in her throat and she started to cough.

"Are you okay?" Miles made as if to get up to pat her on the back.

Penelope waved a hand. "I'm fine," she said in a strained voice.

She didn't know how she felt. Yes, she had planned to break it off with Miles, but to be unceremoniously dumped instead . . . She had to admit that it stung just a bit.

"I'm very happy for you and Sloan," she finally said in a small voice.

"So you understand?" Miles's face brightened and Penelope could hear him sigh with relief.

"You're a great gal, Penelope," Miles said, as he dug into his Welsh rarebit with gusto.

I just don't play tennis, sail, or enter triathlons, Penelope thought.

TWENTY

꧁ꞏꞏ꧂

Penelope hesitated, unsure of how to say good-bye to Miles. Should she kiss him? Shake his hand? He solved the problem by leaning in quickly and giving her a peck on the cheek. He squeezed her shoulder.

"You've been just great," he said, as he turned and headed toward his car. "I'll see you when you get back to New York."

He all but dove into the driver's seat of the Jaguar and within seconds had started the car and pulled away from the curb.

Penelope gave a half-hearted wave and opened the door to her cottage.

The bottle of wine was still sitting on the coffee table in the living room and she decided to pour herself a glass. She got the fire going again and curled up on the sofa with a knitted throw over her lap.

Her emotions were all jumbled up and she couldn't decide how she felt. Certainly she was grateful that she hadn't had to be the one to tell Miles she wanted to break up. On the other hand, having Miles safely tucked away in New York while she was living in England had felt so comfortable. If anyone asked, she could say she had a boyfriend back in the States and that would be that. And without the necessity of actually having to spend time with Miles.

The sting of having been dumped by Miles was slowly being replaced by an overwhelming sense of relief. Her spirits began to lift—although perhaps that was the wine, she thought.

It wasn't all that late, but she was getting sleepy. Penelope stood up, yawned, stretched, and looked around for Mrs. Danvers.

Odd. She hadn't seen the cat since that afternoon. Mrs. Danvers enjoyed her time in the garden—sunning herself on nice days and stalking nocturnal creatures after dark—but she rarely ever stayed outside this long.

Penelope opened the back door and stood on the mat. She shivered. A cold wind had picked up and it sliced through her sweater and whistled down her neck and back.

"Mrs. Danvers," she called. The words didn't come out very loud—she was unused to shouting—shouting had been frowned upon by her mother and grandmother. She cleared her throat and tried again. "Mrs. Danvers!" That was better.

Penelope looked around expectantly. Surely Mrs. Danvers would come slinking around the corner, her slit eyes alight with satisfaction over a night well spent. Penelope wrapped her arms around herself and rubbed her arms. Where had that cat gotten to?

Finally she was forced to give up—driven inside by the cold. Obviously Mrs. Danvers would return when she was good and ready—or hungry—whichever came first.

Penelope made sure the fire in the living room grate was out, stabbing at the last few dying embers with the poker. She turned out the lights, checked the kitchen again, half expecting to see the cat picking at her food or lapping up water from her water bowl, but Mrs. Danvers was nowhere to be seen.

Finally, somewhat reluctantly, Penelope climbed the stairs to bed.

Her bed was warm and cozy but Penelope couldn't fall asleep. She was worried about Mrs. Danvers being out all night—what if it started to rain?—but then she reminded herself that the cat was perfectly capable of coming inside through the cat door.

Her mind turned instead to the mystery of Regina's death. Was it related to the cold case that Noah had been pursuing? It wasn't beyond the realm of possibility that Regina, with her nose for secrets—particularly damaging ones—might have figured out the identity of the person who had set the fire at Hadleigh House and was hiding in Upper Chumley-on-Stoke under an assumed name.

And if that person had threatened to kill Noah Spencer, it wasn't impossible that they had decided to silence Regina.

A name floated into Penelope's mind. Georgie. Josie said a nurse had called the girl that. Penelope thought she had heard that name recently—but where? And was it even relevant?

Penelope was nearly drifting off to sleep when it came to her and she jerked awake. It had been at the Worthington Fest after Regina had been found murdered. Lady Evelyn Maxwell-Lewis had been at their booth purchasing Charlotte's novel and that woman had come up to them, insisting she recognized Evelyn and that they had gone to school together. She had called Evelyn by the name Georgina. And surely Georgie was short for Georgina?

Penelope began to get excited. It wasn't much to go on but then she remembered other things as well. Josie had said that Georgie's hand had been burned in the fire. She closed her eyes and tried to picture herself standing with Evelyn in Francesca and Annabelle's Boutique. There had been a nasty raised scar on Evelyn's hand—she remembered noticing it at the time.

She rolled onto her side. It still wasn't much to go on—certainly not anything she could go to Detective Maguire with. She felt her face color at the thought. She tried to think back to everything that had happened since Regina had been found dead.

She thought about all the people who might have killed Regina—Charlotte, Worthington himself, poor Nora Blakely, Gordon, or Daphne. Or even Regina's daughter, Victoria, although that had always seemed like a long shot.

She remembered Daphne in the Crown Jewels trying on that handsome gold bracelet while Gordon beamed at her. It had seemed so likely that one or the other of them had done away with Regina in order to be together. But Daphne had an alibi and Penelope honestly couldn't see Gordon as a murderer. He was too kindhearted.

Penelope sighed. She was never going to fall asleep at this rate. She rolled out of bed and went down the stairs.

She had left her phone on the foyer table. She grabbed it and took it over to the sofa, where she curled up with her feet under her and the throw pulled over her legs.

The room was chilly and Pen shivered. Moonlight slanted through the front windows and glinted off the wide-planked wood floor.

She flipped through the photos one more time until she found what she was looking for. There it was—the notation *E = past*. Penelope let the phone drop into her lap. If Evelyn was actually Georgina Hadleigh, then it certainly made sense. Evelyn had a past and obviously Regina had discovered it.

Penelope felt her eyes closing and her head dropped back against the sofa cushions. She jolted herself awake—she didn't want to fall asleep on the couch.

She wrapped her arms around herself as she walked into the kitchen and opened the back door. She stood on the mat and called for Mrs. Danvers again. Nothing moved in the shadows at the corners of the garden and there was no answering meow. Reluctantly she went inside, a sudden gust of wind grabbing the back door and slamming it behind her.

Penelope went back upstairs, dove under the covers, and pulled the blankets up to her chin. Her teeth were chattering slightly and her hands and feet were like ice cubes. The warmth of the comforter finally lulled her to sleep.

She dreamed that Mrs. Danvers was in danger and woke suddenly and sat bolt upright in bed. She was surprised to see the first streaks of light in the overcast sky. Penelope rolled over and tried to go back to sleep but soon realized it was hopeless. She might as well get up. Perhaps she could get a head start on her word quota for the day. It was Sunday and Mabel wasn't expecting her at the bookstore although she thought she might pop in at some point. She wanted to see what Mabel's opinion was on her deductions of the night before—that Evelyn Maxwell-Lewis had quite possibly murdered Regina.

Penelope put the kettle on and dropped some bread into the toaster. She was waiting for the water to boil when her cell phone rang. Miles? she wondered. Was he calling to say good-bye on his way to the airport?

Penelope didn't recognize the telephone number on the caller ID. She didn't recognize the voice either.

"Hello, is this Penelope Parish?" a man's voice said.

"Yes," Penelope said somewhat hesitantly. Was it possible that some telemarketers had tracked her down to Upper Chumley-on-Stoke?

"It's about your cat."

Penelope went still and her hand tightened on the telephone.

"Go on."

"I think I saw it wandering around the grounds of Worthington House. Sweet little thing."

How had Mrs. Danvers gotten all the way to Worthington House? Penelope wondered. She supposed it was possible. Maybe the cat had crawled into someone's car? She'd read of cases where drivers had found cats under their hoods, seeking the warmth of the engine.

"Are you sure it was Mrs. Danvers?" Penelope said.

"It's on her tag, innit? Plain as day."

"Okay, thank you." Did the person expect a reward? "Who is this?" she said.

But even as she said it, she heard a click and the call was cut off. The person had hung up.

* * *

Penelope's first instinct was to throw her coat over her pajamas—actually a sweatshirt and sweatpants—but she forced herself to go upstairs and change into a pair of leggings and a warm sweater.

Her hands were shaking as she did up the buttons on her coat and retrieved her car keys from a bowl on the foyer table.

There was no reason to think any harm had come to Mrs. Danvers. The cat had simply wandered off as cats were wont to do. There was no need to panic. But no matter how many times she told herself that, her heart continued to race and her breath to come in short, sharp gasps.

Penelope slammed the front door behind her and ran to her car, which she'd parked in front of the cottage. It took her several tries to insert the key in the ignition, but she finally got the engine started and pulled out into the road.

She nearly pulled into the wrong lane but corrected herself in time and continued on her way to Worthington House. There was little traffic—it was still early and it would be several hours yet before the villagers began heading to church services or off to visit relatives for the Sunday roast and Yorkshire pudding.

Penelope pulled into the long drive that led to Worthington House, her head swiveling this way and that as she searched for Mrs. Danvers. Some of her fear had evaporated and instead turned to annoyance that the cat had led her on this merry chase on a cold Sunday morning. She should still be tucked up in bed or in front of a roaring fire with a cup of tea and the Sunday papers.

There was no one about that Penelope could see—no

groundskeeper, no dog walker, no security guards. She prayed there wasn't some sort of secret alarm that she was about to set off. She imagined driving into a trap or having a giant net capture her like some pesky insect.

Fortunately nothing of the kind happened, and she made it to the car park without mishap. Penelope got out of the car and looked around. The wind tugged at her coat and blew her hair into her eyes and she brushed it away impatiently.

The grounds of Worthington House were enormous and she hardly knew where to begin. She decided she would walk the perimeter of the castle itself. On such a blustery morning, surely Mrs. Danvers would have sought out a sheltered spot for herself.

Penelope headed out across the front lawn where the Worthington Fest had been held. It now seemed as if the fest had taken place in another lifetime and not merely two weeks ago. The vast lawn was bordered by shrubs pruned into ornamental shapes with tall trees in the distance.

Penelope turned the corner and headed toward the back of the castle where formal gardens were laid out with incredible precision. There was a perennial garden, an annual garden where a few hardy specimens continued to bloom, and a fragrant herb garden set out in a circular pattern. Penelope sniffed—she smelled lavender, thyme, and lemon balm on the perfumed air.

An intricate stone terrace, surrounded by topiary, was the centerpiece of the garden, its furniture shrouded in heavy canvas covers that flapped in the breeze.

Unfortunately, Mrs. Danvers was nowhere to be seen.

Penelope was passing a door set in the thick castle wall when she heard a plaintive meow—or so she thought. She paused and listened hard, her heartbeat speeding up and pounding in her ears as the blood rushed to her head. Had that been a cat or had it been the wind and she'd simply imagined it?

There it was again—most decidedly a cat's meow. Was it Mrs. Danvers? Penelope wasn't sure. Perhaps Worthington kept a cat to chase the mice away?

She moved closer to the door and peered through the window. The glass was thick and wavy with age and she could barely see through it. There was a staircase but no sign of Mrs. Danvers as far as she could tell. She was about to chalk the sound up to the wind whistling through the trees when she heard it again. It was clearly a cat— and to her, it sounded just like Mrs. Danvers.

Penelope tried the door handle. She was surprised when it turned and the door opened. She stepped inside.

TWENTY-ONE

❧❧❧

Penelope stopped short just inside the door. Was she being too stupid to live, like the heroine in a poorly written novel? Why was the door unlocked? Was this a trap? She laughed. This wasn't fiction—this was real life. And there wasn't a bogeyman waiting for her and no sinister plot afoot. The worst that could happen would be having one of the security guards catch her but she could explain about searching for her lost cat and she could always mention that she was friends—even if that was a slight exaggeration—with Charlotte Davenport if need be.

Penelope went down the stairs and found herself in the cellar. The lights weren't on and it was dark and shadowy with only a bit of light coming in through the small windows set high on the wall. She didn't see Mrs. Danvers, although she thought she heard a rustling in one of the darkened corners.

"Mrs. Danvers," Penelope called. The cat rarely ever

came when called but she hoped this time the cat would condescend to listen. "Mrs. Danvers," she called again, not daring to raise her voice too loud for fear of someone hearing her.

She heard a faint meow and cocked her head, listening. She couldn't tell which direction it was coming from but she was positive now that it was a cat. Her spirits lifted— hopefully she and Mrs. Danvers would soon be tucked up at home enjoying a cup of coffee and the Sunday papers.

Penelope felt something furry brush against her legs. She looked down.

"Mrs. Danvers! You naughty girl. You scared me."

She bent to pick up the cat and when she straightened she found she was looking directly into the barrel of a gun.

"I didn't know if you would fall for that telephone call or not," Evelyn Maxwell-Lewis said. "But I thought it was worth taking a chance."

"Was that you?" Penelope said. "But it didn't sound like—"

Evelyn shrugged. "I was in the drama club in school. I was very good at putting on different voices."

Penelope had been too startled to feel fear at first, but now it washed over her, freezing her to the spot and giving her the sensation that she was drowning. Mrs. Danvers squirmed out of her arms, jumped to the floor, and retreated to a corner to groom herself.

"What are you doing with the gun?" Penelope said, although she knew it was a stupid question. Perhaps it would buy her time. Would anyone in the Worthington household be coming down to the cellar? They were unlikely to be searching for a bottle of wine this early on a Sunday.

Evelyn laughed. She was wearing her usual jodhpurs and polished leather riding boots.

"How did you get in here?" Penelope said. "Wasn't the door locked?"

"I borrowed the key the last time I was here for dinner with Worthington and Charlotte. He keeps them in a drawer in a table in the drawing room. I've seen him go in there when we've gone on shoots and he had to get the guns from the cellar. He keeps the keys to the gun safe in there as well."

"If you shoot me here, you'll never get away with it."

Evelyn lifted her chin. "I have no intention of shooting you here. The gun is to persuade you to come with me to my Land Rover, which is parked outside. We'll go out into the countryside where your death will look like a very sad hunting accident. You were out having a ramble and some poor misguided hunter with bad eyesight took you for prey."

Penelope vaguely remembered a personal safety course she had taken in college where they were instructed that you should never let an attacker move you from one place to another. Instead, you were to resist if at all possible. Unfortunately Evelyn was holding a very persuasive gun in her hands. Would she dare to use it here? She'd shot Regina here, Penelope realized, and that pretty much answered that question.

She needed to get away somehow—she needed a distraction. Meanwhile, she needed to keep Evelyn talking.

"Why did you kill Regina?" she said, although she was quite sure she already knew the answer.

"Regina was such a dreadful pest. She actually had the nerve to ask me to pressure my dear Bertram into putting her husband up for a knighthood. Honestly! The man has done nothing to merit a knighthood beyond making a bit of money with that company of his. That's hardly a qualification for a Grand Cross of the British Empire. Of course, Bertram wouldn't hear of it and I can hardly blame him."

Evelyn sniffed. She was quiet for a couple of seconds as if she was mentally somewhere else. Penelope was glad for the delay. Every minute that went by increased the odds that someone would come downstairs and distract Evelyn.

"Somehow Regina found out about my . . . past," Evelyn continued. "She threatened to reveal my identity to the press if I didn't give her what she wanted. She claimed to have the telephone number of a reporter working for the BBC." Evelyn caressed the barrel of the gun she was holding as if she was reliving shooting Regina. "Bertram doesn't know that I was once . . . someone else. I changed my name—I had to because everyone knew who I was—and I created a new life for myself. I couldn't have all of that destroyed because of one silly woman and her ridiculous demands."

Penelope felt a pang of sympathy for Evelyn in spite of herself. Supposedly the years Evelyn had spent in the mental hospital has been considered punishment enough for what she had done. Besides, there had been no trial, no jury to weigh the evidence. Evelyn had been convicted solely in the court of public opinion.

But that didn't alter the fact that she was standing here now, pointing a gun at Penelope's chest.

"Were you the one who set the fire at Hadleigh House?" Pen said, still stalling for time.

Evelyn's head jerked. "Yes, I did. And I've paid a dear price for it—many years locked up in that dreadful psychiatric hospital. They said I had a mental illness called pyromania. I must have been born with it.

"Fortunately in my last years at Arbor View, I met with a new psychiatrist who actually cared if I got better or not. He helped me channel my impulses into riding, which I came to adore. If it hadn't been for him, I'd no doubt still be locked up there."

Penelope had been balancing on the balls of her feet ready to run given the slightest chance. She prayed Evelyn's attention would stray or that she would be racked with sneezing or *something* that would give Penelope a second or two head start.

"By the way," Penelope said, still stalling for the right moment to make her dash—thank heavens she had been a sprinter on the high school track team—something she never thought would come in so handy. "How did Mrs. Danvers get here? I can't believe she walked all this way."

Evelyn tossed her head. "That was easy. I snatched her from your garden when you weren't home and brought her here myself. It was easy enough to lure her with a piece of chicken."

Mrs. Danvers must have sensed they were speaking about her. Out of the corner of her eye, Penelope noticed the cat stand up, stretch, and slowly saunter away from the corner where she had been grooming herself. She sidled closer and closer to Evelyn until she finally brushed up against Evelyn's legs.

Evelyn jumped. "What was that? A mouse?"

Penelope didn't hesitate—she was off like a shot racing through the darkened cellar. She wanted to reach the stairs to the upper level before Evelyn caught up with her.

Footsteps sounded behind her. She hoped the dim light would prevent Evelyn from getting off an accurate shot.

Penelope passed an alcove and darted into it. A cloud of dust arose and nearly made her sneeze. She clamped a finger under her nose to stifle it. Someone was standing next to her and she nearly screamed but it was just one of the Worthington suits of armor.

"Where are you?" Evelyn shouted and her voice echoed around the cavernous space. "I can't have you going to the police. It would spoil everything I've worked so hard to create."

Penelope stayed silent, barely daring to breathe. She thought she was near the stairs. Should she make a run for it? Her legs refused to move—fear had paralyzed her.

A bit of light coming from one of the windows glinted off the barrel of Evelyn's gun.

"There you are," she said in satisfied tones, peering into the alcove where Penelope was crouched.

She had the gun pointed directly at Penelope's chest. Penelope began to shiver. She saw Evelyn's finger move on the trigger and panicked. If she could throw something it might spoil Evelyn's aim.

She lashed out and managed to hit the suit of armor, which teetered unsteadily and finally fell, knocking the gun from Evelyn's hands. It skittered across the floor and disappeared into the shadows. Penelope dropped to her knees and began crawling toward the spot where it had landed.

She snagged her leggings on a rough patch of floor and scraped her knee. It stung and she had to bite her lip to keep from making any noise.

The gun had to be here somewhere. Penelope had heard it land. She stretched out an arm and swept her hand across the floor. She had to find it before Evelyn, who was also down on her knees, did.

Her hand touched something cold—something metal. It was the gun. Penelope grabbed it and struggled to her feet. She was breathing heavily and her heart was still pounding furiously. She hoped she didn't have a heart attack and die of fright.

"Give me that," Evelyn hissed.

Penelope raised the gun and trained it on Evelyn. She'd never shot a gun in her life—or even touched one for that matter—but Evelyn didn't know that. Penelope tried to act cocky—as if she knew what she was doing—and hoped that Evelyn wouldn't notice that her teeth were chattering.

Evelyn scrambled to her feet. Her jodhpurs were covered in dust and there was a hole in the right knee. She looked down at them in disgust.

Penelope leveled the gun at Evelyn, trying to keep it as steady as possible in her shaking hands. She patted her pocket with one hand. Her cell phone must have fallen out while she was crawling around on the floor looking for the gun. On to plan B, she thought.

She motioned to Evelyn with the gun. "We're going to go upstairs where someone will call the police."

Evelyn gave a cackling laugh. "Do you seriously think Worthington is going to believe you? Some upstart American he doesn't even know?"

That had never occurred to Penelope. She suddenly realized how strange it looked—her walking into Worthington's cellar as if she owned the place—even if the door had been unlocked. Evelyn was a frequent guest of Worthington's and presumably a friend. He'd be far more likely to take Evelyn's side and call the police on Penelope!

Evelyn gave a smile that sent a chill through Penelope.

"I was having breakfast with Worthington and Charlotte. I excused myself to visit the bathroom. I'll tell them I heard a noise and came down to investigate and found you breaking in."

"I didn't break in," Penelope said, even as she realized it was ridiculous to argue with Evelyn. "The door was unlocked."

"Of course. I unlocked it. But we won't be telling Worthington that."

"And if I do tell him, he won't believe me—I get it," Penelope said. "Come on." She gestured toward the stairs with the gun. "I guess I'll have to take my chances."

Evelyn made a face but when Penelope waved the gun at her menacingly, she turned and began walking.

Evelyn was halfway up the stairs and Penelope was on the first step when the door at the top of the stairs burst open.

"Police!" a man in uniform shouted, waving his billy club.

Penelope didn't know which of them was more surprised.

"What's going on here?" the policeman demanded, his face creased in confusion. He looked from Penelope to Evelyn and then back again.

"She tried to kill me," Penelope and Evelyn said at the same time.

Penelope had a moment of panic. Would the policeman believe her or Evelyn?

Suddenly Worthington appeared on the stairs. "What's going on?" he demanded. "I heard a noise and called the—"

He stopped short when he saw Penelope and Evelyn.

"Looks like we've got some sorting out to do," the policeman said, scratching his head. "I think I'd better take these two down to the station." He gestured to Penelope and held out his hand. "I'll take that gun now."

TWENTY-TWO

❧

Penelope and Evelyn were taken in separate cars to the police station, where Penelope was put in a small room with a metal table and chairs, a clock on the wall, and bars on the window. A tape recorder sat out on the table. She supposed Evelyn was in a similar room. Penelope could hear her protesting through the wall.

The clock ticked off every second passing with a loud click. An hour passed and it was beginning to get on Penelope's nerves. She was sure she would be hearing that sound in her nightmares for days to come.

How long were they going to keep her here? Surely they had done all the checking necessary and found her record to be free of blemishes—well, except for that one time she was arrested for throwing her shoe during a protest over animal rights. She'd never been convicted and the charges had been dropped, so surely that wasn't still on her record?

Another fifteen minutes went by and Penelope's palms began to sweat. Was this some sort of police technique to wear her down? If so, it was working. She was ready to confess to nearly anything at this point if it meant she could get out of this room.

A horrible thought occurred to her—she would leave this room eventually, she knew that, but would she then be going to a jail cell?

She was nearly dozing when the door suddenly opened. She jumped and banged her knee against the table—the one she'd scraped in the Worthington cellar. She grimaced.

It was Maguire. He was carrying a folder, which he slammed down on the table, making Penelope jump again. She would have been more alarmed if it wasn't for his expression—it was clear he was trying hard not to laugh. His blue eyes twinkled and one side of his mouth curved up in spite of himself.

Surely he couldn't be taking this seriously if he found it so funny?

He sat down opposite Penelope and folded his hands on the table. "So."

Penelope sat up straighter and tried to comb her hair with her fingers. She must look deranged after crawling around the Worthington House cellar.

"How on earth," Maguire began, then scrubbed his face with his hand. "Do you want to tell me what happened?"

Penelope took a deep breath. Where to begin? Should she tell him Evelyn had confessed to murder or simply stick to the story about rescuing Mrs. Danvers? Which was more likely to get her out of this trouble?

Penelope squared her shoulders. "My cat, Mrs. Danvers, had gone missing."

Maguire raised his eyebrows. "Mrs. Danvers as in the novel *Rebecca*?"

In spite of herself, Penelope was pleased that Maguire got the literary reference.

She nodded. "She went out into the garden yesterday and didn't come back. I assumed she'd be home by morning but there was no sign of her. Then the telephone rang."

She shivered. "He said he had seen Mrs. Danvers wandering around Worthington House. I couldn't imagine how the cat managed to get all the way over there, but I needed to check in case it was true and not some other cat that someone had mistaken for mine."

"Did the caller identify himself?"

"No. I thought that was suspicious but I was worried about my cat. I checked as much of the grounds as I could manage and then I heard Mrs. Danvers meowing. It sounded like she was trapped in the cellar." Penelope paused for breath.

"We've got Mrs. Danvers safe and sound here at the station. Constable Cuthbert got quite a nasty scratch trying to corral her." Maguire smiled.

Penelope felt a rush of relief. "I found the cellar door unlocked. Evelyn—Lady Maxwell-Lewis—admitted to having unlocked it."

For a moment Penelope was back in the dim basement facing the barrel of Evelyn's gun. She shuddered.

"Take your time," Maguire said. "Would you like a cup of tea?"

"Yes," Penelope said, suddenly realizing she was absolutely freezing. It was probably from the shock because the room was overheated with a radiator gushing out steam in the corner.

Maguire returned a few minutes later with a tray with two steaming mugs and packets of sugar and creamer.

Penelope stirred some sugar into her tea and held it between her hands, letting the warmth seep into them.

"Where were we?" Maguire said.

"Well, I was in the Worthington cellar," Penelope said with a bit of spirit. "And I was facing Lady Maxwell-Lewis, who had a gun trained on me."

"Why would she do that?"

Penelope's heart sank. Did Maguire really not know that Evelyn had killed Regina? Maybe he wouldn't believe Penelope's story after all.

Penelope reminded him of Regina's notebook and told him about her trip to Birmingham, the fire at Hadleigh House, and all the other bits and pieces she had put together to come to the conclusion that Evelyn was Regina's killer.

Maguire's chair creaked as he leaned back and steepled his fingers.

"That's quite clever," he said. "And I hate to disappoint you or to minimize your detecting prowess, but I'm afraid we've been one step ahead of you. We were on the way to pick up Lady Maxwell-Lewis and bring her in for questioning when we discovered she wasn't at home and Sir Maxwell-Lewis had no idea where she'd gone. She'd been wearing jodhpurs, so he assumed she was out riding somewhere. As we were leaving, we got the call that there was a disturbance at Worthington House. And lo and behold, there was our suspect being held at gunpoint by you." He shook his head. "I guess we owe you one."

"Does that mean you believe me?" Penelope said, her hopes rising.

"It does," Maguire said. "But how about next time you leave the detecting to me, okay?"

Penelope was more than happy to agree. "So I'm free to go?"

"Yes." Maguire fiddled with the folder on his desk. "We may have some more questions for you as we build our case against Lady Maxwell-Lewis. I assume you don't have plans to leave town in the near future?"

Penelope shook her head and stood up.

"Then there's no reason for us to keep you."

W hen Penelope awoke on Monday morning, she was convinced she had dreamed the whole episode. She'd been surprised to fall into a deep and dreamless slumber as soon as her head hit the pillow.

Mrs. Danvers had obviously been tired out by her escapade as well. Normally she would have been fussing at Penelope to get her breakfast as soon as the sun began to rise, but this morning she was still curled up asleep in her bed when Penelope woke up.

Penelope couldn't wait to tell Mabel and Figgy about her adventures of the day before. By the time she got to the Open Book, the open sign was already hanging on the door and Mabel was behind the counter ringing up a customer.

"There you are," Mabel said when Penelope walked in. "Laurence Brimble was just in. He said there was quite a commotion at Worthington House yesterday. He volunteers as a docent there on weekends. He saw several police cars pull into the drive. Have you heard anything about it?"

Figgy wandered over with a plate of freshly baked

Chelsea buns and put them on the counter. India suddenly appeared from around the shelf of biographies and joined them.

"I heard you talking about police cars at Worthington House," India said, helping herself to a bun. "I do hope it wasn't anything serious."

Penelope explained about Mrs. Danvers's escapade and being held at gunpoint by Evelyn.

India gasped and turned white. "You could have been shot!"

The idea made Penelope feel slightly weak in the knees.

"So Lady Evelyn Maxwell-Lewis is really Georgina Hadleigh," India said. "I wonder how Regina figured that out."

"Who knows?" Figgy said, licking a bit of sugar off her lip. "Regina was top-notch when it came to ferreting out other people's secrets."

Penelope noticed the diamond ring sparkling on Figgy's finger.

"Have you told your parents that you and Derek are engaged?" she said.

Figgy made a face. "Not yet. I want them to meet him first. I'm hoping he will be able to win them over."

"Times are changing," India said. "And we must all accept it, I suppose. It's not like in the old days where royalty married other royalty like Queen Victoria and Prince Albert. Look at Worthington and Charlotte, and she's not even British. For that matter, our royal family isn't purely British—the House of Windsor is originally of German descent."

Figgy didn't look particularly consoled by India's statement. "We shall see," she said.

* * *

It was late morning and the shop was quiet. Penelope was helping Mabel set up a display of books to read more than once that readers of the Open Book's newsletter had suggested.

Mabel put down the copy of *The Great Gatsby* that she was holding and looked at Penelope.

Penelope had the odd feeling that Mabel was about to say something important—maybe even profound.

"You know, don't you?" Mabel said. "You figured it out."

Pen was tempted to feign ignorance but decided against it.

"Yes."

"I don't know how Regina found out about Oliver." Mabel placed the book on the display table. "Yes, I was having an affair with a married man. I could make the usual excuses—his wife was distant, consumed by her career—but the fact remains that he rightfully belonged to someone else." She grimaced. "I suspected that your curiosity would get the better of you eventually and you wouldn't rest until you had figured out whose those initials were and what that cryptic note—the one word *wed*—meant."

"I . . ."

Mabel waved a hand. "Let's forget about it, shall we?" Her manner became brisk. "Now. Where shall we put the Hemingway? With Fitzgerald? They were friends, after all."

I'm running across the street to see if the Pig in a Poke has any pasties left," Penelope said around noon. "Does anyone want anything?"

Mabel looked up from the pile of invoices she was going through.

"Can you see if they have any black pudding?"

"Pudding?" Penelope said.

Mabel laughed when she saw the expression on Penelope's face. "It's not pudding actually," Mabel explained. "It's sausage made from blood, herbs and spices, and a filler like rice or barley."

Penelope shuddered.

"If they have it, I'll take a pound. It's quite good, actually."

"I'll take your word for it," Penelope said as she headed toward the door.

The Pig in a Poke was empty when Penelope got there and Gladys was the only one behind the counter.

"Good afternoon, Gladys," Penelope said. "Do you have any of your delicious pasties left? I've become quite attached to them."

"I'm glad you like them, and I'm sorry to disappoint you, my dear." Gladys leaned on the counter. "But since I'm all on me own, I haven't had the time to make any. We had quite the rush this morning—first day of the week and the ladies all out doing their shopping. Cleaned me out of veal kidneys, they did. I was run off my feet the whole time."

"Where's your husband?" Penelope looked around.

"Ah, poor Bruce," Gladys said with a twinkle in her eye. "He had a stroke, poor thing. He got to screaming over his tea—I'd overcooked the roast he said—when it suddenly hit him. His face went all red like a beet and then he clutched for the chair and pulled it down with him. I do feel sorry for him."

Penelope noticed that Gladys didn't look in the least bit sorry. As a matter of fact, she looked practically gleeful.

"I'll be hiring someone to work in the shop with me. I can't do it all on me own."

"Won't Bruce be coming back?"

Gladys shook her head. "At the moment the doctor has recommended further treatment. After he left hospital, we transferred him to the Chumley Care and Rehabilitation Home. He's having what they call occupational therapy."

"Will he be coming back to the shop eventually?" Penelope said.

"We've agreed he should retire," Gladys said with a slight smile. "I can handle the store along with some help. Bruce is looking forward to working on his model railway—he never had much time before." She looked around. "I'll be making a few changes to the shop now that he won't be here to object." She shook her head. "The stroke did something to him. He's changed. I think it humbled him. He's kinder and more considerate." She laughed. "I hope it lasts."

Penelope hoped it lasted, too—for Gladys's sake.

Penelope was leaving the Pig in a Poke with Mabel's pound of black pudding in a bag just as Maguire was walking down the street. He waved and headed toward her.

"I'm sorry about yesterday," he said. "And I'm embarrassed that we put you through that. I hope it wasn't too awful, and I hope you'll let me make it up to you." He looked Penelope in the eye.

"Y-yes," she stammered.

"Great." Maguire smiled. "Pierre's is due to reopen Saturday. Will you let me take you to dinner?"

Penelope's eyes widened and her breath caught in her throat. Was Maguire asking her out on a date? She felt absurdly pleased by the idea.

"What time?" she said.

ACKNOWLEDGMENTS

I have to thank my agent, Jessica Faust, who helped me nurture this idea for a series into a reality and my superb editor, Sarah Blumenstock, who worked with me to make the manuscript the best it could be.

Don't miss the next Open Book mystery

A FATAL FOOTNOTE

Coming Summer 2021 from
Berkley Prime Crime!

Penelope Parish's mother had told her, when she'd accepted the writer in residence position at the Open Book bookstore in Upper Chumley-on-Stoke, England, not to expect to hobnob with the nobility.

But here she was doing exactly that.

It was the night before the wedding of American romance writer Charlotte Davenport and Arthur Worthington, Duke of Upper Chumley-on-Stoke who, despite being well down the line of succession to the throne, was the red-haired favorite of the queen.

The nobility did not wed without a certain amount of pomp and circumstance. In the case of Worthington and Charlotte that consisted of an afternoon polo match where the players graciously allowed Worthington's team to win; a casual dinner buffet for all the guests staying at Worthington House for the duration of the festivities; the wedding ceremony itself the following day; the ceremonial carriage ride through town; the wedding breakfast (more lunch than breakfast if truth be told), and finally, that evening, a ball complete with fireworks and a bonfire on the lawn of the castle.

Thanks to her acquaintance with fellow writer Charlotte Davenport, Penelope was invited to all the festivities, which caused her no small amount of consternation given that her wardrobe was considerably sub par, consisting mainly of jeans, leggings, and shapeless but comfortable sweaters—hardly the sort of sartorial splendor expected when hobnobbing with said nobility.

Charlotte always looked impeccable whether she was wearing a pair of jeans and a crisp white button-down shirt or a priceless designer ball gown, and Worthington's vestments were all carefully bespoke by a legion of devoted tailors in London.

There was nothing for it, Mabel Morris, the proprietor of the Open Book, told Penelope—she was going to have to make a trip to London and do some dreaded shopping.

With the help of Lady Fiona Innes-Goldthorpe, aka Figgy, the manager of the Open Book tea shop and Pen's best friend in Upper Chumley-on-Stoke, Penelope managed to acquire a wardrobe appropriate to the occasion—or, in this case, occasions.

Thus it was that Penelope found herself sitting in the drawing room at Worthington House, dressed in an unaccustomedly elegant gray pencil skirt and black V-neck cashmere sweater rubbing elbows with the likes of the Duke of Upper Chumley-on-Stoke, Lord Ethan Dougal, Lord Tobias Winterbourne, and Lady Winterbourne—the former Cissie Emmott and onetime girlfriend of Arthur

Worthington. The two had remained friends even after their romantic relationship ended.

It was clear that Worthington had a "type." Both Charlotte and Cissie were tall, willowy, and graceful blondes with great style who could almost be mistaken for sisters.

The drawing room, while quite large, felt as snug and cozy as a cocoon with a fire burning in the grate and the dark red velvet drapes drawn across the windows shutting out the chill of the dark night.

Worthington was standing in front of the fire, one elbow resting on the mantle and one leg elegantly crossed over the other, a champagne glass in his hand.

Tobias, a short, stocky man with a red face and thick black eyebrows, approached Worthington and slapped him on the back.

"Good show today, old man. Leading your team on to victory like that."

Worthington assumed a modest expression. "You're way too kind. I played miserably. Now if I'd had my lucky polo stick. . . . Darned if I know what happened to the blasted thing. Last I saw it, it was leaning against the wall in the boot room."

Tobias chuckled. "You're being too humble. You played brilliantly. No one can hold a candle to you on the polo field."

Worthington, it should be noted, did not demur further.

The women were clustered at the opposite end of the room—Penelope, Charlotte, Figgy, Jemima Dougal, Cissie and Yvette Boucher, a petite, dark-haired French woman with a pixie cut who looked effortlessly elegant in a black jumpsuit and black suede kitten heels.

Penelope was perched on the edge of a chintz-covered

sofa attempting to maintain her balance even as its soft, enveloping cushions threatened to swallow her. She had a flute of Moët & Chandon in one hand and a water biscuit with a dab of potted mushrooms in the other, and had come to the realization that if she bit the hors d'oeuvre in half, she was likely to wind up with crumbs all over her skirt. Eating the whole thing in one go wasn't an option either—it was far too large for that. Not for the first time in her life, she wished for a third hand with which to deal with the situation. How incredibly convenient it would be to be able to whip one out on occasions such as these.

Figgy, who by virtue of being the daughter of an Earl had also been invited, was sitting next to Penelope and with a knowing look came to her aid by offering to hold her glass.

Penelope ate her canapé, one hand held underneath to catch the crumbs, and vowed not to accept any more from the butler who was circulating with a silver tray of tempting looking morsels.

"Do give us a hint about your wedding dress," Jemima said to Charlotte in a teasing tone, one hand smoothing down her long plaid skirt. "I'm imagining something regal with a train that goes on forever."

Penelope thought that at the moment Charlotte looked as regal as ever in a pair of wide-legged cream-colored trousers and a matching cream-colored ruffled blouse. The spectacular diamond on her left ring finger sparkled in the light of the chandelier above.

Cissie, who was sitting cross-legged on the floor in front of the sofa, wagged a finger at Jemima. "It's a state secret. You'll find out soon enough."

Cissie owned Atelier Classique and had designed

Charlotte's wedding gown herself. She'd been born in Upper Chumley-on-Stoke but had moved to London after having been sent down from university due to a singular lack of academic achievement.

Her mother had been a sort of royal hanger-on—her great-grandmother having been a lady-in-waiting to the Queen Mother and claimed a distant relationship to the royal family. Her father had no pretentions—royal or otherwise—and had made a fortune in toilet paper thus earning Cissie the nickname of "the Loo Paper Princess" in the British tabloids where she appeared at least once a week.

"Just a tiny clue," Jemima wheedled. "I'm dying of curiosity. Is it satin or taffeta or lace?" She raised her eyebrows.

Cissie stretched out her legs in their slim trousers. A gold crest was embroidered on the toes of her black velvet smoking slippers. "It's one of my best designs yet," she said. "I *will* tell you that."

Penelope noticed Yvette shoot Cissie a look that was decidedly ominous. She nudged Figgy and Figgy whispered back.

"I saw that, too. I wonder what's eating her?"

A butler, in a uniform glittering with gold buttons, stood in the doorway and cleared his throat.

"Dinner is served," he said in solemn tones.

"I'm starving," Cissie said, getting to her feet. She patted her stomach. "Mustn't eat too much though or I won't fit into my ball gown tomorrow night." She glanced at Charlotte over her shoulder. "And you shouldn't eat too much either. There's no time to alter your gown again. Right, Yvette?" She shot Yvette a look.

Yvette gave a small nod.

The gentlemen followed them into the dining room where the table had been set with a fine linen tablecloth and the Worthington china and monogrammed silver. Three ornate silver candelabra marched down the center of the table flanked by flowers clustered in low vases.

Food was spread out on the buffet—roast beef, asparagus, silver gravy boats filled with hollandaise sauce and fondant potatoes. A magnificent chocolate biscuit cake stood on a stand off to one side.

Throwing protocol to the wind—the evening was meant to be casual—the men agreed to sit together on one side of the table with the women on the opposite side. Penelope was seated between Yvette and Figgy.

She turned to Yvette and introduced herself. "How do you know Charlotte?"

Yvette took a sip of her wine. "I work for Atelier Classique. I was part of the team that worked on Charlotte's dress."

Penelope couldn't help but notice that her tone was rather bitter and she had rolled her eyes at the word *team*.

"I'm only here in case last-minute adjustments need to be made," Yvette said, picking up her fork.

Penelope began chatting with Figgy and by the time the main course was finished, she felt as stuffed as a Thanksgiving turkey.

The butler was serving the dessert when Cissie pushed back her chair and excused herself.

"I'll be right back. Don't wait for me," she said, waving a hand at the table.

Penelope had her back to the entrance to the dining room but she was able to hear Cissie talking to someone.

"I'm afraid I have no idea who you are," Cissie said in

the sort of tone one would use with a recalcitrant child or a servant who had gotten out of line.

"What was that all about?" Figgy cocked a head toward the door. "That was quite the put-down."

"I have no idea," Penelope said. "But it was certainly curious."

Ready to find
your next great read?

Let us help.

Visit prh.com/nextread